No In Between

The Inside Out Series
by Lisa Renee Jones

No In Between

Lisa Renee Jones

Gallery Books

New York   London   Toronto   Sydney   New Delhi

Gallery Books
A Division of Simon & Schuster, Inc.
1230 Avenue of the Americas
New York, NY 10020

First Gallery Books trade paperback edition August 2014

GALLERY BOOKS and colophon are registered trademarks of Simon & Schuster, Inc.

For information about special discounts for bulk purchases, please contact Simon & Schuster Special Sales at 1-866-506-1949 or business@simonandschuster.com.

The Simon & Schuster Speakers Bureau can bring authors to your live event. For more information or to book an event contact the Simon & Schuster Speakers Bureau at 1-866-248-3049 or visit our website at www.simonspeakers.com.

Interior design by Ruth Lee-Mui

Manufactured in the United States of America

10 9 8 7 6 5 4 3 2 1

Library of Congress Cataloging-in-Publication Data
Jones, Lisa Renee.
No in between / Lisa Renee Jones—First Gallery Books paperback edition.
pages cm (inside out series)
1. Man-woman relationships—Fiction. I. Title.
PS3610.O627N73   2014
813'.6—dc23
2014013005

ISBN 978-1-4767-7241-7
ISBN 978-1-4767-7249-3 (ebook)

To Diego, for sharing this journey with me, and making it better.

Acknowledgments

A special thanks to my agent, Louise Fury, and my editor, Micki Nuding, who have been as passionate about this series as I have been. I'm looking forward to the limo ride in our future, ladies!

Dear Readers:

If you haven't read the novella His Secrets, *which is in Chris's POV and is a look at what Chris really wanted to tell Sara in Paris, it's only 99 cents at all e-tailers. While you don't have to read it to enjoy this story, it's a great prelude.*

I hope you enjoy No In Between!

Lisa

Prologue

November 2012, Journal Entry #1
On a plane from Paris to San Francisco

I will soon be Sara Merit instead of Sara McMillan. I can barely believe it's true, or that Chris Merit, the amazing, talented, gifted man in the leather seat next to me, is about to be my husband. I should be snuggled against him, resting and reveling in our amazing bond that only seems to get stronger, but I cannot seem to relax. My mind is too much of a jumbled mess over last night, and everything that happened in those few hours before we left Paris. All the craziness of the past month is playing around in my head, twisting me in knots one moment, and causing me to break out in a spontaneous smile at others.

And so here I am, writing in a touristy journal etched with the image of the Eiffel Tower (isn't everything you buy in Paris!) that I picked up in the airport, penning my thoughts just the way Rebecca used to. Used to. I feel sick to my stomach, writing about her in the past tense. She is a stranger and she is gone, and yet she's completely a part of me. It's impossible to explain how deeply and profoundly her life, and her words, have spoken to me.

Since reading Rebecca's journals I've often thought of starting my own, and finally doing so makes me feel like I haven't lost her—that there's still hope I might meet her. Maybe it's my form of denial, my hope that Ava didn't kill her. I feel an almost desperate need to discover that she's still out there somewhere, still traveling the world with the hot, rich man I'm told she ran off with to forget Mark. And if I feel these things, I can only imagine what Mark must feel and how deeply this must cut him. I saw the heartache in his eyes after Ava confessed to killing Rebecca; the kind of heartache that leaves a person weak and bleeding—the way the loss of my mother had left me.

Only a week ago, when I'd first arrived in Paris and learned that Ava had turned her confession into accusations against me and Mark, I'd been terrified and overwhelmed, worried about where it would lead, and what it would mean. Now, though, my fear has transformed into anger, and defeat into a readiness to fight. I think I needed the time to deal with the rawness from the news of Rebecca's death, and the attempt on my own life, right on the heels of losing Dylan and then nearly losing Chris with him.

As much as I'd fought going to Paris, I'm so very glad I went. It was on our last night in Paris, only hours before we left, that Chris and I made a real breakthrough in our relationship. I still can't get the memory of the midnight phone call to rescue Amber out of my head, and even more so, the way we'd found her tied up in Isabel's "playroom" with welts all over her skin. But as horrific as that was, it finally got her into rehab. It also convinced Chris that he hadn't fully revealed everything he should have to me, before his marriage proposal.

I can't believe how wrong I'd been about his secret, and I blame myself for not looking deeper inside the man I love. I know how heartache and damage run in deep layers, not easily peeled away. I'd accepted too easily that his big reveal in Paris was about his reasons for seeking out the whip years ago. About the teenage boy he'd shot and killed when he and Amber's family had been mugged, and how he'd been unable to save her mother and father. And it wasn't even about the once a year meltdown he confessed to having during the week of that anniversary.

His real secret, that deeper layer, was that Dylan's death had shown him how much control the whip still has over him. Last night he'd confessed that while he was away for Dylan's funeral, he'd sought that kind of relief over and over again. Chris can no longer say he'll never need the whip again, so we will face that monster together and win. I'll show him that I am strong and won't crumble. He will not destroy me, as he swears he did Amber and now fears he will me. How can he? He's saved me many times over.

It's my turn to save him.

One

~~~

"We're home, baby."

I place my hand in the warmth of Chris's and he helps me out of the black sedan he'd hired to drive us from the airport to our San Francisco apartment. "Finally," I murmur, feeling like we've been traveling for weeks, not sixteen hours.

"Finally," Chris agrees, guiding me out of the chilly November wind and under the canopy at the front door of the building while we wait for our bags to be unloaded. "And you know what 'home' means," he adds, dragging me close, his hand flattening over my trench coat in the exact location of my jeans-clad backside.

"Yes," I assure him, all too aware that he's referencing his planned "punishment" for my refusal to join the "Mile High Club" despite the private jet he'd chartered for our travel. "You've made your intentions *quite* well known."

He lowers his head, his mouth finding my ear, spiky strands

of his blond hair teasing my cheek. "You were afraid we'd get arrested for having sex on the plane. We wouldn't have, but if we had, I would have made sure it was worth it."

"We don't do audiences," I remind him, pushing away from him before I drown in that earthy, rich scent of his that defines temptation.

Not about to allow my escape, he encloses my waist with his arm, trapping my body against his, and my hands settle beneath his leather jacket on the hard wall of his chest as he says, "I offered to order the flight attendant to get lost."

"Do you want me to take your bags up now, Mr. Merit?" the doorman asks.

Chris's lips curve. "Now would be good." The heated look he gives me before releasing me says he's not talking about the bags.

I stand back and watch as Chris generously tips several staff members, returning to drape his arm over my shoulder. With our hips fitted snugly together, I'm warm all over as we pass through the sliding doors to enter the lobby—and not just with the certainty of all the naughty things Chris has dancing around in my head. I've successfully tuned out all the troubles we'll face tomorrow with the police over Ava, and I'm reveling in the memory of my first visit here and how far we've come since then. It's a memory made complete when we spot Jacob waiting for us on this side of the front desk, looking every bit the unapproachable security person, in his dark suit and earpiece, as he had then.

"Welcome home, Mr. Merit," he greets, glancing at me to add, "Ms. McMillan."

I grin at him and he arches a brow. "Something I missed?"

"No," I assure him. "Something *I* missed: you, greeting us all stoic and formal in that way you do. It feels like home."

"I wasn't aware I was being stoic," he says, looking positively stoic.

"Like the Terminator, but you don't have a big gun," Chris jokes.

I give a snort of laughter that Jacob doesn't seem to notice. He levels Chris with a stare and with a completely straight face says, "It's against company policy to utilize big guns at work. Though while I'm doing contract work with Blake, anything goes."

Barely holding back another snort, I lift my hands. "Way too much man talk for me."

Chris chuckles and kisses my cheek.

The name of the private investigator, who's been looking into both Rebecca's and Ella's disappearances, ties my stomach in knots. "Speaking of Blake," I say, trying to sound nonchalant, though I suddenly feel anxious about tomorrow's appointment at the police station, "anything new from him on Ava, Rebecca, or Ella while we were airborne?"

"Nothing I've been made aware of," Jacob says.

Chris angles me toward the elevator and tells Jacob, "We need sleep. Pretend we aren't here."

I turn to say, "Unless you hear from Blake."

"But it had better be important," Chris adds as the elevator opens and we step inside.

Suspicious that Chris knows something he isn't telling me, I wait until the door closes to confront him. "If you or Jacob know anything and you aren't telling me—"

He cuts me off by shackling my wrists and pulling me to him, aligning our hips and legs with an intimate caress down my backside. "I know nothing you don't know," he promises. "Remember what we said in Paris, baby." He spreads his fingers on my cheek, his thumb stroking a seductive line along my jaw, his voice lower and deeper as he adds, "No secrets. No in between."

The air around us thickens, and Chris is the driving force. His mood has darkened, doing one of those wicked one-eighty shifts I've come to know and expect from him. No longer is he playful and light—but I'm no longer those things, either. Now we are electric, with a dark current running between us that is raw and carnal, yet soft and sensual.

Chris strokes my hair, dragging his hand down my neck, my shoulder, my arm, and I can almost feel the nerve endings in my body flickering to life, welcoming him and the pleasure he so masterfully arouses in me. But when my eyes meet his, there's more than the punch of awareness I expect. In the depths of those gorgeous deep green eyes, I find something I don't understand; something even more intense than the thrum of arousal burning in my belly.

Uncertainty maybe? Vulnerability? Yes. No. I'm confused, yet I know that I see nothing that Chris doesn't choose for me to see.

The elevator dings, and I jerk around to face the exit that leads directly into our apartment. Like the first night I came here, I have an inescapable sense that once I pass through the door, I'll never be the same again. Life will never be the same.

I realize Chris isn't touching me anymore. He wasn't touching me that night, either. It's as if he feels I have to make the decision to move forward on my own, and some part of me knows why. He needs to know now that home with him is still home to me. It reminds me of why we connect, why we are those missing pieces of a puzzle that have found a perfect fit. No matter how perfect his being imperfect makes him to me, he will never see himself as I do. He will never feel he is not flawed. He will always need me to be his eyes, and he is mine.

I walk into the apartment, the glossy, light wood beneath my feet. Our suitcases are already sitting by the entryway, brought up from the service entrance. Intentionally repeating what I'd done during that first visit here, feeling that's what he wants, I travel down the steps to the sunken living room. I drop my purse on top of the coffee table as I pass and keep going until I stand in front of the floor-to-ceiling window. Flattening my hands on the glass, watching the orange glow of the sun fade into the water, I see the stars begin to illuminate a city as shrouded in secrets as Chris and I once were. But now our blank canvas is inked with colors, not fears, and love has blossomed where there was once only passion.

Music begins to play and I smile when I hear "Broken" by Lifehouse, amazed that Chris would actually remember the song he'd played that first night we were together. *I'm falling apart,* the lyrics say. *I'm barely breathing.* I'm not falling apart, but as Chris steps behind me, his heat radiating through me, I am definitely barely breathing.

He caresses my coat off my shoulders, and this replay of the past sends an erotic thrill down my spine. As his hands fall away from me my lashes lower, my breath hitching as I anticipate his touch, waiting, wanting, until finally his hands settle possessively on my waist. He leans into me, and the feel of the thick ridge of his erection against my backside is impossibly arousing. A delicate, enticing brush of his fingers sweeping hair from my neck follows and rolls over me like a warm sun expanding through a newly open blind.

"Put your hands on the glass above you," he orders softly.

The command thrills me, and the temptation to do as he bids, to relive our first night together, is a powerful one. Yet I have the unnerving sensation of also reliving the uncertainty I'd thought we were beyond. I don't understand this feeling, and I don't like it.

Desperate to drive it away, I turn to face him, momentarily overwhelmed by how tall and broad, how perfectly male he is. And as I blink instead of speak, he claims control again. He presses me against the window, his powerful thighs frame my legs, his hands brand my hips.

His head tilts, the stubble of his jaw rasping deliciously on my skin, as he announces, "I'm going to fuck you against the window again."

Please. Yes. Don't make me beg, I think, and the rest of the world begins to slide away. There is only this man, the blistering heat he creates in me, and the foggy certainty that I'd had something important to say. He nips my earlobe, erotically licking away the pinch he's created, his hands traveling upward, over my rib cage, his fingers brushing the curves of my breasts.

My nipples tighten and the low thrum he's created in my sex, over hours of verbal teasing, blossoms and intensifies. "Chris," I whisper, a plea for more in my voice. For him. I want him, all of him.

"Hands over your head," he orders again.

No In Between

I want to obey. Being at this man's mercy is the biggest adrenaline rush of my life, but that feeling is clawing at me again, the sense that all is not right. Leaning into him, I ball my fingers around his shirt, and search his handsome, unreadable face. "Are we okay?"

Surprise flashes in his eyes, followed by that indefinable emotion again that I want to call vulnerability but isn't. I don't know what it is. He cups my face. "I need you too damn much for there to be any other answer."

"Then why do you feel just out of reach to me?"

"I'm not. I'm right here, and I'm bleeding for you every which way."

I don't understand the deep cut in his words, even less than I understand whatever emotion he's battling. "What does that mean?"

He drops his head back between his shoulder blades, tension rolling off of him. Seconds tick by like hours and he finally lowers his tormented gaze to mine. "I'm still thinking about last night. I'm still living it."

"What does that mean?" I say again.

"I don't know what it means," he confesses. "That's the problem. That's my fear."

"Chris, you're confusing me. Make me understand."

"When you came to the club after Dylan died, I was out of my own skin, damn near out of my head. Had I stayed, I don't know what I would have done to you—or with you."

"So that's it." I remember him telling me he used to be like Amber, that he still is, in many ways. "Amber's meltdown made you worry that you might melt down again."

11

"I will. I'm a ticking time bomb. Eventually it's going to happen."

"You don't know that."

"I do. I always knew, but I denied it. But no more. We're going to have to eventually deal with it."

That "we" relaxes my spine. My hands settle on his arms, my eyes seek his. "I'm not afraid."

"I know."

But he still is, and that's the real problem. We still have that damn whip trying to split us apart.

The intercom buzzer sounds and Chris straightens, running a rough hand through his hair. Curious and concerned about the reason for the interruption, I listen anxiously as Chris punches the intercom button and growls, "This better be important."

"Detective Grant is here," Jacob replies. "He's insisting I let him come up."

Adrenaline surges through me and I rush up the stairs to stand by Chris. "Why is he here? We aren't supposed to be at the police station until tomorrow afternoon for questioning."

Chris holds up a hand to me and replies to Jacob, "Tell him we'll see him tomorrow. And call Blake to make sure there isn't anything new I need to know about."

"Consider him handled," Jacob confirms.

Chris releases the intercom and turns to me, his hands sliding down my arms. "Deep breaths, baby. It's okay. Most likely he was trying to corner us to get more details without David present."

"Why would he want to avoid our attorney? And don't we look suspicious if we don't talk to him?"

"That's what he hopes we'll think, but we don't have anything to hide, so why would we care what he thinks? He expects smart people with good attorneys to decline to talk to him."

"And that's my point. We did nothing wrong. *I'm* the one Ava attacked and tried to kill. Why would he try to corner us?"

"Probably pretty normal with any high profile suspect, but I'm calling David to be sure."

He tugs his cell phone from his pocket, returning to the living area to face the window, and I force myself to sit down on the edge of the couch. Though I listen closely, hoping to understand his conversation with David, I can't.

Finally, he ends the call and sits next to me, dragging my legs over his lap. "David says there's a bail adjustment hearing set for Ava this Friday. They'll likely ask all available witnesses to testify."

I rest my elbows on the leather arm behind me. "What's a bail adjustment hearing?"

"Her counsel is asking to have the bond reduced, and this format allows them a little more room for testimony than a standard bail hearing."

"She could get out?"

"Let's hope not."

My heart sinks. "So yes."

"They held her the first time. Hopefully they'll have the ammunition to hold her this time. We should learn more at the police station tomorrow."

"Does that mean we should have talked to the detective tonight?"

"No. David wants to be with us. They haven't told him enough for him to feel comfortable with where the conversation is heading. He also stressed that this is an election year, which means the DA is in reelection mode."

"Which is motivation to solve the case and get a conviction."

"Yes. It is."

I wait, expecting him to say more and when he doesn't, reality slowly comes to me, turning my stomach as it does. "A conviction at all costs—even a fall guy."

"I'd like to think the DA is more ethical than that."

His phone beeps and he answers it, once again listening intently. "Just call me when you reach him," is all he says before he sets his phone on the coffee table. "Jacob can't get ahold of Blake. He'll call us when he does. He's also trying to reach Mark for us since the bastard won't return my calls."

"So we're in limbo, waiting for answers."

"Yes, but at least we do it together." He drags me to him and I snuggle against the hard lines of his body, my head resting on his chest, my mind counting the beat of his heart. *Together,* I repeat in my mind. I close my eyes and repeat those words over and over.

Two

Blinking awake, I find myself captured in Chris's beautiful green-eyed stare, slowly becoming aware of my back against the couch cushion, and the intimate way our jean-clad legs twine together. "Hey," I murmur, trailing fingers over the sexy stubble shadowing his jawline.

"Hey."

"I could really get used to waking up next to you every day."

He closes his hand over my fingers and kisses them. "I hope you already are."

My lips curve. "I want more practice. Lots more. How long did we sleep?"

"About twelve hours."

"What?" I jerk upward onto my elbow, swiping the messy dark brown veil of hair from my eyes to squint against the sunlight beaming through the wall of windows. "How is it even possible that it's daylight and we never made it to bed? We still have our clothes on."

"I took our shoes off about three hours ago, when you woke up and went to the bathroom."

"I went to the bathroom?"

He laughs. "Yes. I planned to move to the bedroom when you got back, but apparently I fell asleep."

"I don't remember any of that. Did I sleep through any callbacks from Blake or Mark, too?"

"No calls from anyone." He reaches to the coffee table and double-checks his phone before setting it back down. "Nope. Nothing."

"Why hasn't Blake called you?"

"I'm guessing he has nothing new to tell us and didn't want to wake us up for no reason. It's only eight in the morning."

"I suppose that makes sense—but Mark's ignoring us doesn't. We've been trying to reach him for days now. I was really hoping he'd give us some insight on how the police are handling the case before this afternoon." I half climb over Chris to grab my purse from the coffee table.

"Knee, baby," he grumbles, grabbing my leg. "Knee."

"Oops, sorry," I say and quickly snatch my phone, checking the caller ID as I settle back beside him. "No one called me, either. Hmmm. The only two full-time staff members left at the gallery are Amanda and Ralph. Maybe I can catch Ralph, and he can tell us what is going on with Mark." I start to punch in the gallery's number but hesitate, worried about what I'll say if he asks questions when he calls back. *If* he calls back. No one seems to want to talk to us right now. "How much do you think the gallery staff knows about what's going on?"

"I talked to David and Blake right before we left Paris, and both confirmed that nothing outside of Ricco and Mary's arrest has gone public."

"I thought this kind of thing always made the press."

"The police can seal the file in the public relations department, and apparently they've done that here. David says the DA doesn't want an unsolved missing person's case with the word 'murder' floating around, until they have a certain conviction."

Murder. My heart twists and I quickly shove the word aside before it starts messing with my mind, too. "I wonder what Mark has told the staff, if anything. I guess I'll leave a message for Ralph and hope that by the time he gets in, we hear something more from Blake or Mark."

"Leave your message," he says. "I'll stay busy while I wait." He drags me to the center of the couch, the deliciously heavy weight of him settling on top of me.

"Hmmm," I murmur, as the thick ridge of his erection presses into my belly, "apparently my knee didn't hurt you all that badly." I indicate my cell phone and hit the auto-dial. "Behave. I'm making my call."

"Whatever you want," he promises, and I'm pretty sure he's not talking about my call when his hands caress from my waist to my breasts.

"Stop that," I chide. "The line is ringing."

Undeterred, he shoves my T-shirt up my belly, his fingers teasing the delicate skin he's exposed.

"Stop," I demand, shoving my fingers into his wildly sexy blond hair to hold him steady, and dragging the burn of his stare to mine.

"No," he replies simply.

"Yes."

"Yes is a good answer," he agrees, and despite my grip on his hair, he manages to slide his thumb between my thighs and turn the seam of my jeans into an erotic distraction.

My lashes flutter with the heat licking at my sex, and I can't help but think of *him* licking me there. Somehow I still hear the options for the answering service menu, and I release Chris to hit the button to bypass them and get to Ralph. Chris embraces the opportunity to unsnap my jeans and tug down the zipper. And when his mouth comes down on the newly bared spot, his tongue dipping into my belly button, Ralph's voice comes on the line at the same time, and I can't manage to form words, let alone coherent speech.

Chris reaches for my phone and I grab it. "No. I have to call back."

"Call back when they open." He takes my cell from me and tosses it onto the chair to my right. "We have too many hours to kill before the meeting for you to stress this much."

"Time we need to use to get some answers."

"And that answer will be 'yes' when I cue you to say it." He pulls my jeans down my hips, taking my panties with them.

"Try to call Blake first, Chris."

He tosses my jeans as he had my phone, and starts skimming my T-shirt up my rib cage. "When we're done here." He unhooks my bra, covering my breasts with his hands, his fingers teasing my nipples, bending down to lick one of the stiff, aching peaks. "Any problem with that plan?"

"Problem?" I ask breathlessly. "What problem?"

His lips curve and he rolls my T-shirt the rest of the way up and over my head. I try to lower my hands but he holds them over my head. "Keep them there. Move them and I'll dish out that punishment I never did last night." He drags his hand over my bare breasts, plucking roughly at my nipples, and I feel the spikes of pleasure all the way to my sex.

Adrenaline rushes through me, part fear of the unknown, part white-hot arousal. "Punish me how?" I demand, my legs clenching around his hips of their own accord.

His gaze does a hot swipe of my puckered nipples and heavy, swollen breasts before lifting to mine. "We covered the list of possibilities on the plane yesterday."

Heat zips through me with the memory of those whispered promises, all of which had been intimidatingly out of my comfort zone, and ever so arousing. "Yes. We did."

He widens my legs, his fingers sliding into the slick, wet heat of my body, his thumb stroking my nub. "Do you want my mouth here?"

"Yes," escapes my lips.

"What if I tell you that if you come before I say you can, the price will be me choosing one of those punishments I'm considering?"

I laugh, a throaty, nervous rasp and remind him, "We've been down this path before. I'll fail. In fact, at this very moment, if you breathe wrong—or right—I'll come."

That sexy, evil mouth of his curves with satisfaction. "Then maybe we should move right to the punishment."

Nerves rush through me, mixed with enough adrenaline to make me tremble. Or maybe, that's just *him* making me tremble. "I deserve the orgasm if I'm getting the punishment," I manage to argue.

He laughs, and it sounds naughty and dominant, as if he's already decided which of those wicked promises he made to me on the plane he's going to fulfill. "Let's see how ready you really are," he murmurs, slipping a finger inside of me, then another, and stroking a line of pleasure as he does. I fight the arch of my hips, the burn of release, and he seems to understand, to know. "You can have your orgasm, baby," he promises, "but if you move your hands, then I'll punish you." He curves his hand around my backside and lifts me into the pump of his fingers. "Understood?"

"Yes," I pant. "Yes." I barely know what I'm agreeing to, for the tiny darts of pleasure the stroke of his fingers are shooting through every part of me.

"Good." He leans down and kisses my belly, then I feel the flicker of his tongue on the swollen buds of my nipples. "There is only punishment," he murmurs against my skin, pausing for a moment to add, "Or no punishment."

Punishment or no punishment. The words replay in my mind, and unbidden, so does Rebecca's journal entry. *You know I have to punish you.* I never understood why she'd describe Mark saying this to her as being so addictive, but I do now. I feel the same dread and desire she'd described with him, the ache that is fear and lust in one breath.

Chris's shoulders nudge my knees, his hot breath rasping over my swollen clit, and the anticipation inside me is almost too much to bear. I actually start to move my hands and pull him to me but catch myself. If I defy him, I know my punishment will begin with the denial of his mouth, and I want his mouth. Desperately.

More of his hot breath strokes over me and his tongue whispers over my inner thigh, and I have to dig my fingers into the leather arms to keep them in place. He's taunting me, trying to get me to do what he has forbidden me. But I don't. I won't. I am waiting for the ultimate reward, and finally it comes.

His warm mouth closes down over my clit and it's as if the hard ball of tension nestled inside me is unleashed, only to snap back in place all over again. Now I have his mouth, his tongue, but I crave that sweet, perfect moment when everything around me explodes into pleasure. And it's close, so very close. His tongue is magic, rolling my clit, licking and swirling, while his fingers pump into me. I am without inhibitions, panting, moving with him, so on edge I feel I'll crack into pieces. He's keeping me there on purpose, slowing when I need him to speed up, moving when I need him to stay. I can't take it anymore. I reach for him, my hand coming down on his head, and just like that, he stops what he is doing. I gasp, reaching for him, but it's too late for me to turn back, to change what I have done.

He hovers over me, his eyes meeting mine. "I told you not to move."

"I know, but—"

"No buts. Punishment or no punishment. Those were the options." Surprising me, he turns me over and drags me to my knees, pulling my backside up into the air. My heart races and adrenaline surges with the certainty that the punishment is coming.

Suddenly his bare hand smacks my bottom, the sting of it shocking me, radiating over my skin and up my spine. I gasp and arch my back, and it's a mistake. I move into the next smack of his palm, creating more impact, more burn. Somehow I remember what he'd taught me, and I start counting with the next smack of his hand. Three, four, five. I hold my breath for the sixth that never comes.

Chris flips me over again, pressing me into the couch with the weight of his body, his fingers wrapping the long strands of my hair. For several seconds we breathe together, the air charged around us, electric, powerful. I can feel this man in every part of me, in every pore, every nerve ending. And when his mouth slants over mine, hot and hard, an unapologetic reprimand that says he has absolute control, I have never wanted to be kissed so badly in my entire life. He owns me and there is no part of me capable of denying him that claim. No part of me that rejects it or believes it to be untrue. There is simply only what he can take from me. My submission.

I'm panting when he tears his mouth from mine and releases my hair to slide down my body. He settles between my legs and I whimper as his mouth comes down on my clit. He sucks and licks, sending tantalizing sensations to every part of me. And this time he takes me where I want to go and I am lost, ripe for the release almost upon me. He licks me one last time and my sex clenches around his fingers, every muscle in my body tensing before the pleasure finally rolls over me.

Everything is a wash of sensations where nothing else exists. I slowly come back to reality, gasping with the aftermath of what he has just done to me.

Chris starts to move away and I reach for him, trying to pull him back. "Wait. Please." And just like that, I'm picked up and thrown over his shoulder, his hand settling on my backside, where he squeezes my cheek roughly. My heart races with the certainty that he intends to spank me again, and my breath stops in my lungs.

He enters our bathroom, flips on the light, and deposits me on the white-tiled counter. Then he walks to the shower and turns it on, pulling off his shirt in the process. My gaze devours the ripples of his muscular back, and the way his dragon ink flexes with the movement. He is power and control. He is pure male dominance. He is my future husband, and there's something so damn sexy about the idea of being this man's wife.

He turns to face me, his eyes pure, white-hot lust. He unbuttons his jeans and slides them down his powerful legs, and I am aware of every inch of his perfect, rock-hard body.

"Come here," he commands, and I don't even hesitate. He's accused me of enjoying his control, and he's right. I not only like it, I crave it, freely offering him the submission I would never consider with anyone else.

Pushing off of the counter, aroused by the slight sting of my backside, I cross the space between us and when I stand before him, my body trembles with how much I need his touch. It feels as if I haven't had it in years, not mere seconds.

I expect him to deny me, to make me wait, but in one of those mood shifts, tenderness softens his eyes and face. The next thing I know, he's dragging me into the shower and into an embrace.

My hand flattens on his chest. "You spanked me. And you didn't warn me."

He presses me against the wall. "Why do you think that is?"

He is dark again, on edge, and taking me with him and I stumble over my reply. "I . . . I don't know."

"Because if I melt down again, there won't be a warning. You have to be prepared for that. *We* have to be prepared."

My heart squeezes with understanding. He's not pushing me away because of Amber. He's pulling me closer. I wrap my arms around him. "We will be."

"We *have* to be," he stresses again, molding me to him, holding me a little too tightly, as if he's afraid of losing me. So I hold him a little too tightly because he needs me to.

It's nearly noon when I emerge from the bedroom to find Chris staring out of the window while he talks on the phone. He's in black Diesel jeans, a matching Diesel T-shirt, and biker boots I helped him pick out in Paris, and he's holding a cup of coffee. The stiffness of his spine and the tension in his shoulders make me wonder if he slept much less last night than he'd let on. And if he's worried a whole lot more than he lets on about our meeting today.

I move to sit on the overstuffed brown leather chair across from him and he turns, ending his call. His eyes light on me, the sunlight capturing the flecks of amber in his eyes and turning them golden. He moves toward me, his stride casual, his scalding inspection of my black skirt and V-neck sweater pure predator.

He claims the ottoman in front of me, his hand settling on my knee, fingers resting at the top of my boots. "You look good, baby," he says, heat roughening his voice.

Some of that heat seems to rush to my cheeks. "Thank you. I thought I should be professional for the meeting."

"Dress to impress yourself, not them." His eyes twinkle with the mischief I so adore and he says, "Undress to impress me." I try to smile, failing miserably, and Chris notices instantly. "Hey," he says, caressing my cheek. "Ease up, baby. This meeting is nothing to worry about."

I search his face, looking for tension, but it's not there. Maybe I'd imagined it. "We're going into this blind, and that bothers me. Mark won't call us back. Neither has Ralph, though I left him two messages. Blake and David had nothing new to tell us. There *has* to be a reason the detective came here last night. And please tell me that was David on the phone."

"Obviously I need to cut you off at two cups of coffee, you're going a million miles an hour," he teased. "And no, it wasn't David. It was the jeweler I told you about. I sketched a ring design I plan to show you, but I wanted to be sure he could work with what I had in mind."

"You sketched a ring for me?" I ask, thrilled. "I'll have a Chris Merit original on my finger!"

"And in your bed," he teases. "But yes. I sketched a ring. I have a few finishing touches to put on it and then I'll show you."

A glow comes over me. Somehow, Chris has managed to wipe away everything wrong and make everything absolutely right. I lean in and press my hands to his cheeks. "Designing my ring is the most amazing gift you could give me."

His lips curve and he covers my hands with his, drawing them between us. "Let's hope you think so when you see it."

"You know I will. I don't want to wait to see it. Can I just have a peek? Please? I don't care that it's not finished."

He stands up and pulls me with him. "After the meeting with the police."

The announcement is like a blast of winter air. "Right," I say, swallowing a knot of reality. "The meeting."

"David wants to meet with us at a coffee shop by the police station beforehand, but we still have plenty of time before we have to head that way. Why don't we run by the gallery and see what we can find out about Mark? Maybe that'll put you more at ease."

"Yes," I agree quickly. "I think that's a good idea." And *it is* a good idea, so why is my stomach suddenly twisting and turning?

"Ralph and Amanda are going to ask questions," he warns.

"So are the police. It'll be good practice, and I'll feel better going to the station as knowledgeable as we can get."

He gives me a keen inspection. "You're sure?"

"Yes," I say. "I'm sure." He doesn't look convinced and my stomach gives an extra jolt. Some part of me doesn't want to return to the gallery, and I don't know why.

Like the thorns on the roses he loves to give me, I welcome the pain of the flogger biting into my back. It is the escape from all that I've lost, all that I've seen and done, and regret doing. He gives this to me. He is my drug. The pain is my drug. It ripples through me and I feel nothing but the bitter bite of leather and the sweet silk of the darkness and pleasure that follows.

Rebecca Mason

Three

I can't tell if Ava's coffee shop is open as we turn down the alleyway behind the gallery. I don't know why I even care, but considering the way my stomach starts flip-flopping at the sight of the Cup O' Café sign, I obviously do. Maybe *it's* the reason some part of me didn't want to come here—or rather, Ava is. She's the reason we're all living through hell. She's the monster who murdered Rebecca and who almost put me in my own grave.

Fortunately, it's only a few moments later that Chris parks the 911 in the lot behind the gallery and gives me other things to think about. "That's Ralph's car," I say, indicating a black Camry, the only other car in the lot. "Amanda takes the bus, but any interns would park back here, as would any sales staff. I wonder who's running this place in Mark's absence?"

Chris shoves open his door and sets one booted foot on the pavement. "I'm guessing that with all that he has going on, your departure, and Mary in jail, there isn't much to run. Blake says the gallery's been closed to the public all week. Can you call the reception desk and see if they can let us in?"

I punch in the number and get the answering service. Chris walks around the Porsche and opens my door as I leave Ralph yet another message on his private line. "No luck," I say, letting Chris help me out of the car. "Maybe my security code still works."

Looking less than optimistic, Chris shoves the sleek black leather of his jacket aside, resting his hands on his hips. "Under normal circumstances, I'd say there's no way in hell Mark would make that kind of a slip. But there's nothing normal about any of this."

A gust of cold wind blasts us and I huddle into my black trench coat. "I'm ready to be inside," I exclaim, making a dash for the building. At the door Chris steps close, using his big body to block the wind, and I key in my code—to receive a beep of rejection.

"The front door it is," Chris concludes, taking my elbow. "Hopefully we can flag someone through the glass."

We cut down the side of the building, thankfully out of the torture of the wind, to find the Closed sign in the gallery window. There are no lights on the showroom floor or any sign of life, but I start knocking and Chris joins in.

After ten frustrating minutes I'm ready to give up, when I see Amanda dash through the gallery inside. I wait at the door to greet her and the instant it's open, she flings her arms around my neck and bursts into tears.

I hug her, not sure what to make of the outburst. Amanda's young and rather timid, but she's never been overly dramatic or

emotional. "What's wrong, honey?" I ask, exchanging a concerned look with Chris.

Releasing me, she swipes at her damp cheeks. "Sorry.
Just . . ." Hesitating, she seems to register something important.
"Come inside," she says, grabbing my hand and pulling me for-
ward. "Before the press reappear and swarm us."

I enter the showroom with Chris on my heels, and my
stomach is remarkably calm. Amanda rushes to the door to lock
up again, and when she faces us again, she's a frazzled mess as
she swipes her long dark hair from her face. "You have no idea
how crazy it's been. We need to move away from the front. The
press take pictures from outside the window." She rushes toward
the back, and Chris and I fall in step behind her.

"I saw Ralph's car," I comment. "Is it just the two of you
here?"

"Yes," she confirms. "It's been just us for the whole week."

Chris moves ahead and holds the door to the offices open
for us. "Has Mark been in at all?" he asks as she starts to pass
him.

"No," she says. "His mom got a blood infection from her
cancer surgery. She's better now, but it was bad, I think."

Amanda enters the office area and I pause beside Chris,
whose grim expression isn't comforting. "You've heard of a
blood infection like that before?"

"Yes. I've seen it a few times since I started volunteering at
the Children's Hospital. It's never good."

"How not good?"

"It's always a fight for your life, with either full recovery or
no recovery at all."

"It sounds like she's out of trouble, though, right?"

"The way it would have lowered her immune system, when she's fighting cancer, could be an issue."

"That sure explains Mark's silence."

He nods and we step into the U-shaped office to find Amanda hovering by the reception desk to our right. "Ralph!" she shouts. "Come out here!"

Ralph appears in the doorway of his office just off of the main lobby, and the minute he sees me his eyes light up. "Sara!" he exclaims, holding his hands out and rambling in what I think is Chinese, before he rushes forward and hugs me. "Please tell me that you're here to help."

I lean back to give him a critical eye, and nowhere is the Ralph I know. His thick dark hair is rumpled, his royal-blue trademark bow tie is falling off, his white shirt is wrinkled, and his dark-rimmed glasses are tilted. "This is a first," I say.

His brow furrows. "I've hugged you before."

"I mean the messy clothes and the Chinese. And why didn't you return my calls?"

He scrubs his head. "My voice mail's backed up. It's been a bitch around here. We're just trying to survive."

"Tell them why you're talking in Chinese," Amanda encourages, but doesn't give him time to reply. "When he talks to the press, he alternates between senseless fortune cookie sayings and Chinese."

Ralph shrugs. "It makes them hang up." He glances at Chris, his tone glowing with appreciation. "Hello, Mr. Merit. So nice to see you. I hope you didn't come to pull your art, like others have. Of course, Ricco doesn't count."

"No," Chris says, crossing his arms in front of his chest. "I'm not pulling my art, but I do want to get this place up and running again. Ricco stopped by? He's out of jail?"

"His attorney called," Ralph explains. "I'm not sure where Ricco himself is. I can't keep up with things here, let alone anything past our doors."

Amanda drops dramatically into the chair behind the reception desk. "It's been the worst week of my life."

I frown, still focused on Ralph. "But Ricco didn't have any work at the gallery. He pulled it all after Rebecca left."

"I know," Ralph confirms. "That's what made the whole thing strange. His attorney didn't seem to know the facts."

"You said the press keeps calling?" Chris asks, and he's obviously thinking what I am. That wasn't Ricco's attorney that called. It was a member of the press.

"And coming by," Ralph adds. "Everyone wants to know about Mary being arrested for selling counterfeit art. Having our salesperson do such a thing doesn't exactly instill confidence in the public. Having a famous artist like Ricco Alvarez help her? Even less. Our customers and the talent are both dropping like flies."

"It's the Rebecca questions that are the hardest for me," Amanda adds. "The press is asking about her. They push hard, and even if Mark would let us talk about her, I really can't. All I know is that she left and she's supposed to return. I guess they think she was involved, too."

Unbelievably, Mark has left them completely in the dark. "I know it's hard," I say. "Isn't the phone set on the answering service? Why are you talking to reporters at all?"

"They trick us," she replies. "They leave messages and pretend to be customers."

This seems to confirm my suspicion that Ralph talked to a reporter, not Ricco's attorney.

"Has Mark given you any idea when he'll be able to return, or bring in help?" Chris asks.

Ralph snorts. "He's not even returning our calls. We have to talk to Crystal Smith now."

"Who's that?" I ask.

"The name sounds remotely familiar," Chris comments. "I think I might have talked to her regarding one of my auction items at some point."

"I'd never heard of her before this week," Amanda replies. "She's the acting manager of Riptide while Mark's mother is out sick. She's the one who told us about the blood infection. He didn't. The last thing Mark told us was to organize a grand reopening party, but Crystal told us not to."

Chris scrubs his jaw, looking as puzzled as I feel. "She's overriding Mark?"

"He doesn't even let anyone else choose the coffee in this place," I add.

"Exactly," Ralph agrees. "King Bossman seems to be MIA. We have Queen Smith instead."

Just how hard had the past week hit Mark?

Chris's hand rests on the back of my neck. "Let's go talk a minute." He glances between Ralph and Amanda. "If you have any problems while we're here, come get one of us. We'll be in Sara's office."

He urges me forward, drawing my hand into his as he pulls

me into my old office. *Rebecca's old office.* I can smell her rose-scented candles that should long be faded, like a part of her lingers here.

"I'm concerned Mark's mother is far worse than they know," Chris says, after he shuts the door. "There's no other explanation for him letting the gallery spin out of control like this."

"That, and grief over Rebecca."

"I'm not going to pretend to understand the relationship he had with Rebecca. The end result is the same, and it's not good. This place is falling apart. I'm going to go to his office to look around."

"I'll call this Crystal Smith person."

Pausing at the door, he glances at his watch. "We need to leave within a half hour for our meeting with David."

I nod and he leaves, shutting me inside. Shrugging out of my coat, I toss it on the visitor's chair and sit behind the desk, already reaching for the phone when my gaze catches on a painting to the right of the door. The brilliant painting of roses by local artist Georgia O'Nay is from Mark's personal collection, chosen for Rebecca's wall for reasons representing their Master and submissive bond.

Emotions swell in my chest and I force them aside, grabbing the phone and punching the auto-dial to Riptide. "I need to speak to Mark Compton," I say when the receptionist answers.

"Just a moment," the woman replies without hesitation, and I hold my breath, waiting for that steely, commanding voice of his, only to hear a female say, "This is Crystal Smith. Can I help you?"

Disappointment fills me. "Ms. Smith. Hi. This is Sara Mc-Millan, and I—"

"Sara." There is a lift to her voice that almost sounds like excitement, though I can't understand how that could be. "Are you back in the States?"

"I . . . yes. You know who I am?"

"Of course. Though we didn't work together directly, I was very aware of your replacing Rebecca and taking her role with Allure."

Replacing Rebecca. The choice of words stabs me with such guilt that I slump forward and press my hand to my face. Replacing Rebecca. I took her life. I lived her life.

"Sorry," she says softly, seeming to read my discomfort, or perhaps I'd been silent longer than I realized. "That was a poor choice of words."

"You said nothing wrong," I say, and it hits me that her sensitivity has to mean she knows more than the rest of the staff, but I'm afraid to say more and assume incorrectly. "The reason I'm calling is that I'm here at Allure. I've been trying to reach Mark and had hoped he'd be here."

"He's been by his mother's side pretty much around the clock the past few days. She's doing better now, but it was a rough ride."

"So she's okay?"

"As okay as someone battling stage-three cancer who just recovered from a blood infection can be."

Recovered. That's a good word. "Right. Of course. Do you know his plans here? He's not even talking to the staff."

"No." She hesitates and there's a weird tension in the air

before she says, "I offered to switch places with him and run Al-lure while he's here in New York, but I guess there are reasons he has to be there as well. He won't really talk to me."

"Mark doesn't talk to anyone."

"Yes. I can see that." She hesitates again. "Look, Sara. I don't want to pressure you. Actually"—she laughs awkwardly—"I really *do* want to pressure you. I know you quit the gallery, but will you please come back to work for a few weeks?"

I blink, confused. "Did Mark ask you to talk to me?"

"No. I meant it when I said he's not talking to me." There's a strain in her voice that rings oddly personal, when Mark is personal with no one. But then, Mark is doing a lot of things I don't expect this week. "Please help," she adds. "He needs to heal and so does his mother."

"How well do you know his mother?" I ask, curious about what feels more and more like her personal bond with the family.

"She hired me, and she's—" her voice cracks—"she's a spe-cial person. And a stubborn crazy woman when she wants to be. I have to handle everything well or she'll be trying to work through her chemo treatments.

"Amanda and Ralph are in over their heads," she continues, "and I've been handling all the angry artists, crazy reporters, and customers who insist on talking to management. I need help. I can't run Riptide and Allure at the same time."

Mark's checked out. Totally, completely, checked out. His mother must be worse than we know. Maybe even worse than Crystal knows. "I can't make any promises," I hedge, wanting to help but unsure of what I can do with this investigation going

37

on. "I have to go to a meeting. Do you have a number I can call you back at?"

"Of course, but Mark is headed out there tonight. We should talk before he arrives and come up with a plan that he'll accept."

So Mark *isn't* just handing her the power. She's taking it, and the two of us teaming up are destined to go toe-to-toe with Bossman in a big way before this is over. "I'll call you back tonight," I promise. "What time do you leave?" A knock sounds on my door and Ralph pokes his head in, holding up a newspaper.

"Let me give you my cell," Crystal offers as he dashes to my desk, sets the paper down, and leaves again. "And I don't care what time it is. Whatever works for you," she adds, "I don't sleep much anyway."

We exchange numbers and end the call. Setting the phone back into the cradle, my gaze lands on the newspaper headlines Ralph obviously wanted me to see: Local Art Gallery Paints a Masterpiece of Scandal. I grab the paper and begin to read.

One employee is deep in the midst of a counterfeiting scandal, with renowned artist Ricco Alvarez her partner or perhaps the mastermind of her efforts, while another employee of the gallery is completely missing. Where is Rebecca Mason? Did she flee involvement in the scandal, or is she a victim of a darker, more menacing cover-up?

I quickly scan the article. There's no mention of Ava at all, or of her attack on me. In fact, it's a rather uninformed article that says little to nothing. But what breaks my heart is the photo of Rebecca. It's the same shot of her that's on the Allure website, her long brown hair shiny and sleek to her shoulders, a huge, happy smile on her face. She was so like Ella, young and just starting out in life, and now she is gone . . . like Ella. I'm afraid for Ella, and with each day that passes, I worry more that she will never return. I don't want her to end up dead like Rebecca.

Dead. There is that word I've avoided and out of nowhere, it throws me into a memory I don't want to relive. I'm back at the hospital after my mother's heart attack, and I stand in the waiting room, waiting for the doctor. I can see the blue cloth seats lining the wall, hear the cartoons that some man has been watching for hours. There's a woman with her knees to her chest in a seat in the corner, and some sort of flute music comes from the speakers. The doctor enters the room and all of us stand up, but his eyes are on me. His eyes are brown. His hair is black. He is pale as he walks toward me.

I'm sorry. We tried everything and she fought hard, but your mother didn't make it.

My eyes burn with a memory I haven't relived so completely in years, and suddenly the sweetness of the rose scent clinging to the room is overwhelming, and I feel like I'm about to be sick. I grab the trash can, desperately willing the sickness to pass. What's wrong with me? I never get sick.

The door opens, and I don't have to look up to know it's Chris. Even like this, I feel that current that he brings with him into a room, but I can't seem to lift my head.

He kneels beside me and his hand settles on my knee,

feeling warm and deeply right. "Hey," he murmurs softly. "What happened, baby? Are you okay? Talk to me."

Talk to me. He says that often, and I like that. I like that he listens to me and he cares. He's so a part of me that I don't know what I'd do if I lost him, like my mother. Like I fear I've lost Ella.

"Sara, baby. I need to know you're okay."

"I am," I manage to whisper. "I just suddenly felt sick. It came out of nowhere, but it's passing."

"Do you need a drink?"

"No." I manage to straighten. "I'm okay."

His gaze catches on the desk and he grabs the newspaper, reading what I had minutes before. "You got sick suddenly, huh?" He tosses it back on the desk. "After reading that article?"

"I was supposed to be filling in for her." My voice trembles. "She was supposed to come back."

He takes my hand and draws my knuckles to his lips. "I know. Believe me, baby. I know."

"I know you said the DA is keeping most of this under wraps, but I worry that means there's a problem we don't know about. Did you find anything in Mark's office?"

"He cleaned out his files, so either he's not planning on coming back anytime soon or he's protecting his records in case anyone digs around." He glances at his watch. "We need to go if you're able?"

"Yes, I'm okay now. I don't know why reading that affected me like it did."

Pushing to his feet, he helps me to mine. "Jet lag and stress can be a wicked combination."

"I talked to Crystal. Mark's on his way here tonight. She says he's been by his mother's side constantly. She asked me to come back to the gallery for a few weeks, and I need to do it. It feels like the right thing to do."

Chris studies me for a long moment, before he reaches up, gently sliding hair behind my ear. "Then we'll come back."

"We?"

"I'm not leaving you here alone with Mark."

"If this is about what I told you in Paris—"

"It absolutely has everything to do with it. I want to help him, and we will. But I won't forget that when I was at my weakest, he tried to convince you that he could fuck me out of your system. I don't trust him."

I give a choppy nod. "I know. He's broken."

"I am, too, but at least I admit it. And I know how powerful pain is. It can drive you insane and it can make you do things you never thought you were capable of doing. Never, *ever*, underestimate it. Never, Sara." He molds me close. "Do you understand what I'm saying to you?"

He's not talking about Mark anymore. He's talking about him, and us, and where he's been and fears he will take me. "Yes. I understand."

41

Four

―――⁓―――

Our attorney looks like Vin Diesel in a suit. As he sits down at our table at the coffee shop by the police station he says into his phone, "Hell no, we aren't coming at two fifteen." He glances at his Rolex. "It's one forty-five now and our meeting is set for three. This is a power play meant to make my clients feel unsettled, and I'm not in the mood for this shit. And don't ask them the bullshit questions we talked about." He pauses a second and then snorts. "Yeah right. Whatever, Detective."

"Assholes. All of them," he grumbles, tucking his phone into his pocket and glancing at Chris. "I'd shake your hand, but I wouldn't want to break your magic maker."

"You mean your moneymaker," Chris jokes back.

"Exactly," he agrees with a grin before turning to me and shoving his very large hand in my direction. "I'm David, but I guess you figured that out. Hope my crankiness didn't scare you."

"No," I say, shaking his hand. "You didn't scare me, but this whole process does."

"Leave it to me, sweetheart, and you'll be fine. I'll go Rocky on them if I have to." He waves down a waitress and orders some triple-venti concoction. Then he says, "Let's get right to it. Ava has a bail adjustment hearing Friday morning. She hasn't made her bond, and she wants it reduced so she can be free until the trial. Of course, no one wants that to happen."

"But it could?" I ask.

"The police have a quandary," he explains. "They never want to let a murderer out of jail, but they can't charge a case they aren't sure will stick in court. And without a body, the odds of that are pretty low. So I predict they'll drop those charges and focus on the attack on you, Sara."

"She admitted she killed her," I argue. "How can that not be enough?"

"Crazy as it sounds," David replies, "a lot of people confess to crimes they didn't do. My insider at the station tells me that the police believe Ava is guilty, and they fully intend to hold her. They'll just need to prove she tried to kill you, and is therefore a danger to you and to society in general."

He pauses to chug a big gulp of the beverage the waitress set in front of him. "Bail hearings aren't overly complex, but at a hearing like this one, more details are allowed than usual. If the murder charges are dropped, Ava's people will say the attempted murder case has no more merit than the murder case did." He opens his briefcase and removes some sheets of paper, handing one to each of us. "This is my hot topic list that I think you might be asked about today, or in future interviews. Expect to be recorded."

I scan the list and feel like I've been punched in the stomach.

1. What is your BDSM involvement?
2. How intimate was Sara with Mark?
3. What about with Mark and Ava?
4. Was Chris intimate with Ava or Rebecca at any point?

This is going to feel like a public flogging.

At ten minutes to three, I'm sitting between Chris and David at a rectangular metal table inside a police interrogation room. Remembering David's warning that we'll be recorded, I say nothing as he and Chris talk sports. All the while, David sips from his third triple-caffeinated concoction from the coffee shop, and his foot and knee never stop moving up and down. He's making me a little nervous. Or maybe it's the unseen eyes I can feel staring at us from behind the one-way glass in front of us.

My cell phone beeps and I grab it, noting the text is from Amanda. She's tried to call me three times in the five minutes since we sat down, but the reception in here is horrible and the call keeps dropping.

"Amanda again?" Chris asks.

I nod. "A text this time." I hold my phone so that we can both read the message. A strange man is outside and he won't leave. He's sitting by the door. Ralph and I are afraid to go to our cars.

Chris reaches for his phone. "Tell her I'll send Jacob over, but she should also call the police."

"I could tell them here," I suggest, watching as Chris types a message to Jacob.

David axes that idea. "These guys won't be a help. It's faster if she calls."

I punch in Amanda's number and get yet another broken signal message while Chris's phone beeps with a text.

"It's the room," David says. "I find I can text but not talk. Step outside but be quick about it. They're making us squirm for a few minutes, but they'll be here anytime now."

I push to my feet and Chris shackles my arm. "Don't let anyone draw you into conversation. Tell them you can't talk without David present."

I nod and he releases me. Stepping outside the door, I enter a bullpen-like room that hums with voices and electronics, where about a dozen desks, some occupied and others not, fill the space. Random people mill around, some noticing me, most ignoring me.

Claiming one of the metal chairs lining the wall, I dial Amanda, who answers on the first ring, sounding breathless and urgent. "Sara."

"Yes. Are you okay?"

"Yes. For now. I'm sorry to bug you, but Crystal is in some meeting and this guy is creeping us out. I was afraid to call the police and bring more media attention."

"Chris is sending the head of security from our apartment building to you. His name is Jacob. Let him in when he gets there, but if you feel you're in danger, call 9-1-1."

"I'm not sure. He might just be a reporter. I don't want to make a big deal out of nothing, but Ralph and I are both creeped out."

"How long has he been there?"

"Not long after you left. "

I don't like how that sounds. "Don't take any chances. Jacob is only five minutes away. Text me when he gets there so I know you're okay."

"I will. Thank you."

I end the call and dial Jacob. "Please tell me you're almost at the gallery," I say when he answers.

"About a block away."

"Good. They say this guy has been hanging by the door since we left."

"I'll handle it," he assures me and when we end the call, I stand up, intending to return to the room. My skin prickles and a familiar surge of power I know can be from only one person washes over me. My gaze lifts and collides with the steely gray stare of Mark Compton. I am frozen, unable to move, unprepared to see him, though Crystal told me he was headed back here. But I am, and my blood is racing in reaction, my heart skipping random beats.

Another man in an expensive fitted suit, much like Mark's gray one, steps to Mark's side, his features ruggedly male, whereas Mark's are of a classical male beauty. And where Mark's classically clean-shaven and handsome, his short blond hair always neatly groomed, this man's thick, black hair is long enough to be tied at his nape, and the stubble on his jawline is much heavier than a shadow.

The man says something to Mark, and I get the feeling the stranger is his attorney. Mark barely acknowledges what's said to him, closing the distance between us with predatory grace: beautiful, powerful, impossible to ignore, and I am his prey.

I'm not immune to Mark's certain flavor of power and mas-
culinity, but being affected by his larger-than-life presence and
wanting him are two different things. It's a way Rebecca and I
differed, and I can't help remembering her words. *He was magnificent. Really, truly the most gorgeous man I've ever known. Instant
lust exploded inside me. I wanted to feel him close to me, to feel him
touch me. To touch him.*

She'd started out infatuated and then fell in love, and suddenly
I'm angry with Mark for not seeing what he had with her, before
he lost her. Even more for trying to push her away by involving
Ava and Ryan, and possibly others, in their intimate moments.

I step forward, stopping when we are toe-to-toe, but he
speaks before I do. "Ms. McMillan," he says in that low baritone
that's both sultry suggestion and hard steel.

I lift my chin and meet his stare, and I see the barely masked
heartache in the depths of those shrewd gray eyes. I see love lost,
and my anger is ripped right out of my chest. "Mark," I whisper,
bleeding for him, with him. "It's good to see you." Without any
conscious decision, I wrap my arms around him and press my
cheek to his chest. He doesn't hug me back but I don't care. It
kills me to realize that Rebecca finally taught Mark what it is to
love, and she'll never even know.

"Ms. McMillan," he warns tersely. "Now is not the time for
affection."

I step back and put my hands to my hips. "Why don't you
return our phone calls?"

His expression is unreadable, the pain I'd seen minutes before carefully banked. "I'm certain you're aware that I've had my
hands full."

The stranger joins us, his piercing blue eyes finding mine. "This is Tiger," Mark says. "My attorney."

"What is it with you men? Do you have a problem using a person's actual name?"

"You must be Sara," Tiger comments. "It's a name I earned, so it's the one I favor."

Taking the bait, I ask, "And how exactly did you earn it?"

"I'll rip your throat out if you cross my clients," he replies, and I don't like the subtle threat, real or imagined.

I narrow my eyes at him. "You said 'you must be Sara.' How did you know that?"

Mark answers, "I told him of your propensity for too much conversation."

"Does he know of your propensity for arrogance?" I challenge.

"He does," Mark confirms, his jaw flexing tightly.

I realize that I've hit a nerve of self-blame, a nerve that has to be raw. "I'm sorry," I say quickly. "It slipped out. I wasn't trying to hurt you."

He gives me one of those heavy-lidded looks. "Not a problem, Ms. McMillan. I also warned Tiger that you tend to be painfully honest."

"There's nothing wrong with honesty," Tiger comments.

I cut him an irritated look. "There is if it hurts someone." I turn toward Mark. "Can we talk alone for a minute?"

"No private conversation," Tiger replies.

I gape at Tiger. "You're protecting Mark from *me*?"

"I'm protecting you both from prying eyes," he says, his tone all business. "Save the hugs and personal conversation for elsewhere." He glances at his watch. "It's three. We need to get to our meeting room."

Three. It hits me now why the police wanted to move us to two fifteen. They were trying to prevent us from running into Mark, and I wonder why. Was it by Mark's request? I open my mouth to ask, but Mark's gaze has gone beyond my shoulder, staring intently.

I turn to find Chris standing in the doorway of the interview room, locked in an intense staredown with Mark.

When his attention shifts to me, his eyes are unreadable and his expression stone. He says nothing, but I know what he wants. I walk forward and stop in front of him. "Chris—"

He gives a short shake of his head and then backs into the room. Inhaling, I steel myself for what is to come, and follow him inside to discover two detectives sitting at the table.

Five

~~~

Chris and I reclaim our seats, and the relief I feel when he reaches for my hand under the table is immense. This interview is daunting enough without worrying that whatever just happened between him and Mark out there will affect us.

"Nice of you both to finally join us," the detective directly across from me says. I don't need to see the badge clipped onto his shirt that reads "Grant" to recognize the sarcastic, cigarette-roughened voice of the man I'd spoken to on the phone while in Paris. His wrinkled white shirt, loose black tie, and rumpled salt-and-pepper hair have that hard-edged, hard-living look that completes the package.

"I told you not to go there," David warns. "She was attacked. She deserved a fucking one-week escape from where the shit went down."

The second detective, a woman with Barbie doll good

looks who sits across from Chris, glares at David. "Do you have to talk like that?"

David snorts. "Afraid someone might find out you like it, Detective Miller?"

I suck in a breath at the smart-ass remark. Chris is stone-faced, but the slight quirk to his mouth says he's amused, and I try to be comforted by his lack of concern.

Detective Miller makes a disgusted sound, crossing her arms over her navy-blue blazer and white silk blouse. "You're a real asshole, David."

I blink in disbelief.

"Language, Detective," David chides her.

The look they give each other seems more like a simmering connection than scathing distaste.

Detective Grant levels me with a stare that brims with accusation. "Running off to another country is not something a victim does when they want to put a potential murderer behind bars, Ms. McMillan."

Chris's fingers flex tightly on my leg. "You know," he begins with that lethal nonchalant sarcasm, "it really is outrageous, the way victims think you actually give a damn about their emotional trauma. We certainly wouldn't want you to be inconvenienced by such things." He sits up, lacing his fingers on the table. "Here's an idea. Why don't you get retailers and restaurants to post public service notices? It could read: Attention: victims of violent crimes. You are not really a victim until we say you're a victim. Do not leave town or you risk punishment."

David barks out approving laughter and downs his coffee.

Grant and Miller stare at Chris like he's grown an extra head, and Chris's lips curve with undisguised amusement.

The room falls into a silence that seems to stretch eternally. Just when I think the empty space is intolerable, and I'll have to fill it with words, David does the most bizarre thing. He starts singing a Christmas song: *"You better watch out. You better not cry."*

Detective Grant snaps, "Enough, David. And stop with all the venti coffees, damn it. Every time you come in here with one of those things, you drive me to the bottle."

"That's the idea," David assures him, and I realize that he has a well-established relationship with both of them. I also start to see him as a calculated loose cannon. He intentionally keeps everyone off balance and out of control, thus *he's* the one in control.

Not surprisingly, Detective Grant turns his reprimand from David to Chris with a scathing "As for you, Mr. Merit, I was aware you were an artist—"

"An incredibly rich, brilliant artist," David inserts, and I almost laugh.

Grant continues, "But no one warned me you were a comedian."

Chris leans back easily. "I was going for smart-ass."

"So you intended to be a smart-ass to a police officer," Detective Miller says tartly.

"Exactly," Chris agrees. "Just like Detective Grant intended to be a smart-ass to the victim he's supposed to be protecting. Not exactly the image of public service the campaign stickers I've seen all over the city are preaching, now, is it?" There's a subtle threat beneath the words, a promise that he'll be outspoken about our treatment if it continues, which is made more powerful by David's reminder of just how deep Chris's pockets reach.

"You know," David chimes in. "I guess we do have to sympathize with law enforcement in election years. The public wants to feel they are being well served and all. The pressure to get a conviction any way you can has to be intense."

Detective Grant leans closer to David and all but growls, "Don't throw that election crap at me. We aren't elected officials in this room. We do our job no matter what year it is."

"Then do it," David says. "Get to the questions and save the head games for someone else."

A muscle ticks in Grant's jaw but he grabs a folder and opens it. "Ms. McMillan, referencing the police report on the night of the incident, you stated you went to Mr. Compton's home because you and Mr. Merit had a fight. You felt Mr. Compton could give you advice. You were talking to him in his living room when the trouble broke out. Ryan Kilmer, whom you knew from a work project with Mr. Compton, and the defendant, Ava Perez, whom you knew from the coffee shop she owns, exited the back room, both in half-dressed disarray. Ava saw you and went nuts, attacking you. Mark grabbed her to protect you and told you to leave. You exited the house and Ava followed you, first trying to run you down with a car, and then holding a gun on you."

"Yes," I manage weakly, cotton gathering in my throat at the grimness of those memories. "That's all accurate."

"Did she ever say she'd kill you?" he asks.

"Inside the house when she launched herself at me, she shouted that she'd kill me like she did Rebecca."

"And why do you think she wanted to kill you, or even Rebecca for that matter?"

"Considering she went nuts over me simply talking to Mark, I can only assume jealousy."

This earns me a quick and uncomfortable question. "Were you having sex with Mr. Compton?"

"No," I say firmly, hyperaware of Chris by my side. "I was with Chris then, as I am now."

Detective Grant's look is as cynical as they come. "Did you want to?"

My defenses prickle. "No. Not that night, and not ever."

"Did he want to have sex with *you*?"

"I . . . I don't know."

Detective Miller scoffs. "Please, Ms. McMillan. A woman knows if a man wants to have sex with her."

"Yes," Chris supplies. "Mark wanted to have sex with Sara." Cringing, I squeeze my eyes shut as he adds, "I knew he did. I'm sure Ava knew as well."

"But you, Ms. McMillan," Detective Grant says, "didn't want to have sex with him."

"Move on," David orders.

Detective Grant changes the subject. "Do you believe it was her intent to hit and kill you with the car?"

I inhale, those horrible few seconds returning with vicious force. I can almost feel the night air, hear the car engine and my own breathing. "Yes. She wanted to kill me. That tree saved my life. I darted behind it or I wouldn't be here now."

"When she failed, she held you at gunpoint?" he presses.

I nod. "That's right."

"And she ordered you into the car?"

"Yes."

"So she had the chance to shoot you, but she didn't."

It's not a question and my anger is sharp and instant. "She intended to kill me." I lean in closer. "She tried to kill me with the car. And if not for Chris risking his own life to disarm her, I wouldn't be here right now."

Chris's fingers slide under my hair to my neck, an act he normally reserves for those intimate moments when he is in control. The effect is jolting, and I realize instantly that's his intent. As I focus on him my anger levels off, and I inhale a calming breath. Chris's hand slowly slides from my neck, settling back on my leg.

After a short count of ten, I open my eyes. The two detectives have turned away, heads lowered as they whisper between themselves. They straighten and Detective Miller takes over the conversation.

"I'm sure everyone here is aware that Ms. Perez retracted her confession to the murder of Rebecca Mason. It's difficult to secure an indictment in a murder charge without a body, and we are going to temporarily drop those charges to build a case. We have until Friday morning to decide if we're going to proceed with the attempted murder charges."

Abruptly, David scoots his chair to the head of the table, firmly grabbing both sides and smiling. "*Damn,* I'm good." He motions to Chris and me. "Aren't I good? Go ahead. Say it."

"That's why I hired you," Chris assures him.

Detective Miller grimaces. "Please, David. Tell us why you're gloating. We can't *wait* to hear."

"Don't mind if I do," David says, looking as pleased as he sounds. "I knew you were going to bluff on the attempted murder charges. It's all part of your head game to get information they'll willingly give you anyway. And it's really as low as it gets, considering the defendant tried to kill Sara."

"Innocent until proven guilty," Detective Miller comments.

My anger returns like a swish of a now-sharpened blade. "She *tried to run me down with a car*. It was smashed into the tree when the police got there. How much more proof do you need?"

"And what about the four witnesses?" David asks. "Should I count them out?" He raises a finger. "One." Then another finger. "Two. Should I continue the demonstration?"

"We can count," Detective Miller snaps.

David scoffs. "Apparently not, because you keeping 'forgetting.' Let me be clear. Ms. Perez is a danger to my clients and to society. If you and your people aren't good enough to convince a judge she needs to stay behind bars, protection orders for Chris and Sara must be in place before that woman leaves custody. And she'd better have a leg monitor that's watched nonstop. You don't want to *know* how deep I'll cut if anything happens to one of my clients."

"It's not as simple as you make it, Counselor," Detective Grant says tightly. "There are complicated relationships involved in this case and the ever-changing stories have given me whiplash."

"We haven't changed our stories," David points out. "If Ms. Perez has, that makes her look even more unstable, and unstable is dangerous."

"We aren't at liberty to say more at this point," Detective Miller informs him. "We'd like to continue our questioning and go from there."

David leans back in his chair and taps his pen on the table a few times before he agrees. "Five minutes. Make the time count."

Detective Miller immediately turns to me. "Who's Ella Ferguson?"

"My neighbor and friend, who bought Rebecca's storage unit. She eloped and left me with the unit."

"And she's where now?"

"You know she filed a missing person's report," David answers irritably. "Get to the point or we're done here."

"Her point," Detective Grant says tightly, "is clear. We want to know where Ella is."

They've hit a raw nerve, and I say heatedly, "So do I. Where *is* she? I've filed a report here, and in France, but no one seems to be looking for her. Just like no one seemed to care about Rebecca, even after I started looking for her."

"And when *exactly* did you start looking for Ella?" Detective Miller asks, ignoring my inquiries.

"It's all in the reports," David says irritably.

"I want to hear it again," Detective Miller counters.

I jump in, ready to get out of this tiny cage of a room. "Ella handed me the key to the unit the night she eloped, along with the journals. I started reading them and got concerned for Rebecca's safety. I decided to try to find her. When I was told she was on extended vacation it heightened my concern, so I went to the gallery."

Detective Grant tilts his head. "And then ended up taking her job."

"Temporarily. I was off for the summer, and since I have an art degree I thought I'd look for Rebecca and earn extra income."

"You basically started living her life." His tone is pure accusation.

I make a disgusted sound, fed up with their lack of action, which they blame on everyone else. "That job, and the connection reading those journals gave me to Rebecca, is what drove me to look for her. I'm the *only* reason anyone was looking for her." Chris squeezes my hand in silent support. "I couldn't save her, but I can at least see justice done for her. Ava has to be stopped before she hurts someone else."

Detective Grant dismisses me, turning his attention on Chris. "Are you a member of Mark Compton's club, Mr. Merit?"

"Yes," Chris replies without hesitation, appearing unfazed by the abrupt change of topic.

The detective cuts a look back to me. "Are you, Ms. McMillan?"

"No," I say, following Chris's lead of less is more.

"Have you ever been to the club?" he presses me.

"She's been twice," Chris replies on my behalf. "Both times with me."

That earns Chris another of Grant's accusing questions. "Were you ever at the club when Rebecca was there?"

Chris doesn't give him so much as a blink of hesitation. "Not that I'm aware of, but I stuck to my private room. I had no interest in the rest of the club."

Grant studies him for long seconds, then cuts sharply to me. "Did you ever see Rebecca at the club, Ms. McMillan?"

My pulse leaps with the accusation, but David never gives me a chance to defend myself. He gives the table an angry pound and declares, "No games. She never met Rebecca. Refer to the date the storage unit was purchased. She'd already left town."

"What about after Rebecca returned to San Francisco?" Grant argues and then turns his wrath on me again. "Did you meet her then?"

"I never met Rebecca," I say, and I swear my heart has moved to my throat. "The reason I had a job was to fill in for her."

"So if Rebecca returned, you would have lost a dream job, right?" he says.

"What? No." I pull my suddenly trembling hand from the table to my lap. "I could have kept my job. I talked to Mark about that."

"Rebecca's return date was before Sara started at the gallery," David reminds him. "So game over and move on. Stop taunting her."

"Actually," Detective Miller says, "we aren't prepared to disclose Rebecca's specific travel dates at this point."

David eyes her for several seconds and makes that snorting noise. "Let me get this straight. You've now decided Rebecca Mason came to the city, left again, and came back?"

"What I'm saying, Counselor," she replies tartly, "is nothing. We aren't prepared to release what we know about her travel at this point."

"Of course you aren't," David says with acidic sarcasm. "How else would you victimize the victim?" He sighs heavily and motions with his hand. "Move on to another subject, or this interview is over."

"Gladly." Her attention lands on me. "Back to the club, then. Ms. McMillan—"

"I'll spare us all some time," Chris interrupts, leaning forward. "Sara was not, and is not, a part of the club."

"Let her tell me," she insists.

I repeat Chris's words. "I have not been, and am not, a part of the club."

Chris continues, "I took Sara to the club for one reason only: to show her what I'd been involved with, and why I didn't want her to be a part of what I considered my past. We didn't have sex while we were there. We didn't go to the public areas. I didn't even allow her to talk to anyone on the way in."

"You didn't *allow her*?" Detective Miller asks, sounding appalled.

"To protect her," Chris explains.

Detective Grant scoffs. "We've heard that before."

"What does that mean?" I ask, my defenses flaring for Chris.

David intervenes, demanding, "How is any of this related to Ava trying to kill my client?"

Again Detective Miller answers. "There's a personal relationship between the defendant and the witnesses. We need to understand that dynamic."

"Not for the bail hearing," David counters.

Detective Grant replies, "You know as well as we do that we have to be prepared for anything."

"Furthermore," Detective Miller adds, "if Ms. Perez is awarded a lower bond and she's released, it's in everyone's best interest that the DA feels comfortable putting his neck on the line to even take it to the grand jury to indict her."

David's brow wrinkles and his lips twist. "I smell a bad fish and it stinks to high heaven. I don't like it when things stink. So fair warning. I gave you five minutes; you have about two left."

Detective Miller instigates a back and forth with Chris. "You don't want Sara at the club because you think it's what? Dangerous?"

"Far from it. Mark Compton takes his responsibility to protect the members of the club seriously, or I would never have stepped foot inside. It's simply not right for me or Sara."

"Meaning BDSM, or the lifestyle, or . . . ?"

"There's nothing wrong with the lifestyle, if that's what you're getting at. BDSM is like anything else. It's right for some and not for others. It can be a way people cope with things they might not otherwise deal with. It can be a simple escape from everyday pressures. It has many healthy, pleasurable purposes, but like anything, it can be taken to unhealthy extremes."

Her lips curl. "Did you take it to an unhealthy extreme, Mr. Merit?"

I dig my fingernails into my leg, worried about where this is going, but Chris doesn't miss a beat. "A couple of pieces of chocolate every day is safe for one person, but for a diabetic, it's life threatening. Unhealthy is defined by the person."

"That's a nonanswer," Detective Grant says, sounding more than a little displeased. "But if you don't want to talk about you, let's talk about Mark Compton. Does he take this BDSM thing to an unhealthy extreme?"

"Asked and answered," David interjects. "He said *extreme* is defined by the individual."

"And I said it's a nonanswer," Detective Grant snaps, focusing on me again. "Ms. McMillan, when you were reading the journals did you find Mr. Compton's behavior to be extreme?"

"She's not answering," David says. "That would be opinion, which is nonadmissible in court, and we all know the journals don't even mention Mark Compton's name."

Detective Grant cuts him a look. "Since when are you Compton's attorney?"

"I didn't like your question." David motions with his hand again. "Move on."

Lips thinning, Grant removes two journals from his accordion folder. "Did you read *all* of the journals you turned in to us, Ms. McMillan?"

"Yes. I was trying to find clues that would tell me how to find her."

"Did you read the entry where Mr. Compton used a knife to taunt Rebecca during sex?"

"Again," David interrupts. "We don't have any proof the man in the journal is Mark Compton."

Grant doesn't look at him. "Did you read the scene, Ms. McMillan?"

My throat thickens and I nod, fearing a squeaked out reply will show some kind of guilt during this witch hunt.

"Is that why you went to look for her?" he presses. "Because you were afraid for her?"

"We didn't come here to discuss Mr. Compton," David interjects.

"We need to know what Ms. McMillan's motivations were so we know she's rock solid in front of a jury. If she looks bad, the defendant looks good."

"It wasn't about the journal entries," I offer honestly. "I hate the idea of people losing their belongings to an auction, which is why I didn't get involved in auction-hunting when Ella did."

He pulls one of the journals from the accordion file and holds it up. "You know this journal, I assume?"

I nod. "That's her work journal."

"Did you read this note she wrote?" He opens it to a page and flips it around, showing me a passage highlighted with a pointed sticky note.

I read the familiar passage out loud. *"Riptide auction piece. Legit? Find Expert."* I glance up at him. "I brought this note to the attention of the private eye we hired to help find Rebecca. I was concerned that it might have somehow led to her disappearance. That's how Mary and Ricco's actions were discovered."

"The private eye would be who?" Detective Miller queries.

"Blake Walker of Walker Security," David supplies. "Which you know since you questioned him."

"Simply making sure there wasn't another private eye," Detective Miller states, the tension between her and David palpable.

Detective Grant stays focused on me. "Were you concerned they might have killed Rebecca?"

"In my interactions with Ricco, it was clear that he was in love with Rebecca. I didn't believe he would hurt her."

"And Mary?" he presses.

"She was prickly with me, and my understanding is that's how she treated Rebecca."

Grant arches a brow. "Why was that?"

"We both worked with Mark on Riptide auction items, and he trusted us over her."

"Did you ever sleep with Mr. Compton or engage in any form of sexual activity?"

"Asked and answered," David says sharply.

Despite his objection, I say, "Never."

Detective Miller shifts in her chair. "You seem to rule out Ricco as having anything to do with Rebecca's disappearance. What about Mary?"

"She's mean-spirited," I say, "but Mary knew Ricco cared about Rebecca. He was vocal about it to everyone. And in my opinion, Mary's more of a revenge kind of person. She'd want to hurt Rebecca and Mark—not kill either of them."

Detective Grant moves the journal in front of Chris. "She marked out your name and her notes about you. Why?"

My heart starts racing. Do they know Chris fought with Mark over Rebecca? How would they know? Would Mark have told them?

"I don't begin to assume I know why another person does anything," Chris answers, in full avoidance mode.

The journal is scooted back in front of me. "Any idea why she marked out Mr. Merit's name?"

Where is this going? Are they accusing Chris of something? "I saw no notes that indicated why in anything I read." Somehow my voice is steady, though my knees aren't.

David slaps his hands on the table. "And on that note, I'm going to ask my clients to leave so I can talk with you alone." He pushes to his feet. "This interview is over."

"I'm scared, Chris," I say as we exit the police station into the parking lot, still reeling from the interrogation.

He stops walking and faces me, his hands settling solidly on my arms. "That wasn't about you, baby. They're using you for information. Think about them like you do Mark. Don't let them intimidate you."

"Mark can't put me in jail."

"They can't, either," he assures me. "You have an alibi."

"But they implied that Rebecca came back and left again. They made it sound like I killed her to keep my job."

"Blake would have seen another travel date. It's all a head game. I'm confident you're in the clear." He scrubs a hand through his hair. "And I'm hoping like hell I was in Paris the day Rebecca returned. I never checked the date. I didn't have a reason to until now."

I blanch. "Do you think they're going after you?"

"No. I think they're going after Mark. And they'll use any intimidation method they can to put the knife in our hands if we let them."

"They do seem to think he's involved in her disappearance, don't they?"

"Yes. They do."

"Do you?" While I know in my heart that Mark's innocent, I find myself holding my breath.

He will never belong to me as I do to him. I will never control him as he does me. I play by his rules and I never know how they will change, or what or who will be part of the new game each of our encounters becomes.

Rebecca Mason

Six

Rather than answer my question, Chris ushers me into the 911, where he shuts us inside. He sits with his wrists on the steering wheel, staring forward, tension rippling off of him. I hold my breath, still waiting on the answer to my question.

Finally, he turns to face me and says, "No. I don't think Mark had anything to do with Rebecca's disappearance."

"Then why did you have to think about your answer?"

"Because he made decisions that led her to the place she ended up. I've tried not to blame him, but he has a responsibility and he has to own that, or he'll repeat it with another negative outcome. I'm not sure he has that in him."

Like Chris has owned what happened to Amber. "I was angry with Mark, too, but for all his sins, and he had plenty with Rebecca, he didn't make Ava kill her."

"No, he didn't. And had Ava been someone else, Rebecca might have simply ended up like Amber. But he put both of them in situations that led to that kind of hate and anger. You say he loved her. I say he didn't. Or he wasn't *in love* with her like I am with you, any more than I was with Amber. You don't drag someone you love into that kind of hell, and play the kinds of games he did with her mind and body. You climb out of hell to be with them."

My eyes prickle and I lean into Chris and cup his cheek. "I love you. And Amber's going to be fine, Chris."

"Fine? She's lost years of her life, and I let it happen."

I realize now why I was so determined to save Amber. She's not one of his scars. She's an open, bleeding wound. "No. You didn't."

"I did. And that's why I get Mark. I get his mistakes. I get the guilt he feels. And now, he's living with the fear of his mother's death. So we'll help him get through this, but I need to be sure I know his state of mind, so I know how to navigate the situation. If he keeps denying his role in what happened, and refuses to make changes, this could be the end of the line with him."

He kisses my hand and turns away, starting the car. I want to say more, but Chris's cell phone rings and the opportunity is lost for now. By the time we near our apartment, Chris has confirmed that Jacob handled what turned out to be a reporter at the gallery and set up a meeting with him to talk about security concerns and options.

He ends the call and drives around to the back of our building to the garage. "I'm going to take my Harley to my meeting with Jacob, so you can have the car."

"I thought I'd go with you."

He shakes his head. "I'm going to try to connect with Mark

after my meeting with Jacob and get a feel for where his head is, and I want to do that alone. And Jacob says Amanda is ready to quit after getting spooked today, so I assume you'll want to go talk to her."

"Oh no, that's not good. There are only two of them as it is. Yes. I'll go talk to her."

Chris parks the 911 and leaves it running. When I join him on the driver's side to take over, he says, "We'll go pick out a car of your choice next week."

"I have my Ford."

"Give it to Amanda. You said she doesn't have a car. We'll get you a new one."

"I don't need a new car."

"Yes." He pulls me to him. "You do. One you feel is yours and meets my standards, which are high where you're concerned." He doesn't give me time to argue. "Tell Amanda we'll have security in place at the gallery by tomorrow. That should make her feel better. I'll tell Mark when I see him." He strokes my hair from my face and tilts my face to his. "Try not to worry too much. We're okay." He kisses me soundly and then crosses the parking garage to his Harley.

We're okay, I repeat in my head, thinking about what he'd said about Amber and Rebecca. Why do I think he said that more for himself than me this time?

When I arrive at the gallery's back parking lot, I'm surprised to see Ryan Kilmer's silver BMW parked near the door, not far from Jacob's black sedan. Locking the 911, I head toward the building and call Jacob to let me inside.

"What's Ryan Kilmer doing here?" I ask when he opens the door.

"From what I can tell, comforting Amanda," he says as I step inside. "He arrived about ten minutes after I did."

The mama bear in me flares to life, determined to protect Amanda. "That's what I was afraid of."

"I take it you don't approve of him?"

"Not a bit. She's too young for him, and he's—" I stop myself from saying "a Master," unsure of what Jacob knows about that side of Chris's life, "too old for her."

Jacob's eyes flicker a moment with what I am almost certain is understanding, but he says only, "I tend to agree. Will you be okay if I leave while he's still here?"

A memory of Ryan and Mark cornering me at the open house for Ryan's property is uncomfortable, but not frightening. "I'm fine," I assure him. "It's Amanda I'm worried about."

"Understood." He hesitates a moment, before adding, "Just a general warning about the investigation, speaking from experience. Anyone involved could decide to protect themselves by throwing someone else under the bus."

"I know," I assure him, thinking of my father and Michael. "I'll keep my guard up. And thank you for everything, Jacob. I know it's your job to be here for me, but you do it well, and it's appreciated."

His stoic features actually soften. "It's my absolute pleasure, Ms. McMillan." He pushes open the door to depart, pausing to add, "Walker Security is arranging for a man to be here by morning, but in the meantime it's better to be cautious. If you leave after dark and Mr. Merit isn't here, either have someone walk you out, or call me and I'll come over."

"Absolutely. Thank you."

He exits and the automatic locks click into place behind him. I start to turn and hesitate a moment as a thought hits me. If there are cameras inside and outside the building, then any visit from Rebecca would have been recorded. If Rebecca came here, there would have been footage. And why wouldn't she just come here or go to Mark's house? How did she end up with Ava, whom she didn't even like? There's only one answer that makes sense. She came here, found out Mark was out of town, and went to the coffee shop. Mark said he never knew she had returned to the city. Maybe she went next door to muster her courage to come here, not knowing Mark was out of town? *Somehow,* she ended up with Ava.

I'm still considering the possibilities when I enter the business office to a ringing phone and an unmanned desk. Crossing to Ralph's office, I find him packing his briefcase. Glancing at my watch, I note it's barely six o'clock, early for the gallery to close. "Everything okay?" I ask, worried that Amanda isn't the only one who might be ready to quit.

His eyes lift to mine. "As okay as we get around here, these days. I didn't expect you back tonight."

"Chris had a meeting, so I thought I'd stop in and check on things after your problem with the reporter. Where's Amanda?"

"In the break room flirting with Ryan." He leans on his desk, his crooked bow tie at half-mast. "He showed up about the time she was ready to walk out over that reporter stalking us all afternoon. Fortunately, she's drawn to rich and good-looking men, and he convinced her to stay." He lowers his voice. "And while I'm grateful he worked his mojo, she's so over her head with him, it's scary."

He's so right. "I know. I've tried to warn her away from him in the past. Obviously it didn't work."

"Try harder."

He's right again. "I will."

"Good. Because she won't listen to me." He straightens. "Did you hear Bossman's back in town?"

"I saw him at the police station. Did he call or come by here?"

"No. Ryan told us he's here, and we're hoping it means we can get back to some form of order."

I'm irritated that Mark would communicate with Ryan but he won't return my calls. Has this investigation become Chris and me against Mark and Ryan? Is it worse than that—against Mark, Ryan, and Ava?

No, that's silly. Mark isn't aligned with Ava. I pray Ryan isn't, either.

Ralph slides his briefcase strap onto his shoulder. "Crystal has us closing at six since we aren't operating the showroom. Are you coming in tomorrow?"

I won't know until Chris has talked with Mark. "No decisions yet, but I'm just a phone call away, no matter what. And there will be security here starting tomorrow. No more reporters stalking you."

"That's welcome news. Shall we go herd Ryan and Amanda out of here, so we can all leave?"

"I think I'll stay and try to talk to her, while I have a chance."

"You sure? I don't like leaving you here alone."

"I'll be fine. I think our talk will go better if it's just her and me."

He nods, giving me a hug on his way out. Pausing at the reception desk on my way to the break room, I'm stunned by the pages and pages of messages by the phone, though I suspect many are repeats. I *have* to help out here. There's no way Crystal can handle Riptide's massive operation and juggle Allure, too.

Since Amanda still hasn't returned, I drop my coat and purse on her desk and head toward the break room. The soft murmur of voices has me peering cautiously around the doorway. Ryan and Amanda stand on the other side of the small kitchen table, facing each other.

He's leaning close to Amanda, his head dipped low, and he murmurs something that I can't make out.

Amanda leans away from him, giving me a partial glimpse of her face. "I'm not ready," she whispers. "I can't."

Pretty sure I know what they're discussing, I curl my hands into fists and it's all I can do not to shout out my agreement. Of course she's not ready. She's a kid, an intern. He's in his thirties, a Master with a depth of sexual experience.

"You *are* ready," he insists, and I've had enough.

With a deep breath, I step into the room, and dare the deep muddy waters of butting into someone else's life. "Ready for what?"

Ryan turns to face me, his light brown eyes skimming my body a bit too intimately. My stomach drops and I'm back in the moment when he and Mark tried to seduce me; when they trapped me, touched me. "Sara," Ryan says softly, his voice almost as intimate as his inspection had been. "Good to see you.

The last time we saw each other was in less than favorable circumstances."

Is *that* what he calls Ava trying to kill me?

"I've been worried," he adds. "How are you?"

"As good as any of us can be, under the still *unfavorable circumstances*."

His mouth slips into a grim line. "Indeed. It's not our best year, is it?"

His nonchalance over Rebecca's death, and almost mine, makes me so angry, I decide no reply is better than what would come out of my mouth.

I focus on Amanda instead. "You're not ready for what?"

She twists her fingers together in front of her. "Oh, I . . ."

"She wants a promotion," Ryan offers, "and she's afraid to ask Mark."

His explanation is so fast and smooth, his stare so steady and unwavering, that I almost believe him. But I know Amanda almost walked out today and when I look at her, she cuts her gaze away, unintentionally telling me he's lying. "I can talk to Mark for you," I offer, pushing for the truth.

Her gaze jerks to mine. "No. Please no. I'm not . . . ready. Not yet. Please. Promise, Sara. Don't say anything."

"I'll wait until you're ready," I say. "Just let me know."

Her shoulders slump with relief. "Thank you. Yes, I will." She casts Ryan a tentative look. "I'm going to go gather my things."

She seems to wait for his approval, and he gives it with a nod. Then, and only then, does she rush from the room. Everything about the exchange screams Master and submissive.

I advance on Ryan. "Are you crazy?" I hiss softly. "Rebecca's dead, and a million eyes are on the gallery and on Mark. This is *not* the time to be playing Master and submissive with one of the staff members."

He arches a brow. "Mark? Not Mr. Compton?" He laughs. "He was crazy to think you'd ever call him Master."

Unease ripples through me at the implication that they'd talked about turning me into their submissive, as they had Rebecca. "No," I say, my tone crisp. "I wouldn't, and neither is Amanda. She's too young and too innocent, and frankly too immature, to take either of you on."

"No woman in my life has to take me on, Sara. I'm not Mark. I know you read Rebecca's journals. I can't believe anything she wrote about me would have said that I was."

More unease slides through me. He's just admitted that he's the other person in the journals. Then Jacob's warning flickers in my mind, and I wonder if Ryan's baiting me for information, trying to find out if he's in the journals. I'm not sure why he'd care, though. Ava killed Rebecca. Didn't she?

"My point," I say, "is that now is not the time to bring your lifestyle into the gallery."

"*My* lifestyle? Look in the mirror, Sara. It's yours, too, and if you must know, I called Riptide looking for Mark, who hasn't exactly been returning anyone's calls. They told me he was headed here. I called the back-up line, and Amanda started rambling about some strange guy by the door. I was a few blocks away, so I came over to help. Now I'm going to give her a ride home. No games; just me being a gentleman. If Mark shows up, tell him I came by."

He disappears into the hallway. No matter how he frames the story, I don't believe his intentions are honorable toward Amanda. I've always thought he was less aggressive than Mark, but I'm not so sure anymore. Perhaps he's the biggest game player of all.

Seven

He shoved me against the wall and then tore my panties off. His lips pressed close to my ear, his breath was hot on my neck, as he said, you know the rules, you know I have to punish you.

Rebecca Mason

Being alone is a unique opportunity to look around—perhaps for the security feed from the camera outside. I don't know what I'm looking for, but it feels like there's a missing piece to this puzzle that no one knows. I double-check the security system, then go to my old office. Settling behind the desk, I'm oddly drawn to the haunting painting of the roses again, as if my mind is trying to tell me something. A shiver races down my spine, and I dial Jacob to give him a heads-up that I'm alone.

"I'm going to stay awhile, but I'll definitely want an escort when I leave."

"Is the security system in place?" he asks.

"Yes, I checked."

"Good. Call me in an hour to check in, or I'm going to come check on you."

I let out a sigh of relief. "Thanks again, Jacob."

"Thank me by not forgetting to call in an hour."

We hang up, and the fact that Jacob feels I'm safe enough with the security system eases some of my nerves. But then, he also thinks Rebecca's killer is in jail.

I frown at that random thought. She *is* in jail. Of course she is.

I'm just about to start nosing around the gallery when Chris calls. "Hey, baby."

His deep voice radiates through me and I feel the tension from my encounter with Ryan melt away. I sink deeper into the soft leather of my chair. "Hey."

"Are you still at the gallery?"

"Yes. Can you meet me here?"

"No. Mark finally called me, and I'm meeting him in about twenty minutes."

"Did you hear from David after he left the police station?"

"We texted. I'm supposed to meet him after I talk to Mark for a full update. Did Jacob leave?"

"Yes, but he's coming back to get me when I'm ready to go. Is there any word on Rebecca's travel dates?"

"Blake confirmed Rebecca returned before you started at the gallery, and I confirmed I was in Paris that entire week, but he's backtracking to make sure there isn't another date he missed."

"Does he think that's possible?"

"He checked all the public transportation logs and saw nothing, but he's double-checking anyway. He's looking into private flights as well, but he won't have any way of finding travel by car."

My heart sinks. "That's true. And it gives the police a tool to manipulate and scare us."

"They can only do those things if we let them. We won't, and neither will David."

"Did Mark say anything helpful when you talked to him?"

"No, we only spoke for a minute—speaking of which, I need to leave for my meeting with him. Call me if you need anything, and don't leave there without Jacob."

"I won't."

"Try not to stress too much, baby. David's good at his job. He's arrogant, loud, and obnoxious, but it works for him, and he's working for us."

"I know."

"Keep knowing, and I'll see you soon." He lowers his voice. "I know a certain window that has your name on it." He hangs up and I let the phone slide away, a smile touching my lips, but it's a sad smile. I love that man. I want to marry him. I just don't want to do it in the middle of this nightmare and I have to do anything I can to make it end. We know the ending isn't going to be a happy one, but at least it will be an end.

Pushing to my feet, I head out into the hallway and decide to start my search in the supply room, where I look for file boxes or security records, but find nothing. I search Mark's barren office for the security feed and find nothing. Maybe it streams directly to his computer? I suddenly realize then that the feed will show me sitting in his office and searching around the gallery, but I shrug. The worst he can do is fire me.

An hour into my exploration, I call Jacob and check in. Afterward I search the four offices used for interns, then the cabinets in the break room. Next up is Amanda's desk, then I spend a long time scavenging Ralph's files.

Finally, I end up back in my office. I've already searched the files and desk, and my gaze now lands on the bookshelf. I settle myself onto the floor and turn on the radio on my cell phone, the music making the emptiness more bearable.

I start flipping through books, looking for notes or any other clue that might tell me something of importance. A name. A number. Anything. I don't know. As I search I pile up the books, making sure nothing's underneath them on the shelves. Just as I've restored order to the mess, the door to the outer office buzzes and I freeze.

Holding my breath, I wait for who will appear, and a crackle of familiar energy stirs in the air a moment before Mark fills the doorway. I've barely had a moment to blink from the impact of his power and devastating good looks before his steps swallow the space between us.

He towers above me, pinning me with an unreadable steely gray stare. "I wasn't aware that breaking and entering was one of your skills, Ms. McMillan. What are you doing?"

Either he didn't meet with Chris, or he's just trying to put me on the spot. "Your staff was freaking out over a reporter who'd parked himself outside for two hours, and Amanda almost quit. I rushed over, but Ryan beat me here. He did his Magic Mike routine on her and she stayed."

"Magic Mike?"

"It's from a movie that has a lot of naked men and dancing, so it's probably not your thing."

He holds out his hand. "Get off the floor, Ms. McMillan."

He pulls me to my feet and I'm suddenly toe-to-toe with him.

"Thank you," I pretty much croak out, and the slight narrowing of his eyes tells me he notices. It's power to him to affect me, another game—and I'm very tired of games.

I tug my hand away and step backward. "Did you meet with Chris?" I ask.

"Yes."

"And?"

"And I'll let him tell you."

I sigh. "Of course. Why would you tell me, since you're standing right here? But okay."

He looks amused, I think.

"In case he forgot to mention it," I say, "you've rehired me. Well, technically Crystal did, and before you get upset with her, she did it because she cares about you."

"I'm not even going to ask how you presume to know what Ms. Smith feels, since you barely know her."

"She told me."

He just stares at me. "Is that how you know Chris cares about you, Ms. McMillan? He *tells* you?"

I'm not sure what he's implying, but I'm pretty sure it's a slap to Chris, and I don't like it. "Show *and* tell, Mark. It's a good combination."

Something dark flickers in his eyes, gone in a blink, but his probing questions are not. "How exactly does he show you?"

My lips purse. "In my book, privacy is like a great pair of high heels. To be cherished."

"Good answer, Ms. McMillan. I'm sure Chris would approve. It means he can trust you, and trust is not an easy thing to give or receive."

Is his remark about Rebecca? Or Ava? Maybe Ryan? Or perhaps it's deeper. Perhaps it's about what made him who he is today, the way Amber is a part of what made Chris who he is today.

"Mark—"

But his eyes shut, and he inhales deeply, emotions he rarely allows anyone to see rippling over his face. He abruptly turns and exits the office, leaving me staring after him. Then the song playing on my phone insinuates itself into my ears. *Say something, I'm giving up on you. Say something, I'm giving up on you. I'll be the one if you want me to . . .*

"Say Something" by A Great Big World is always haunting, but gut-wrenchingly so tied to the months of silence from Rebecca. I can only imagine how much Mark must crave the sound of her voice, how much hope he must hang on to the possibility she might still return. How much he must wish he could tell her what he never dared—that he loved her.

Shutting off the radio, I go down the hall toward Mark's office. His hands are against the wall, his head tilted forward, tension tightening his body. This isn't the controlled man I know. This is the man I saw falling apart that night under the tree, after Ava confessed to murdering Rebecca.

I want to go to him, but my gut says he doesn't want me to see him like this. I'm backing away when he says, "Is there something you need, Ms. McMillan?"

"Just . . . goodnight."

I don't move. I need to say or do something to help him.

"*Go home,* Ms. McMillan," he snaps.

Sighing in defeat, I turn and leave him alone, but it's not easy. Not when I know how badly being alone hurts.

As I wait for Jacob to arrive to escort me out, Chris calls and asks me to meet him and David at the pizza joint next to our apartment building. I arrive home fifteen minutes later and hand the 911 off to the attendant. I wave at Jacob, who'd followed me over here, and head toward the restaurant. I know it has great takeout, but I've never been inside.

Turns out it's far more Italian eatery than pizzeria, with dim lighting, soft music, and cozy booths beyond the hostess stand. A tall, husky man with brown hair streaked with gray greets me with an extended hand. "You must be Sara."

I tentatively shake hands. "Yes, I'm Sara. And you're . . . psychic?"

He chuckles low and deep. "Wouldn't that come in handy? But no. Chris described you with artistic detail, and you're as beautiful as he said. I'm Marco, the owner here."

I blush. "Thank you. I remember Chris talking about you. Don't you own a chopper shop, too?"

"Custom choppers, motorcycle repair, you name it. Chris and I tinker on his Harleys occasionally." He winks. "Nice to see he's no longer a lone rider." I smile, warmed as always by the way Chris is genuinely liked by so many.

Marco motions to my coat. "Let me take that for you." I shrug out of my trench coat and hand it over, then with a grand gesture he waves us forward. "Come, I'll show you to your table."

I follow him around a corner where there's a row of six booths several steps above the floor, all draped with curtains for privacy. "I love this setup," I murmur. He smiles his pleasure at the compliment, and then pulls one of the curtains back to reveal Chris and David, each with a beer in hand. Chris's eyes light on me, and the heat and tenderness in his gaze makes the craziness of the day fade away for a moment.

Setting his beer down, Chris draws my hand into his. The heat of his stare and the sizzle of his touch send a wave of warmth up my arm and over my chest, and the tension in my spine finally relaxes.

As I slide in next to Chris, he lifts his chin at Marco. "I see you met Sara."

Marco winks at me and then answers Chris in what I think is Italian. I really can't be certain of much when Chris's fingers are lazily caressing my thigh, sending darts of electricity straight to my sex.

Chris smiles, answering Marco in English. "You're right, Marco." His hand discreetly slides under the tablecloth, beneath my skirt, his warm fingers flexing against my bare thigh. "Sara *is* beautiful and save your Italian Don Juan routine for someone else. She's *mine*."

I blush and not from the compliment or his words, but from the way Chris's hand is climbing higher and higher until his fingers sweep my panties. "She blushes," Marco observes, kissing his fingers, as if it's the conversation creating my reaction. "Bella." His tongue rolls with an Italian accent, and unbidden,

I am reminded of the Spanish version of the endearment for *beautiful* Ricco Alvarez often uses. Marco points at Chris. "Watch it. I like a challenge." He leaves Chris no time for rebuttal, disappearing as he tugs the curtain shut and then surprises me as he peeks back inside and adds, "Your pizza should be up any minute," and winks at me.

David's phone rings and he answers the call, giving me the chance to grab Chris's hand and softly hiss a warning. "Behave."

He laughs, his eyes warm with wicked promise that softens into tenderness, and his hand, thankfully, flattens on top of my thigh. "I missed you."

I soften at the sweet, unexpected confession, officially melting inside and out. "I missed you, too." My lips curve and I dare to taunt the proverbial tiger. "And you've certainly made me wish we were home."

"Soon, baby," he promises. "Soon."

"Assholes," David complains, drawing our attention back to him. He sets his phone on the table and looks at me. "And so we meet again, Sara McMillan."

I smile, amused by his odd way of speaking. "Yes indeed," I say. "We meet again."

Chris hands me his beer. "Here. He makes more sense when you're drinking."

I laugh, and despite not being a beer kind of girl, I take a swig, then hand the bottle back to Chris. "I needed that. You scared the crap out of me with the police today, David."

He snorts and tips up his beer. "You can't let the badge go to their heads. That's dangerous for them and us."

"You sang a Christmas song," I remind him. "I'm still in disbelief."

He wiggles his brows. "Creative shift of energy. It pulled the attention from Chris."

Chris chuckles. "I think you finally convinced them you're crazy. And speaking of crazy. I think Detectives Grant and Miller both need to be reminded of the meaning of their badges."

David loosens his tie. "The nature of law enforcement is 'us, them, and everyone else.' You never know what they are really doing or thinking. The objective of the interview is to get you to say something you don't want to say." He rests an elbow on the table. "I'm of the opinion that the journals, and anyone mentioned in the passages, have become their primary focus."

"That would be Mark, Ryan, and Ava," I supply, "but Rebecca never gave names."

"Mark did say that Grant was all over him," Chris says. "He's even pulled away from the club to try to protect the membership."

"You'd think that would mean Mark and Ryan would be communicating," I observe, "but Ryan stopped by the gallery this afternoon and said Mark won't return his calls."

"Ryan had better not hold his breath for a returned call," Chris suggests. "Mark's attorney seems to be of the opinion that Ryan is going to do whatever is necessary to make sure he's in the clear, including throwing Mark under the bus."

"I met Tiger at the police station today," I remind them. "So forgive me if I don't put a lot of merit in his opinions. He acted like Mark needed a bodyguard to protect him from me."

"Tiger didn't get his name for nothing," David assures us. "He'll rip your throat out to keep his client on top, but in this case he was probably worried you'd make it look like Mark was asking you to prep him for his interview." He takes a swig of his beer. "And that wouldn't be good. Which brings me to your working at the gallery. I don't recommend it, and I seriously doubt Mark's attorney will, either."

"I have to help out," I insist, straightening. "It's falling apart. The staff is scared. And I saw Mark tonight and he said nothing about it being a problem." I turn to Chris. "He stopped into the gallery right before I left, and he wasn't doing well."

"I already had this argument with Chris," David interjects before Chris can answer. "Mark isn't my concern. You two are. He needs to hire someone else."

I turn to Chris to state my case, but he says, "Relax, baby. I already told David we're helping Mark out until his mother stabilizes. No one deserves to fear for a parent's life while fighting for their own."

"How is she?"

"She's barely started her battle to beat cancer. The blood infection she got after surgery almost killed her."

"When I talked to Crystal she said she was improving, so I assume that means stable?"

"From what I gathered."

"My position on Mark is this," David says, sounding like he's starting a lecture that's going to grate on every nerve I own.

"Save it," Chris tells him. "Move on to another subject. Didn't you want to talk about the bail hearing?"

The curtains are opened just then, and a waiter appears

with a piping hot pizza and my diet soda. When we're alone again, I ask, "What about the bail hearing?"

David picks up a slice of pizza. "Before I answer, just know this. I don't approve of *either* of you spending time with Mark, let alone at the gallery." He sets his pizza on his plate.

"The bail hearing, David," Chris urges.

"Right," he says. "The bail hearing. There will be no witness testimony, so you can both rest easy there."

I blink in confusion. "I didn't know it was even an option."

"Bail adjustment hearings allow limited testimony in the interest of public safety," David explains. "But the DA doesn't seem to want to complicate the situation, which I think is smart. He has four witnesses including you, Sara, who say the defendant tried to kill you. We don't need the defense to start character assassinations now. They'll get to that later."

Chris fills my plate, but food is the last thing on my mind right now. "What character assassinations?"

David swipes a napkin over his mouth. "Your honesty and character will be tested. It's expected, but I think it's going to get nasty in this case. I have an insider at the DA's office who tells me the defense threatened the DA."

Chris abandons a bite of pizza halfway to his mouth. "Threatened?"

David nods and swallows nearly half a slice in one bite. "Apparently the defense said in a not-so-subtle way that the press would"—he makes quotations marks with his fingers—"'accidentally' get a story about a seedy sex club, murder, and some kind of other bullshit mayhem. My insider's choice of words, not mine."

I'm reeling at the prospect that Ava could be set free. "You think they're so worried about the press that they'd let her walk?"

David shoves aside his pizza, which tells me we're now in serious territory. "Easing up on Ava at the hearing won't stop her defense from going public after the bond is in place. That's what I came here to talk about tonight. Even if they don't like it, the DA is prepared for Friday to become a press frenzy. My guess is Ava's folks will throw every name and diversion into the hat they can find."

"Meaning me and you, baby," Chris adds. "And being at the gallery is only going to put us more in the spotlight." He turns to me, and there's no missing the grim set to his jaw. "We're witnesses against Ava, and because we aren't involved in the four-way that group had going on, we're the most credible. They could very well attack us. You have to be ready for this to be all about headlines. The club. BDSM. Me. You."

"Right," David concurs. "And while I can protect you from everything in the court system, I can't protect you from the press unless they slander you."

My heart lurches. Suddenly the scandal seems like a much bigger worry than it did moments before. "What about Chris and his charity work? This could ruin him."

"Baby, I'm fine. I can handle my charity."

"You can't be sure of that," I argue. "Lance Armstrong created Livestrong and they had to break free of him to survive." I turn to David. "Can we threaten them with slander charges now?"

David grimaces. "That's not an option."

"Why? They could ruin Chris, and—"

"Sara, sugar," he interrupts, his tone as condescending as it gets. "The detectives were wrong. *You're* the one who needs to lay off the caffeine. Let me do my job."

My jaw drops. Did he really just call me "sugar," and tell me to let him do his job? I'm officially at my threshold for arrogant assholes today. Then his phone rings again, and he answers it without so much as a raised finger.

"Sara," Chris says, squeezing my leg to get my attention.

I tear my gaze from David and look at Chris. "His *job* should include protecting your reputation and your career."

"Baby—"

"Don't 'baby' me right after he called me sugar," I snap. "I'm going to the bathroom to deep breathe."

His grip tightens on my leg. "He's just high-strung."

"If you try to keep me here, be warned that I have a very vivid fantasy in my head right now, which involves me dumping a pitcher of beer over David's head."

He grins and lets go of my leg.

"I thought you'd agree." I head toward the restroom sign, go down a narrow hallway, and lock myself in the small room, where I lean on the sink. David's dismissing the real danger the press could do to Chris. We can't wait until it's already happened to come up with a plan.

I've barely had time to think when a knock sounds on the door. "Sara."

I unlatch the door and Chris enters, locking the door behind him. Certain he's here to sing David's merits, I say, "He's an asshole, Chris. The press cyclone is going to hit, and we have to be ready. We have to get you cleared, and you have to go to

Paris and do your charity event, away from all of this. Distance yourself from this nightmare. You *have* to."

He backs me against the counter, his hips pressed to mine, and the teasing, sweet lover of moments before is nowhere to be found. His jaw is tight, his eyes hard. "Did you really just suggest I leave you to deal with this alone?"

"Yes, but—"

"You still don't trust me."

"What? That's crazy, Chris."

"It's accurate. In the back of your mind, you still think that if something punches my buttons like Dylan did, I'll leave. I told you. I'm not leaving, and I'm not letting you doubt us anymore."

"I don't doubt us."

"You do. But we're going to fix that and I've already figured out there's only one way to do that, aside from me melting down and you realizing that I'm here to stay. I've taken things slowly to protect the trust between us, but we're ready for what comes next, and I'm going to push you and push you hard. I'm going to tear down every inhibition you own until I own them. I'm going to make you crazy wondering what will be next and even crazier when it comes. I'm going to take you to places you think you can't go, and find out you can. And when you say 'I do' to me, there won't be any doubts or any barriers left. Are you prepared for what that means?"

"Yes," I whisper. "It's what I've been asking for."

"Then we start now." He turns me to face the counter, shocking me by yanking my skirt up and palming my cheeks. His eyes meet mine in the mirror. "I'm going to spank you.

There won't be any foreplay or fucking after. It's going to sting. You will not cry out. When I'm done, I'm leaving, and you will bring your pretty little backside and sit down next to me like nothing happened. And when I'm ready, I'll fuck you. Choose now. Accept it or not."

The idea is horrifying and sexy, and I'm wet and aching and so many things at once that I can barely breathe. "I . . . yes. Yes, I do."

He yanks my panties off and stuffs them in his pocket. His hand comes down on my backside and it's such a shock, I barely swallow my yelp. Already his palm is on me again. I try to count. Three. Four. Five. Oh God. Six.

He turns me to face him, his hands going to the counter, not touching me. I'm panting in pain and pleasure, my knees weak. "Pull your skirt down and come back to the table. I want you there in two minutes. If you take one second longer, I'll bring you back in here and spank you again. Understand?"

"Yes."

He turns and leaves the bathroom.

Eight

⌘

It hurt in a bittersweet, arousing way, and while I felt exposed
and vulnerable, I've come to know those things arouse me in ways
I never thought possible.

Rebecca's words replay in my mind as I grab the sink to steady
myself, the ache in my backside radiating down my wobbly
legs. I'm warm all over, wet between my thighs, and so aroused
that Chris's absence hurts far more than his hand. Until now, I
had never understood what drew Rebecca to this kind of encounter. It's like I am spinning terrifyingly out of control, and
yet somehow it's delicious in a forbidden, fantastic kind of way.
Chris is pushing me. I want to be pushed.

His warning plays in my mind. *I want you there in two min-*
utes. If you take one second longer, I'll spank you again. While the
spanking isn't such a horrible threat, my bottom is still ripe

from Chris's palm, leaving other parts of my body eager for the rewards of meeting his demands.

I yank open the door and rush down the hallway, stopping at the curtain, where I have a moment of apprehension and not because of what's happened with Chris. Because I'd left here angry with David, who is too observant for my own good right now. Silently I lecture myself about being cool and unreadable, like that will suddenly change how transparent I am. Chris ends my fretting by dragging the curtain back and I am instantly captured in the smoldering embers burning in the depths of his hot stare. He studies me for a moment, satisfaction slowly lighting his eyes, and I can feel the heat of my cheeks that matches the burn of my body. He knows I liked what he did. *He liked* what he did. And he really likes that I followed his orders.

He reaches for my hand, pulling me into the booth, his touch downright scorching. "You're late," he reprimands softly, and this time I am happy to discover that David is, once again, on the phone.

"I was standing right here," I point out as he reaches around me and shuts the curtain, then settles back in his seat, his body angled intimately toward mine.

"Good try, baby," he says, pinning me in a sizzling stare. "But I know you know that isn't going to work." His lips hint at a curve and if a tiny part of me worried that a spanking in a bathroom would make me feel awkward with Chris, it hasn't. In fact, as he brushes my hair behind my ear, his fingers linger on my skin and he says, "But I promise to kiss it and make it better," there is a warm sense of expanding intimacy between us. As if we've climbed a wall and we're finally standing on top.

"Get back to me," David says loudly, ending his call.

Chris's gaze lingers on mine a moment, and with evident reluctance that pleases me, he leans back against the cushion to face David, who is staring at us. And staring at us. Seconds tick by and my fingers curl into my palms with the sudden fear he somehow knows about my burning backside.

"I was a dickhead, Sara," David blurts out, reminding me of what Chris had successfully made me forget. He's right. He is. But thankfully he's a dickhead who doesn't seem to know my panties are in Chris's pocket.

"Because you say you were a dickhead or because Chris says you were?" I challenge.

"Both," he replies.

I give him a nod. "Then it's unanimous."

"Yeah well, I'm sorry, but that doesn't mean it won't happen again. I get passionate about what I do." He grabs his briefcase. "And right now, I'm going to go do my job and compare case notes with Tiger. I can promise you he won't be ripping this dickhead's throat out."

"You're meeting with Mark's attorney?"

"That's right, sugar." He winks and holds his hands up. "Don't throw anything at me. I'm joking. No more sugar. I'll stick to cutie or doll face in the future." He glances at Chris. "I'll call you in the morning with an update."

"Call me tonight," Chris says.

"It'll be late," David warns.

"That's fine." Chris motions to the table. "I got the food tonight."

David grins. "Like I'd have it any other way." He moves to

the curtain and gives me another keen, unwelcome inspection. "You haven't said much. That makes me nervous."

"That's the caffeine," I counter.

He snorts out laughter and glances at Chris. "Witty, isn't she?"

"Too much for her own good sometimes." David grunts for no apparent reason and then disappears through the curtain.

Chris tosses money onto the table. "Let's go, too."

Chris and I chat with Marco as we collect our jackets, and the way Chris finds every opportunity to touch me makes me smile in ways that reach beyond the laughter his and Marco's easy rapport sparks in me. When we finally step out into the chilly evening air, it's hand in hand, an erotic charge in the connection of our skin, even in the air we breathe. But he doesn't speak and he's stopped looking at me and I know why. This is part of the anticipation of what comes next. He's promised punishment. He *will* punish me. And just as he'd predicted, I crave the answer to what comes next. And while I normally welcome the sight of Jacob in our lobby, tonight I'm pleased to find his replacement is satisfied with a lift of our hands in greeting.

Once we're in the elevator, Chris surprises me by letting go of me, punching in our floor, and then leaning on the wall. I take his lead and lean on the opposite wall. "You were late," he reminds me. "You know what that means."

"Yes. You told me."

"What did I say?"

"That you're going to punish me."

"How?"

"Spank me again."

"Yes," he agrees. "I am." But there is something about the way he says it that tells me this is not going to be "just" a spanking, if there is such a thing. It's going to be more. It's going to push my limits.

The doors slide open to reveal our apartment and Chris punches the button to hold it open, but his eyes stay on me. "Go into the living room and undress, and then sit on the couch."

My lips part at the surprising command. "You want me to—"

"Yes," he says, his tone firm. "I do."

"And so I will," I say. "And you know why?" I move across the elevator and slip my hands under his jacket to rest on the hard wall of his chest. "Because it's not a lack of trust that I have in you, and that you think you see in me, Chris. It's *your* lack of trust in you that scares me." I start to pull away, but his fingers twine in my hair and he kisses me, deeply, possessively, so damn thoroughly that I'm reeling when it's over.

"Go undress," he orders, saying nothing in reply to my confession, and making none of his own.

I want to push him for something in reply, anything really, but the elevator isn't the place. I zip out of the doorway and all but run through the foyer and down the stairs. I begin undressing, the moonlight and stars filtering through the floor-to-ceiling windows, casting the room and me in a soft glow. Stealing a sideways look, hoping to catch a glimpse of Chris, I do not see him, but music begins to play and I recognize the song as "Madness" by Muse. Aware that Chris makes every choice with a purpose, I listen to the words.

I, I can't get these memories out of my mind.
And some kind of madness has started to evolve.
Mmmm. And I, I tried so hard to let you go.

Swallowing hard, I know he's connecting the meaning of this song to the war he wages daily against his inner demons, and to his fight to protect me from the person he believes they make him.

More of the words repeat into my mind. And *Now I need to know is this real love, or is it just madness keeping us afloat.* He's telling me he's afraid I won't love him if I fully know him. It's always there between us. He's fighting it now for me, and for us, and it matters. It matters so very much.

I finish undressing, and then claim a spot in the center of the brown leather couch. Before me is a sea of stars dotting the black canvas of the sky, and I am reminded of the first night I'd come here, when I'd been enamored with the brilliant artist, unwilling to see him as more. We've come so far since then, and yet I feel as if we still have barriers to hurdle. And I want them hurdled.

There's a tingling to my skin a moment before Chris, wearing only his low-slung jeans, appears to my right, and I feel that familiar punch of awareness. It burns and spreads, like warm honey in my blood, between my thighs. He affects me in ways I didn't know another human being could affect another, and in this moment, in this instant where I feel beyond my body, nestled deep in my soul, I know he was right in that bathroom tonight. It terrifies me to think of how deeply him leaving again would cut me. But I also know I've made the decision to take that risk.

He walks to the coffee table and pulls it back several feet, giving us space for what I'm certain will be wicked torture. I see it in his eyes as he steps closer and does a sweeping, seductive inspection of my naked body; my gaze lands on the rectangular box he's holding. He goes down on one knee in front of me and he sets the box on my legs. And while I know our games, and I know not to touch it as surely as I know not to touch him, I still have to curl my fingers around the leather seam of the couch to stop myself.

"Open the box," he orders, and his eyes hold the dominance I'd seen in that bathroom mirror before he'd spanked me. But there's a hint of something more, something that reminds me of the vulnerability I'd seen in him last night. He's opened himself for me to see this, and it's this willingness to give himself to me that spreads hope over my fears.

I reach for the box and my hand trembles with the rush of adrenaline and anticipation pumping through my body. He seems to understand, taking the lid from me and setting it aside. And then I just sit there, staring down at the pink, fluffy paddle inside.

"It seemed much less intimidating on the AdamEve.com website," I comment.

His fingers slide under my chin, lifting my gaze to his, and I feel that tiny little touch in every part of me. I want him. I want him badly. "You can always say 'no.'"

"No. I mean yes. I mean—"

He leans in and kisses me, and there's a soft brush of his lips over mine, a sensual lick of his tongue before his mouth is gone and I am captured in the gentle command of his stare. "Pick it up and hold it. Get used to how it feels."

I inhale and breathe out as I flatten my hand on the paddle, letting the fur tickle my palm. He reaches down and closes my hand around it, moving the box to set the paddle back on top of my legs. "It's a different feeling than my hand."

"Harder?"

"Different. Not harder. Lean back and hold your weight on your hands."

Obeying him has become automatic and I do as he's ordered, the position thrusting my breasts into the air. Chris's gaze rakes over me, a hot sensual stroke I feel everywhere and yet nowhere. He does not touch me. It's the fur paddle that contacts my skin, brushing over my legs, my arms, my belly, and finally, my sensitive nipples. He takes his time, missing nothing, returning to this place or that place. Warmth tingles through me, the tension in my muscles easing. More of that slick honey slides through me to settle heavily between my thighs.

But just when I forget that this is the prelude to what is defined as "punishment," Chris lets the paddle fall away from me and he claims the cushion beside me. "Sit up on your knees and face my lap."

I see where this is headed with a hard smack of realization. He wants me across his lap in the most vulnerable of ways. "Chris, I—"

"No thinking. Just do it."

His tone is hard, sharp, even, and it's as if he removes my options. I don't know how or why it works for me, but it does, and I listen. I turn so that my knees rest against his jean-clad thigh, the muscle flexing beneath my palm where my hand rests on his leg.

He leans in and frames my face, drawing my gaze to his. "Have I ever hurt you?"

"No. No, of course not."

"I'm not going to start now." He runs his thumb over my lips, inching closer to rest his cheek against mine, his warm breath teasing my ear. "This position lets me hit certain spots that will please you."

"And you know this because you—"

"Have experience," he supplies, easing back to look at me.

"So you've done this to other women." I know his past, and I try not to think about how I compare for fear it will drive me, and him, insane.

"I'm no Boy Scout, baby," he reminds me. "You know that, but it's different with you. *Everything* is different with you."

It's exactly what I need to hear and what, even in my most insecure moments, he's made me feel. My hesitation evaporates, and with a deep breath, I lean into his lap, but Chris laces his fingers in my hair and drags my mouth to his. "You don't have to do this."

"I was just nervous. That's all."

"You're sure?"

"Absolutely."

He isn't convinced, his eyes narrowing, probing. "I see fear in your eyes, Sara. I don't like it."

My fingers curl on his jaw. "Fear of being too vulnerable and needing you too much."

"And my fear? It's of *you* not needing *me enough*."

His mouth lowers to mine, and I whisper, "Too late," a moment before his tongue licks into my mouth with a long, drugging sweep that leaves me breathless, before he releases me, and I don't hesitate to answer the question I see in his eyes.

I stretch over Chris's lap, my elbows settling on the soft leather of the couch. My head tilts forward, allowing me the solace of my long, dark hair, though there is none for my bare backside. I am exposed in every possible way.

"Relax, baby," Chris murmurs, his warm hand flattening on my lower back.

"I'm trying."

"Take a deep breath and let it out."

As I suck in air his hand begins stroking up and down my spine. Over and over, I feel the slow, gentle movements seducing me, softening my tense muscles. Time seems to stand still, and it could be seconds or minutes that pass, but the music begins to come back to me. Words meld with his touch, becoming soothingly erotic, almost hypnotic. Gradually his hand moves lower, over my backside, and still he continues the same back and forth motion. Sensations seduce me, draw me in, and I forget to think. Until his hand stills and his fingers flex against my cheek.

I jerk, trying to sit up, and Chris's hand flattens on my back, holding me in place. "Stay, baby. I'll warn you first."

I pant, trying to slow my breathing. "Yes. No. I mean yes."

"Easy, baby," he murmurs again.

I force myself to relax, to sink against him and the couch, and close my eyes. I'm expecting the paddle any instant, but instead, he spreads my thighs and traces down the seam between my cheeks until his fingers slide into the slick, wet heat that defies my resistance and declares I am hot and aroused. And I am aroused, by how completely at his mercy I am. He reaches beneath me, his fingers stroking my clit in a deliciously, oh so right way, but one hand stays on my backside. One hand promises what is to come. But his fingers slide inside me, and the threat of that hand on my ass fades in the shameless lift of my hips, the pump of my hips against his hand.

Suddenly, though, his fingers are gone and I'm left gasping as his hand begins a gentle patting on my backside. I hold my breath, expecting this to be the warning before the sting, but his touch remains light, erotic. Over and over, he drums on me, the sensation an intoxicating vibration, and unbelievably, I'm on the edge again, my sex clenching, aching.

I feel Chris shift and reach for something, and then the music changes. "Listen to the song," he orders. "Focus on the words." The volume cranks to a roar and Muse's "Hysteria" thunders around us. *'Cause I want it now. I want it nowwww. Give me your heart and your soul. And I'm not breaking down. I'm breaking out.*

Adrenaline surges through me and the loud beat consumes my mind, and I know it's my warning. I try to brace myself for what's coming, but I can't think beyond how loud the words are, and I jerk when the fur of the paddle becomes the soft patting on my backside. It becomes faster but not harder. The music lances my mind and every nerve ending is in overload, tingling with every touch of the paddle. A burn begins inside me, an ache for more, for whatever comes next. It's no longer fear, it's need, but he doesn't give it to me.

The music punches into my mind, like it's echoing my thoughts. *I want it now. I want it now.* I do. I want it. "Chris, I—"

His fingers slice into my hair and he tugs my head back. "Now, baby," he warns. One hard blow comes down on my bottom and my back arches with the shock, but I don't have the opportunity to process it, let alone object. Another blow comes down. And another. Four, I think. No, five. I don't count. I can't count. Then he stops, but he doesn't let go of my hair or speak. He doesn't move at all. I lie there, feeling the gentle pull of my hair, the warmth of my cheeks, but then there's an odd sensation in my chest that I cannot escape. Suddenly, that sensation turns to a bubble of laughter. I have no idea why I'm laughing. I don't feel amused; I feel overwhelmed and aroused, and I don't know what else.

Without warning the paddle comes down on me again, and my laughter stops. Three more times I feel the heat of its touch, and then it's gone, and so is Chris's hold on my hair. I gasp and fall forward, and more laughter bubbles from some deep place inside of me, but it's not like any laughter I've ever experienced. It's as if some unidentifiable emotion is being ripped from a deep part of me.

Chris turns me to face him and, embarrassed by whatever's happening to me, I bury my face in his chest, curling into the hard warmth of his body. "Sara, look at me."

"No." I choke on more stupid laughter. "I can't."

He strokes my hair. "Laughter is like crying. It's a normal reaction to the endorphins. Let it happen."

"So I'm not crazy?"

He nuzzles my cheek. "If you're crazy, then we'll be crazy together."

I'm not laughing anymore, and the emotion in my chest expands into something completely different. Something only Chris makes me feel. Flattening my hands on his chest, I lean back and stare into his eyes, and where I feared I'd feel vulnerable, I don't. "Together," I repeat and the word feels good on my lips, the way he does.

He lowers his mouth nearer to mine and his breath is a sweet seduction, a prelude to the kiss I crave, like I crave him. For long seconds, we linger like this and I swear I can hear my own heart beat. Chris moves first, his hand splaying on my back, molding me to him, and I tangle my fingers in his blond hair, but still we don't kiss. We just breathe together, until the band of need between us snaps. Our mouths come together and we are crazy kissing, tongues tangling, hands all over each other's bodies.

He cups my breasts, teasing my nipples in that rough, delicious way he does and I am on fire, burning up from within, where I need him now. I moan and shift my body to shamelessly, eagerly, straddle him. My arms wrap around his neck. "I really need to be inside you," I confess, then blush to amend, "I mean—"

"You need to be inside me?" he teases, his laugh vibrating through my body, and tightening my sex.

"You know what I mean," I chide. "And now you know why I never flirted with men. I suck at it. Why are your pants still on?"

"So I wouldn't fuck you before you were ready." He reaches for his jeans. "Lift up."

We do some creative maneuvering and finally my hand is around his thick shaft, guiding him to me while he balances me. Then he is stretching me, filling me in ways far beyond the physical, in ways that reach deep into my soul. I take him fully, deeply, as completely as if I can't get enough of him. We are in wild abandon together, the music pounding around us, our bodies swaying, grinding. Somehow we are both making love and fucking and it is perfection. It is right and real and absolute, like my love for this man.

Somehow, I am leaning toward his knees, and his hands are at my waist, shackling me, holding me up, his gaze stroking my nipples, while his cock strokes me to the edge. He drives into me, pulling me down, pushing up. Over and over. Harder and harder. The music filters into my mind again, and the fast beat seems to become a part of our erotic dance, until I feel the rush of release overwhelming me.

"Chris," I plead as my muscles start to tense. "I'm going to fall."

He scoops me up against him, enclosing me in his arms, pulling me down against his hips. He is thick and hard and my body reacts to the feel of him in me, against me. My sex tightens and then the spasms begin to rip through me. Chris buries his face in my neck, a deep, guttural groan escaping him as he shudders and spills warm, wet heat into me.

We collapse together, clinging to each other. Seconds tick by, or minutes . . . I don't know or care. I'm with him. As he reaches behind him and turns down the music, I remember that first song and what he was telling me.

My hands cup his face and for once, it's me forcing him to look at me. "It's real."

"What?" he asks.

"That's what you were asking with that first song, wasn't it? Is this real enough to survive anything, no matter how bad?

The answer is yes—it's real. And I'll tell you what you told me in Paris. If you run, Chris, run fast, because I'll come after you. That's just the kind of bitch I am."

I expect him to laugh, but he doesn't. My name whispers from his lips, a tormented rough growl and his hand comes down on the back of my head, his mouth slanting over mine. His tongue sweeps past my lips, his kiss demanding, fierce, and I taste his need to believe me in it, his need to know we are right and real, and forever.

He doesn't even stop kissing me when he picks me up and carries me to the bedroom. He cleans us both up, and then wraps me in his arms from behind. We lie there in our bed, legs twined together and it's a perfect moment, so perfect that I dare to believe the past cannot rip this from us. Our demons are finally not as strong as we are.

Yet somehow, out of nowhere, I can almost hear Rebecca's voice in my head as she reads her written words.

The rush of fear is far better than the defeat of boredom. The high of not knowing what comes next is so much better than always knowing one day will be like the last. Never anticipation, never feeling anything. No. I cannot go back. So why am I so terrified of going forward?

Nine

The nightmare happened again. I am on the trolley with a crowd of people, but I blink and they disappear. I am left alone with only one other person. My dead mother. I ask her, as I always do in these dreams, how she is here, but she merely smiles. There is something evil in her expression that hurts me and makes me question the love I'd thought she had for me. Is my subconscious mind telling me it was as fake as her stories about my father?

The trolley continues without a driver and we start rolling down a hill toward the Bay. I know how this nightmare goes; I've had different versions many times, but still I cannot control my reaction. I begin to scream and I want to jump, but the car is going too fast. I can't stop the inevitable from happening. I can't and I don't. The trolley crashes into the ocean and icy water seeps through my clothes, piercing my skin like a sharp, painful blade.

I try to swim to the surface but the trolley is over me, shoving me down, down, down. . . . I cannot get to the surface. I cannot breathe. And my mother is nowhere. She is just gone. Like me.

I wake with a gasp, jolting to a sitting position, and it takes me several heaving breaths to realize I'm in bed.

"Easy, baby. It's just the alarm clock."

Chris's voice breaks through the havoc in my mind; his hand on my back calms the tension tightening my spine.

"I had a nightmare," I say, welcoming his arm around my neck, his forehead against mine. "It was . . . it was like I was Rebecca, and I was writing in one of her journals."

He leans back, giving me a curious look, grabbing the remote off the nightstand and sending the shades into motion and a new day's light spilling in as they lift. "I thought her entries were erotic, not scary."

I pull my knees to my bare chest. "Not all of them. She wrote a lot about her nightmares and her death."

"Wait. She wrote about her death? Why haven't I heard about this before now?"

"They were just nightmares. It didn't feel important."

"They were a by-product of her life, so my question is what brought them on? Was she afraid of someone?"

"No. They weren't about a person. She was always drowning in the Bay. They were more about control, I think. About her feeling like something in her life was spiraling out of control and she couldn't stop it."

"Was there anyone else in the nightmares?"

"Her dead mother."

He tilts his head, giving me a keen inspection. "Let me get this straight. Rebecca had control issues, an absent father, a love for art, and was messed up over her mother."

There is a tight knot in my chest, rapidly getting tighter. "And she loved a man she feared she could never truly have. Yes. We were alike. That's why I connected to her writing."

"Sara, where did that come from?"

"I'm sorry. It's not about now. It's about the past, when I was reading her journals, and you left me. I understood her and I didn't even know her."

"I see my instincts to lock those damn journals away were right."

"At the time I locked them away, it was," I grudgingly admit. "But her words were also what gave me the courage to seek out a dream that led us to each other. She changed my life, Chris, and she haunts me beyond those journals. I can't explain it, but I feel like I was always supposed to find her justice." I look upward a moment and shake my head. "I sound like a crazy person."

"No." He wraps his arm around my calves, just below mine. "You sound like someone who cares, and there are too few people who do."

"Like you do," I say. "You help people, Chris, and I love that about you. You're helping Mark even though he doesn't deserve it from you."

"I've found that in life, the times we need help are often the times we deserve it the least."

"Sometimes people like Rebecca deserve it and they never have it."

His phone beeps on the nightstand and he releases me to reach for it. "That reminds me," I say. "Did David ever call?"

"This is from him," he says, indicating his phone, and reading: *"Client emergency last night and this morning. Tied up all morning. Update you later. Just don't say anything I wouldn't say today, and you'll be fine."*

I laugh. "Seriously? Don't say anything he wouldn't say? *No one* says the things that man says. *Sugar.*"

Chris grins. "The next time we go to dinner with him, I'm ordering a pitcher of beer."

Smiling, I shake my head. "I so would enjoy that." It hits me that I forgot something else last night. "You never told me what happened when you met with Mark."

"Not much. He's a cracked brick wall, trying to pretend he's steel. And his normal outlet for maintaining that façade is gone. Tiger made him sign the club over."

"To who?"

"His head of security."

"I'm shocked. That's a major part of who he is."

"It might be the best thing that ever happened to him. It's going to force him to deal with life, not hide from it."

"I'm not sure if I agree or disagree. Mark's hard to understand."

"And to help."

"Did he decline my offer to help at the gallery?"

"No, he's not a fool. He wants to be close to his mother right now, and that means Allure isn't a priority."

"It shouldn't be."

"You're right—and his mother deserves her son next to

her when she fights this monster. We'll help that happen." He glances at his cell phone. "It's eight now. Mark agreed to hire security, and Jacob is meeting us at the gallery at nine."

"Jacob? What about his job here?"

"Blake worked a deal with the building management to have Jacob at the gallery today. Walker Security's working on a plan to carry the gallery through the trial." He motions to the bathroom. "Care to save water with me?"

"Not if you want to be there on time."

He leans in and kisses my neck. "Good point, because I could definitely make you my breakfast and forgo the shower." He throws off the blanket and starts walking toward the bathroom, gloriously, wonderfully naked. My God, the man has a great ass. I drop back on the bed and sigh blissfully as his scent whispers all around me. Things might be bad but they are really darn good, too.

Rolling onto my stomach, I grab the remote from the night-stand and turn on the news, then reach into my drawer and pull out my new journal. Sitting up and resting against the headboard, I stare at the image of the Eiffel Tower on the cover, not overly eager to open it. After the meeting with the police, and seeing how Rebecca's words have become such public fodder, I'm not so sure I want mine documented. Still, I open to a blank page and remove the pen clipped inside, and find myself re-creating the very first entry in Rebecca's journal that I'd ever read.

Dangerous.

For months I've had dreams and nightmares about how perfectly he personifies the word. Sleep-laden, alternate realities where I can vividly smell his musky male scent, feel his hard body against mine. Taste the sweet and sensuous flavor of him—like milk chocolate with its silky demand that I indulge in one more bite. And another. So good, I'd forgotten there's a price for overindulgence. And there is a price. There is always a price.

The word *dangerous* bothers me, just like it had Detective Grant. It has always bothered me. Its use was a big part of what drove me to look for Rebecca.

Chris asked me if she feared anyone. She did. She feared Mark and the power he had to hurt her, but that isn't so odd. I had that same thought about Chris last night.

I glance up and my gaze lands on the television as a photo of Ava appears next to a pretty blond newscaster. Scrambling for the remote, I turn up the volume.

"Guilty or not guilty? That appears to be the question with a woman who first confessed to killing a missing young woman named Rebecca Mason, and attacking another. Now our sources say that in tomorrow's bail adjustment hearing she'll change her plea to not guilty, claiming she was coerced to confess by someone threatening her life."

An image of Rebecca replaces that of Ava. *"The real question becomes 'where is Rebecca Mason?' So far there has been no body found, and without one, police will be hard-pressed to support a murder charge. Could the answer lie in the high-end art world she worked in? Or perhaps a link to underground sex clubs and billionaire clients? Our sources say it might just be possible. Tune in tomorrow night for a special report with Kali Wilson."*

The story leaves me shaken, and when the bed shifts I glance up to find Chris, fully dressed in a black long-sleeved T-shirt and black jeans, sitting next to me. "I guess it's out now."

His lips tighten. "It appears it is."

"What do you think?"

He takes the remote from me and turns off the TV. "I think this is about to get very nasty."

Forty minutes later Chris and I step outside of our building. He hands the attendant a large bill to retrieve our car, and the kid's eyes light up at Chris's generosity before he rushes away.

The instant he's gone, Chris grabs the lapels of my coat and pulls it open, exposing my slim-fitting pale blue suit-dress to his sizzling inspection. My cheeks heat and I yank it shut. "Behave. We aren't alone."

"You look too damn fuckable to be around Mark Compton. Tomorrow you wear a bag. A big, ugly one."

I laugh but I don't miss the underlining edginess to his mood or make the mistake of dismissing it. He's not even close to over being pissed at Mark's attempts to seduce me. I push to my toes and kiss him. "I'll have a bodyguard," I remind him. "Two, actually. You and Jacob."

He seems to have more to say on the matter, but his cell phone rings and he snags it from his pocket. "Amber's rehab facility," he announces grimly. "It's already after nine," he tells me before answering. "Can you call Jacob and tell him we're five minutes away?"

I nod, digging my phone out of my purse while trying to listen in on his conversation. By the time I punch in Jacob's number, I hear Chris say, "Whatever it takes. Money isn't an issue," and I have the impression he isn't getting good news.

"I'm here," Jacob answers, not bothering with a greeting. "Where are you two?"

"Five minutes away."

"I'll be inside the gallery. I got here early. Your 'Bossman' let me in."

I laugh at the nickname the staff uses for Mark, but it chokes out of me, as laden with tension as Chris's body language. "Sounds like Ralph is there and teaching you his gallery slang."

"He is and he did," Jacob confirms. "Apparently 'Bossman' is code for 'Asshole.'"

"I take it he isn't in a good mood?"

"He has moods? I heard he only did 'Asshole' and 'Asshole.'"

"He's normally arrogant and difficult, but fair and rather generous with his employees. But right now, his mother has cancer, and Rebecca . . . she mattered to him."

"Don't worry. I have a high tolerance for assholes. It's a gift my father taught me."

His remark hits a hot spot I've been silently nursing. I almost died last week, and my father doesn't even know. "Your father must resemble mine," I say, my tone cynical.

"I sure as hell hope not," he says. "There's a news truck out front. I'll watch for you at the rear parking lot."

Stuffing my phone back in my purse, I discover Chris is still on his, still listening intently to whatever is being said to him, his gaze cast off to the distance.

If he knows when the Porsche is pulled up beside us, and the attendant holds my door, he doesn't acknowledge it. Concerned, I pause outside the car and wait, and it's a good three more minutes before he ends the call, his jaw flexing as he slides his cell back into his pocket. I watch as he glances up and looks startled that the car is here; he's rarely startled by anything. He heads toward the driver's side and I climb in, allowing the attendant to shut me inside.

"Everything still a 'go' with Jacob, I assume?" Chris asks as he puts the car into gear.

"He's already there and he met with Mark. There's a news truck in front of the gallery, so he wants us to meet him at the back." Softening my voice, I ask, "What about Amber?"

He reaches the end of the drive and brakes, staring straight ahead for several seconds before he looks at me, his eyes dark. "She's turned violent. They feel she needs more attention and a longer stay than initially planned."

"That's not good."

"No. It's not."

I want to comfort him, but Chris doesn't like fluffy words any more than I do, and they won't ease the self-blame eating him alive. I think of how he compared Amber to Rebecca, and himself to Mark, and a bad feeling slides through me. His helping Mark isn't just about Mark. It's about repenting for his own sins.

Chris cuts down the alleyway between the coffee shop and the gallery and says into his phone, "We'll pull up to the back door to avoid the press. I'll let Sara go in, and then park. Right."

"You think the press is going to swarm us?" I ask when he hangs up.

"After that news piece this morning, everyone and their uncle will be after a story. So yes. If not now, soon."

He maneuvers the 911 to only inches from the door, where Jacob stands, looking his normal stoic self in his standard dark suit. "Remember," Chris warns as Jacob opens my door. "Ralph and Amanda are going to know what was on the news. There's been nothing about you yet, but tomorrow will be a different story. You need to figure out what you want to tell them, and when."

I give a short nod and exit the car. *It's about to get nasty.* It had been an odd choice of words from Chris, but so appropriate. Murder is as nasty as it gets.

Jacob shuts the car door and I enter the gallery with him on my heels; then he says, "Stay inside."

I turn to see him going back out. Grabbing the door, I gape at the crush of press rushing the 911, now pulled into a parking spot. Someone shouts and several people start running in my direction. I back up and shut the door.

Stunned, I hold my breath and wait for Chris and Jacob to appear. This is insanity. It's the stuff of fake tabloids, not real lives. Seconds tick by like hours, and I begin to get nervous. Should I call the police on the press for trespassing?

I rush into the office. "Amanda," I say urgently. "I need the number . . ." My words trail off when I discover she's not at her desk.

"She's a no-show so far," Ralph calls from his office. "And she's not answering her phone."

Oh God. What else this morning? Concerned, I go to his doorway to find him looking frazzled, all kinds of files overlapping one another on his desk and a calculator tape dipping to the ground over the top. "Has she ever done this before? I remember her being reliable."

"Never," he says, seeming irritated at the need to abandon his calculator. "But the Ava news this morning could have spooked her."

"You heard," I say, taking the blows as they come.

"I'm sure the whole city heard. Murder, sex scandals, and so on and so on. Amanda's a 'drink beer out of a glass' kind of girl. Hand her a bottle, and she doesn't know what to do with it."

"Ah . . . translation?"

"It's too much for her."

"And you?"

"I'll live, especially since Bossman tells me you're going to be around. But you have sales things to do and I can't do her job and mine, too. Bossman has me running all kinds of financials on the gallery that require focus." He lowers his voice. "The kind of data you put together to put a business on the market."

"What?" I close the distance between us and stop in front of his desk, keeping my tone hushed. "You think he intends to sell the gallery?"

"My mama didn't raise an idiot. He's absolutely reviewing his options. That, or considering a merger with Riptide."

"You must be mistaken." Mark would never sell his pride and joy.

"I'm not."

He says it so definitively that I can't help but pause. If he's right, that leads me to the conclusion that either Mark's mother's health is worse than we know, or the situation with the police is worse than we know. Or both.

"I'll take care of the admin stuff," I promise Ralph. "You just do your thing and buzz me if you hear from Amanda."

"You do the same," he calls out as I leave his office and enter mine, quickly dumping my purse in the desk drawer before walking back into the lobby to hang my coat up on the rack behind the reception desk.

"Soul-sucking bastards ready to destroy a person for thirty seconds of fame," Chris grumbles as he enters the office with Jacob on his heels.

"It went that well, I guess?" I ask, meeting him in the middle of the lobby.

"We're getting a gate put around the parking lot so this won't be an issue again. I don't care if I have to pay for the damn thing myself. I already called Blake and told him to make it happen."

"When's the receptionist due in?" Jacob asks, moving to stand beside us. "I was hoping to look over the messages from the service."

"Twenty-five minutes ago," I supply. "She almost walked out yesterday before I could promise her extra security. But I can clear the messages."

"I'll get the messages," Jacob offers. "You do what you need to do."

"I'm not sure anything else I do will be much help for this place right now. We can't plan a grand reopening with this craziness going on." And after what Ralph told me, I wonder if it matters anymore.

"I'd say focus on convincing the artists on display not to pull their work," Chris suggests. "Use me all you need to. I'll talk to whomever I have to. Is Mark in his office?"

"Yes," Ralph calls from his desk, making it clear he's been eavesdropping. "And Amanda is now thirty minutes late."

Jacob's phone buzzes and he glances at it. "Gotta run. The tech crew's here to install some extra equipment."

He disappears and Chris closes the short distance between us, giving me a sizzling once-over that pretty much strips me naked. "Tomorrow," he says, leaning in near my ear to whisper, "you wear the bag or I keep you in bed." He fixes me in a stare. "Understood?"

I smirk at him and grab the lapels of his jacket as he had mine earlier. "Yes, Master," I whisper.

Chris looks amused. "I dare you to say that later and see what results it gets you." He motions down the hall. "But for now, this 'Master' is going to see 'Bossman.'"

I laugh and call after him, "I dare you to call him that to his face."

The door behind me opens and I turn to see Amanda rushing into the office, her long brown hair tied into a messy ponytail.

"Hi," she says, giving me an awkward wave. "Sorry I'm late. We were driving around the block, waiting for the TV people to get back into their van."

We? Who is we? I consider asking directly but she's so nervous that I stick with, "I hope you didn't make your roommate late to work."

She cuts her gaze, pretty much confirming my fear. She was with Ryan.

"We tried to call you!" Ralph shouts from his office.

"Oh." She flushes and shrugs out of her jacket. "Sorry. I didn't charge my cell last night."

Because she wasn't home. Every instinct I own says she was with him and that he's bad for her. Maybe even dangerous. No. Not dangerous. Where did that come from?

"What should I do today?" she asks, hanging up her coat. Her black skirt is off center and one of her blouse buttons is in the wrong hole.

"If you could get the messages for me and bring them to my office?" I ask, and it hits me that she doesn't seem surprised to see me at all.

"Yes, of course," Amanda agrees. "Is Bossman here?"

"Locked in his office," I confirm.

"And we're in a red zone," Ralph calls out, and I assume by her responding grimace that this must be some new code for Mark being cranky.

"Thanks for the warning."

When she looks everywhere but at me, I ask quietly, "Are you okay?"

Her gaze lifts to mine, her discomfort palpable. I think she's afraid I'll find out about her and Ryan and be upset. Or maybe she's afraid Mark will find out? Unless . . . oh God, I almost swallow my tongue. Please don't let Mark be involved with Amanda, too. Please don't let that be why she's not surprised I'm here.

"I'm okay," she says, but the words come out choked. She delicately clears her throat then adds, "It's just . . . it's the press and Rebecca and . . . just all of it."

It's a logical answer, so why am I waiting for her to say something else? I give her several expectant seconds but she says nothing. Not ready to give up, I ask, "Is there anything I can do to help you get through all this?"

She cuts her gaze again, giving a quick shake of her head. "It's okay."

Okay. I head for my office, and Ralph flags me as I pass his door.

I pause in his doorway as he asks, "Would it be really tacky for me to order coffee from next door and have them deliver it? I mean, I know that coffee shop used to be Ava's, but—"

"Ava's coffee shop is open?"

"It never closed. It's being run by Ava's husband. And yes, you heard me right. I didn't even know she was married, but I guess they were living apart."

Of course her husband would take over the coffee shop. The answer makes perfect sense, just like Amanda's reasons for being late and flustered. And yet, nothing feels quite right at all.

Ten

An hour later Jacob has joined Chris in Mark's office, and I'm reviewing the answering service report Jacob ordered for problems. But every few seconds I keep glancing at the roses in the Georgia O'Nay painting, grasping for something I can't remember. It nags at me, and I reach into my briefcase and pull out my journal. Flipping to a blank page, I cave to the compelling need to write down my thoughts on Rebecca's disappearance:

> *Did Ava act alone?*
> *Could Ava be crazy enough to really claim credit for a murder she didn't commit?*
> *What if Rebecca isn't dead at all?*

I'm irritated at myself for even writing that last question, but it's the one we all are wishfully asking. I start writing again, listing people who mattered to Rebecca:

1. Her mother: She raised Rebecca alone and she died with a secret about her father that tore Rebecca to pieces. I never figured out what that secret was, but I'm certain that Rebecca never knew her father. But what if he knew her? What if her existence was a threat to him, and maybe another family?

2. Ex-boyfriend: I don't know his name, but she wrote about him being stalkerish. He seemed irrelevant, but was he?

3. Mary: Jealous, mean, competitive. I'm pretty sure she had the hots for Mark.

4. Ryan: One of her lovers, though not by choice. Mark brought him into the relationship. I don't know the dynamic of their relationship enough to know what he felt for her. Rebecca didn't express any emotions about him at all, which is odd, considering how intimate they were.

5. Mark: Per Chris, he loved her but wasn't in love with her. I disagree. I saw his eyes the night he heard she was dead. And there's no question she rattled his control like no other person ever had. If there is a fine line between love and hate, where did Mark walk then and now?

6. Ricco: The man who told me there's a fine line between love and hate. He was, and still is, infatuated with Rebecca. He hates Mark for being the one she wanted. As with Mark, I find it hard to believe someone who loves that deeply would kill that person, but what about when they're rejected? What about in a moment of passion?

"Hey, baby."

I look up to find Chris standing in my doorway, and he's a welcome breath of hot, wicked man in denim and leather. He wasn't wearing the jacket a few minutes ago. "Are you leaving?"

"I need to run to the bank and take care of some stuff before tomorrow becomes a bigger zoo than today." He motions to the door. "Walk me out?"

"Yes, of course." I push to my feet and he watches me, tracking my every step, his eyes traveling my body in a hot inspection that I blame for the ache forming in my sex. Or maybe that's the memory of his hand on my backside. He's right; a spanking has a way of making the world fade away.

The instant I'm in front of him, he reaches for me, twining his fingers with mine, and bringing us toe-to-toe. "If you keep looking at me like that," he promises, "I'm going to say 'fuck the gallery' and take you home and fuck you."

"The wait always makes it better," I remind him, as he often does me.

"Ah, my naughty little schoolteacher. You're learning." He leads me into the hallway.

"What was going on in Mark's office?" I ask as we head to the door.

"We Skyped with one of Blake's brothers and lined up the security details."

"Where's Blake?"

"He's on his way here from New York. That's why we had to deal with his brother."

"I thought Kelvin ran San Francisco?"

"I like Kelvin, but we have too much shit going on to not have Blake here in person. He's going to chat one-on-one with Amanda and Ralph sometime tomorrow as well. We want to make sure the press doesn't get to them."

That sets off my alarm bells. "Amanda is acting so odd, Chris. Maybe they already got to her. I hate that I'm saying this, but after what I've seen today, maybe shutting the gallery and funneling sales through Riptide is the way to go for a while."

We near the back exit and Chris halts just beyond several security people milling around. "He may sell it," he says, his tone low, for my ears only.

I move close, careful not to let my voice lift. "Ralph told me he was doing financials to sell, but I thought he was crazy. This is Mark's pride and joy, and it's part of his identity."

"Well, we both know his identity is being shaken up, and I think he's preparing for Riptide to need him full-time."

"Oh, God—his mother? I thought she was better."

"I don't know. He's not saying much, and maybe she's simply going to retire. I'm just guessing." He glances at his watch. "I might be a couple of hours. I need to attend to a few investments." His hand settles on my waist. "I'm going to have the Louvre find a replacement for me for the charity, so we don't have that pressure."

"What? No." I grab his arm. "Chris, if this is about last night—"

He cups my cheek. "I need you to know that nothing is more important than you and this and us."

"Please don't read into last night. I *do* know."

"Not enough, baby, but I'm working on fixing that." His hand falls away. "I need to run. My banker's expecting me, but call me if you need anything. I'll answer. Blake should be here by dinner time to talk through where the investigation stands."

"Did you ask him about—"

"Yes, I've been on him. No word on Ella, though. I'm sorry, but he's trying."

"I want to be there tonight when you meet with Blake."

"I assumed as much. I'll see if we can get him and his team, as well as David, to our house."

Thinking of Ava reminds me of next door. "Did you hear the coffee shop is open?"

"Jacob told me."

"Ralph says Ava's estranged husband is running it."

"Husband? Ava has a husband?"

"That was my reaction when I found out." My brows furrow with a memory and a note to add to my journal. "The day we ran into Ava at the Chanel store, she told me her ex was trying to make her jealous to win her back. Does that make you think what it makes me think?"

"That Ava needed help to make Rebecca disappear and she had it in him."

"It makes sense."

"Yes. It's a logical assumption and I'm sure the police are thinking the same thing."

"If you were that confident about what the police are doing, Blake wouldn't be flying in today on what I'm guessing is your dime. You'd settle for him at a distance and his crew here with us."

He pulls me to him. "Our dime, baby. What's mine is yours and what's yours is definitely mine. *Wife.*" He kisses me soundly on the lips and then heads to the door where he stops to talk to one of the security people.

I stand there, staring after him, and I'm not sure what affects me more. The security of knowing that this amazing man wants me to be his wife, or the fact that he didn't deny the reason Blake is flying here. I was right. He doesn't trust the police department to get the job done. Maybe he even worries, like me, that they'll get the job done wrong.

Back in the office I pull out my list of sales prospects, but I'm still distracted by the painting, and why it's bothering me. Maybe it simply represents what's lost and seems never to be found, and a sense of hopelessness I don't seem able to escape.

Though it feels like I'm spinning my wheels, I finally start the process of highlighting the gallery clients I think will be the most understanding of the circumstances, and thus will be easier sales to close.

Amanda buzzes me. "You have a call on the back line. It's Crystal from Riptide."

I cringe at the realization that I never called her back last night, and the wrath she must have received from Mark. I reach for the phone. "Put her through," I say, rushing to the door to shut it before reclaiming my chair.

"Crystal," I say, answering the line. "I'm so very sorry I didn't call you last night."

"You're there. That's what counts."

"Did Mark give you a hard time about rehiring me?"

"Of course. It started with, 'Ms. Smith—' in that proper authoritative voice of his. And he tried to end it with, 'I trust we will not have this conversation again.'"

"Tried?"

"I was with his mother. She was having a rare feisty moment and wanted to talk to him."

I laugh. "Oh my. He must have loved that."

"Actually, I think he loves anything resembling feisty in her these days."

"I'm sure you're right," I say and not for the first time I have the impression she knows more than Mark's mother well. She knows him.

"How is he?" she asks softly, and something in her tone hints at far more than job duties.

"He's keeping to himself," I reply, "but I don't think he's doing that well at all." I glance down at the messages on my desk, many from reporters. "Has he warned you about the media attention that could be coming in your direction?"

"I know about the Rebecca situation and the news reports this morning. I know it all, Sara. And I mean all of it. You can't shock me. You can't scare me. They can't scare me. *Mark* can't scare me."

There's some sort of loaded punch behind those words that resembles me with Chris too much for me to ignore. "Just . . . be careful, Crystal. Don't—"

"Get emotionally attached? To Mark? I'm smarter than that. To his parents, too late. They're my second family and I'm worried about them. His mother is pretty out of it with the chemo and radiation treatments, and Mark told his father what's going on. He's helping me shelter her, but he's not emotionally equipped to handle much himself."

"I'm wondering about Allure," I start, daring to feel her out about Mark selling the gallery. "Is Mark—"

There's a muffled knock in the background. "Hold on, Sara. Sorry." I hear her open the door and murmur something that I can't make out to someone. Several beats pass and she returns. "I'm afraid I have an auction with complications about to start, but I called for a reason. Newman Riley. Do you know him?"

"I know his work. He's one of the artists on display here at Allure."

"Not after today. He's a bit of a diva and he's on a tirade. He's not pleased that the gallery is closed and that no one will return his calls. Apparently, I don't count as someone since I've talked to him three times. What it comes down to is that he wanted to talk to Mark."

"Did you tell him about Mark's mother and Rebecca?"

"Yes. He doesn't care. I think that's why Mark doesn't care, either. Bottom line, Newman is on a plane to San Francisco as we speak. He plans to remove his work from the gallery personally. I left Mark a message and texted him after he hung up with his mother, but I called because I had a gut feeling he wasn't communicating with you. I didn't want Newman to show up and surprise you."

"Mark's in the gallery, so he must be planning to deal with him when he arrives."

She lowers her voice. "Between you and me, I'm not so sure he has a plan. His mother started crying while she was talking to him, and I'm pretty sure it upset him. She wanted him here for her chemo treatment, and I know he wanted to be here, too."

I press my fingertips to my temple. "No wonder he's locked in his office. I'll handle it. Thank you, Crystal."

"Thank *you*, Sara. Gotta run. Call me if you need me."

The line goes dead and I sit there for a minute, digesting the way she has thanked me, like this is her family she's protecting. She seems emotionally attached, which normally would be a good thing, but now . . . now I think of how emotional attachment has become dangerous. Amber is in rehab over Chris. Ricco is charged with a felony over his attachment to Rebecca. Ava is on trial for murder. Rebecca . . . is dead.

I want to see Crystal's attachment to Mark and his family as good. Instead, I'm worried. And did she know Rebecca? Was she involved with Mark at the same time? Was she someone invited into their play? Does she know Ava? I feel horrible for suspecting her if she's sincere, but I have to be cautious.

I dial Chris and he picks up almost immediately. "Miss me already?"

"I miss our bed with you and me in it, away from all of this," I say. "Is this a bad time?"

"Never. What's up, baby?"

I sigh. "I have a problem. Surprise."

"Does his name start with an 'M'?"

My lips twist wryly. "Yes." I explain what Crystal told me about Riley. "I think I need to handle this, not Mark, but I don't think he'll see it that way. I'm hoping you know Riley and have some insight into his personality."

"Yeah. I know Riley. He's done some charity work with

me. He tends to feel overlooked in the art community. The result isn't always good. I wouldn't put it past him to run his mouth to the press. I'm only a few blocks away. I'll have the security guys on alert and I'll talk to him. I know a few projects coming up that might persuade him to be tolerant."

"Thank you, Chris."

"Thank me later. In bed. Or out of bed. Be creative."

I smile into the phone and respond with what has become our running joke, "I'll use your imagination."

"Even better."

I've barely settled my cell phone back on my desk when Amanda buzzes me again. "Ryan is on the line and he says he's outside to see Mark. They won't let him in."

"Did you tell Mark?"

"He won't pick up his phone."

"Now isn't a good time." And even if it was, I don't think Mark would see Ryan. "He needs to call in advance."

"He says Mark won't take his calls."

"Put Ryan on with me."

"I, ah, he hung up."

No, he didn't. He called her cell phone, instead of contacting her through the security team outside. "If he calls back, put him through."

"Yes. Okay. Thanks."

With the odd dynamics of Mark and Ryan's relationship on my mind, I flip open the journal and I write my own version of Ricco's words. *A fine line between friendship and hate.* I underline the words.

Eleven

Riley shows up at lunchtime, and Jacob quickly detours him to Chris. I order pizza for everyone, including the security crew, who are nearly done with the fence around the parking lot. There's relative quiet in the gallery, and I find myself once again jotting notes in my journal. I've compiled so much information that I decide I should hand it over to Blake tonight.

Flipping to the first entry I'd made on the plane, I pick a random line and begin to read.

He'd thought he'd beaten the need for the whip outside of the one day a year, but Dylan's death proved him wrong.

That's all I need to rip the page out and start tearing it into tiny pieces and I stuff them in my trash can. I will not let my words be a window into Chris's secrets and I wonder now if Rebecca would feel the same if she were alive today.

The pizza arrives and we all decide to eat at our desks. With a slice on my plate, I start to take a bite, then change my mind and buzz Mark's office.

He answers with, "Not now, Ms. McMillan."

"But we ordered—"

"The definition of 'not now' is not now."

I inhale and sit there. And sit there some more. Then I stand up. This man has intimidated me many times, but right now, his grief intimidates me more than the man. He's falling apart. Alone. Exactly what I did after losing my mother. Decision made, I round my desk and make my way down the hallway to his door. I knock and his reply is almost instant.

"Not now means *not now*, Ms. McMillan."

Steeling myself, I turn the knob and enter his office. He personifies every intimidating man who has ever brought me to my knees, yet he is not those men. He is more, or different. He is something I cannot explain.

"Ms. McMillan—"

I snap at the formality of my name, and in a heartbeat I'm across the room, my hands planted on his desk. "Sara. My name is Sara."

He just stares at me, offering not so much as a blink to show he's human. Silence ticks between us, the air charged.

"Think about what you're doing," he warns, his tone a near slap, and I have to remind myself that the stony exterior he portrays is a façade. I've seen glimpses of the wounded man beneath, a man who's bleeding from his soul and alone in his grief.

"I need instructions to deal with some problems."

"Go home. Problems solved."

I'm so over the edge of my comfort zone, I seem beyond fear. I round the desk, invading his space, and he rotates his chair to face me. His stare hits me like a blast of scorching flames. He is angry. Furious even, which is about as intimidating as it gets, but it's also emotion. It's success. It's me tearing through that iron-solid control of his.

He leans back his chair, reclining casually into the leather, but he isn't truly relaxed. "What are you doing, Ms. McMillan?"

"Trying to talk to you."

"Unlike you, I'm not big on conversation." The statement is punched with a blast of ice so cold, it could chill the entire state of Texas.

I don't back down. "I know you're hurting."

The pain in his eyes is gone as quickly as it arrives. "Are you volunteering to help me fuck the hurt out of my system?" he challenges. "Because that's what I do, Ms. McMillan. I fuck things out of my system."

My fingers curl on the edge of the desk and my chin lifts in determination. "I don't intimidate that easily."

"It was a simple invitation. A good fuck shouldn't intimidate anyone. If it does, someone is doing it wrong."

The jab at Chris is almost my undoing, but that's what he wants—and Chris's words about people needing help when they least deserve it come back to me. "I want to help you, Mark. That's why I'm at the gallery. That's why I'm standing here and I'm not asking your permission to be your friend."

"The façade of friendship is a dangerous one."

"You said that about love," I retort, reminding him of how he tried to "save" me when Chris was gone.

His fingers flex into the leather armrests. He doesn't like that response. "Either get naked or get out." His voice is low, seething with anger.

"Stop talking to me like that. Let's get beyond that, for once. And you're just angry with me anyway. I'm okay with that, Mark. At least you're showing me emotion. At least you're being real."

"You mistake me for someone who has emotions, Ms. McMillan. I don't."

"Anger is emotion. Desire is an emotion. Lust and passion. Guess what? Also emotions."

"Those are feelings."

"Emotion is feeling."

"Love. Hate. Sadness. Those are emotions. Fucking is about pleasure. The kind I've offered to show you."

I refuse to let him see how he flusters me. "You feel sadness. I was in the office when that song made you choke up over Rebecca, and I was under that tree with you the night you learned she was gone."

"A night you obviously don't remember well, considering I told you to stay the fuck away from me. You don't listen to instructions well."

"I think that's why you like me," I accuse. "And I think that's why you loved Rebecca."

His lashes lower and this time he doesn't try to hide his pain. Maybe he can't. Maybe that's how deep a nerve I've hit, but I don't regret it. He's about to drown in his own denial. I hope this is a breakthrough, a chance for him to heal.

My hope wavers when the full intensity of his gaze slams

into me and he stands, towering over me, his hands coming down on my shoulders.

"Sara," he says softly, shocking me with more than the use of my first name. "You remind me of her. Did you know that?"

My lips part in shock and confirmation. He hired me, even pursued me, because I was a version of the woman he missed and craved. He turns me toward the door and leans in, his warm breath brushing my cheek. "That's not a good thing for either of us right now. Get out, Ms. McMillan."

He drops his hands, but I can feel him behind me, too close. I'm not going to be a fool, waving a red flag in front of an angry bull. I quickly go to the door, then pause and turn. "Ryan is working his way into Amanda's bed, if he isn't there already. That seems like a serious problem to me."

While his response is slow to arrive, it's precise and sharp. "You would be correct."

"What should I do?"

"Nothing. Let me handle it."

That's not the answer I want or will even entertain, so I don't pretend I will. I turn and exit, leaving Mark alone . . . again.

Three hours later, Chris has saved the day with Riley and calls to let me know that he's dropping him off at the airport. I'm relieved, and exhausted from explaining the gallery situation to clients over and over. The hard work has paid off, though. I have a list of twenty people interested in the grand reopening, and a client who wants to buy one of Chris's paintings.

I'm about to dial another customer when Jacob appears in my doorway and charges toward me. "The police have a warrant. It's legit and I can't hold them at the door more than a few more minutes, if that. I'm going to warn Mark."

"Oh no." I stand up. "What should I do?"

"Prepare the staff and lead them to the front door," he replies. "Law enforcement has it blocked off, so there are no media concerns. You won't be allowed to take more than your coat and purse, and they'll search it before you leave."

"Did you call Chris?"

"Yes. He's about thirty minutes away. The police can't enter the building until certain precautions to protect the art have been taken, which won't take long. I'm going to coordinate with Mark."

As he rushes away, Ralph appears in my doorway. "What's happening?"

"There's a search warrant for the gallery."

Amanda shoves under his arm. "What? They're searching the gallery? Are you serious?"

"I'm afraid so," I confirm. The conversation I'd planned to have with them later clearly needs to happen now. "Tomorrow Ava has a bail adjustment hearing. Her counsel has threatened a media-created scandal if she doesn't get a lower bond, and that will involve the gallery. Grab what you want to take home and then head to the front door, but I can't promise they'll let you leave with anything but a coat and purse."

They just blink at me as if I've grown horns.

I wave them onward. "Go! Get your things."

They disappear and I gather my coat and purse, then remember the journal. If I take it, I'll bring attention to it. If I don't, they might read it. Regretting my detailed notes now, I decide to leave it behind.

Exiting my office, I find Ralph and Amanda waiting by her desk. She casts me an apprehensive look. "Do we just walk out?"

I glance down the hallway to the right at Mark's closed door, wondering if we should wait for him and Jacob, when the door to my left opens. Jerking around, I suck in a breath to find myself face-to-face with Detective Miller again.

"Ms. McMillan," she greets. Her pink-stained lips purse.

"Detective Miller." I motion to Ralph and Amanda. "Can the staff leave?"

She stares at them with such intensity, it would shake far more confident, experienced people than Ralph and Amanda. I've lived all my life around people who glory in intimidating others, so her intent rings loud and clear to me.

"Can they leave?" I press again.

She finally tells them, "The men at the door will instruct you from here. You may leave."

I want to tell her they aren't under arrest, so they "may leave" no matter what, but I think better of it and zip my lips. She steps away from the exit and Amanda and Ralph waste no time departing. I'm now alone with a woman who would hang me out to dry in a heartbeat.

She steps toward me in her sleekly cut black pantsuit; like her makeup and hair, it's a disguise for the predator I see in her eyes. Really, is she all that different from Ava?

She stops a few steps from me, crossing her arms. "I have to say, I didn't expect you to be back here."

"Why's that?"

"You ran to Paris. I figured you'd stay underground."

My defenses prickle, but my voice is thankfully steady. "I

143

didn't run anywhere. And I'm glad I took that week. Shaken by the attack, I wouldn't have handled you attacking me nearly as well as I am now."

"We're just doing our jobs."

"No. *I* did your jobs. I convinced people to start looking for Rebecca, but even with all the attention now, you haven't found her or my friend Ella."

"Ah, yes. Ella."

"Yes. And I still want answers." I broach a concern niggling at my mind. "Ella bought Rebecca's storage unit. What if that put her in danger? What if that's why she can't be found? Two women are missing, and they have a connection."

"*You* could be that connection."

Her fast accusation hits me like a punch. "Are you serious? You're turning this on *me*? No wonder you can't find Rebecca or Ella."

Our eyes lock and hold, the air around us turning downright icy, when I feel a hand between my shoulder blades. "Go outside, Ms. McMillan," Mark commands.

"Yes," Detective Miller agrees, her attention remaining on me. "I need some time alone with the 'Master.'"

"He's not—"

"Ms. McMillan," Mark interrupts, "conversations with Detective Miller are better left to your attorney. My understanding is Detective Miller prefers him to you anyway."

The shock I feel at the surprising comment rolls over the detective's face, too, and the remark and her reaction confirm what I'd suspected during my interview. There's something between her and my attorney, and it's working against me. How

Mark knows this, I'm unsure, but I'm betting Tiger has something to do with it.

As I step around her and exit the office, I hear Mark say, "Let's cut to the chase, Detective Miller. You don't want the lawsuit that damaging any of the art here will bring. There will be—" Then the door shuts, cutting off the rest of his sentence.

Alone in the gallery, I shove a hand through my hair and lean on the wall. Ava's attack, Dylan, Michael . . . all of it happened in just a two-week period, and I *had* needed the time away to be ready for this nightmare. To be ready to fight—and that is exactly what this is. The fact that we're being treated as guilty until we prove we're innocent totally shakes my belief in our legal system.

Fifteen minutes later, I've endured a search that makes airport security look like the candy store, and I exit into the chilly afternoon air, huddling into my trench coat. There are police cars and officers everywhere, but thankfully the street is blocked off and the press is nowhere to be seen.

I see Ralph and Amanda huddled near the alleyway leading to the back parking lot between the coffee shop and us. Ralph waves me over, but my cell phone rings with a call from Chris. Answering, I ask, "Where are you?"

"Outside the barriers. I'm going through hell to get to you."

I massage my forehead. "They won't let me go to you, either. We're stuck here until they release us."

"Just don't answer any questions without David."

"Detective Miller tried to trap me. And do you know she and David—"

"Yes. We'll talk about it in person."

His tone says "end of subject," and I read between the lines. He thinks, or knows, that our phones are tapped. "I feel like we've gone down the rabbit hole," I murmur. "Hurry up and get here. I'm by the alleyway."

"I'll find you."

I stuff my phone in my coat pocket and see that Ralph is still where I expect him to be, but Amanda has disappeared. Going to his side, I glance down the alley and frown. "Where's Amanda?"

"They said we could go." He motions toward the coffee shop, and my gaze follows to see Amanda at the curb. "She's waiting on her ride," Ralph continues. "My car is out back. Joe's supposed to take me back there in a minute."

"Who's Joe?"

As if on a timer, a burly police officer appears. Ralph motions to him and announces, "Joe. My knight in shining armor." The man's stony face doesn't change and Ralph glances at me. "Don't worry, you're still my saving grace. I assume work as usual, tomorrow?"

"I don't know. I'll have to call you."

He hugs me and whispers, "Ryan's picking up Amanda. I think he's a problem." He leans back and looks at me. "You should go find your sexy artist and get out of here."

He and Joe walk down the alleyway while I rush across it to join Amanda, not a second too soon. Ryan's silver BMW pulls up to the curb just as I reach her side.

I step in front of her and knock on the window. Ryan rolls it down. "What are you doing?" I demand.

His brown eyes sharpen but his tone is casual and cool. "She needs a ride."

"You know what I mean. Isn't it enough that one innocent young girl is dead?"

"Rebecca wasn't innocent. She was smart, worldly, and headstrong."

"Which we both know you helped Mark punish her for, over and over."

"Erotic punishment: pleasure, Sara. If you don't know that, Chris is getting something wrong."

Again with the attacks on Chris. It infuriates me, but I'm holding my own today and don't take the bait. "Amanda is young and impressionable. Don't take advantage of her."

"Why don't we let her decide what is right for her."

"She's not deciding. She's under your influence, and *you're* deciding."

"I told you, that's not how it works with me. Look hard and long at whom you're accusing of what. Mark is never involved in anything he doesn't instigate and control, especially where Rebecca was concerned. I wasn't her Master. Think, Sara, and be smart. Be careful."

Those last two words sound more like a threat rather than a warning. We glare at each other, an act I seem to be excelling at with others today.

I turn away and face Amanda, whose hands are stuffed in her long black jacket, her face pale, eyes wide. She looks every bit the frightened mouse, and it drives home my worry that she doesn't belong with Ryan.

"Sara?" she prods tentatively.

Try as I might, nothing I think she'll listen to comes to mind. She's infatuated, and as I know from my days with Michael, that's the kiss of death where good sense is concerned. I step closer to her and soften my voice. "Don't do anything that you don't want to. Understand?"

She frowns. "I'm not. I wouldn't."

Until she's so enamored that "yes" is the only word she knows in the moment, and regret is the only word she knows the morning after. "Charge your phone and call me if you need me, even if it's the middle of the night."

Without a reply, she gets into the BMW and there is nothing I can do but pray she's safe. I watch the car leave, and fight the urge to run after it when it pulls away.

Turning to search out Chris, I find Mark towering over me, his eyes glinting like hot steel. His hand shackles my arm, his touch firm. "Come with me," he demands, and I double step to keep up with him.

"Where are we going?"

He just keeps moving, and the next thing I know he's pulling me into a doorway alcove. The same alcove Chris had once pulled me into, which makes the moment all the more uncomfortable. I don't want to be here with him, or for him to flatten his hands on the wall by my head as Chris had, but I am and he does. And I definitely don't want his big body this close to mine.

"What the fuck were you thinking?" he demands.

I'm confused. "What are you talking about? With Detective Miller?"

"With fucking *Ryan,* Ms. McMillan. I told you to let me handle it."

Unbidden, Ryan's words spring into my mind. *Mark is never involved in anything he doesn't instigate and control.* I shake them off. "Amanda was leaving with him."

"I said I'd handle it," he repeats tightly. "Do you really think Ava made Rebecca disappear on her own? Someone helped her make it happen. Don't go tempting fate."

Another subtle thread weaving through a cloth of mystery. "If you're saying you think it was Ryan, then we *can't* let Amanda leave with him!"

"If I knew it was him, he'd wish he was dead by the time I got done with him. I *don't* know, Ms. McMillan. But he told the police he knew Rebecca was back the night she returned. And he told them Ava took her to me."

"Oh God. Mark, I—"

"She'd fucking be *alive* if Ava took her to me."

I dare to rest my hand on his arm in comfort. "I know."

He gazes at my hand, and I pull it back. "We *don't* know—that's the point," he says. "We know nothing except that she's gone." He pushes off the wall. "I warned you to stay the hell away from me. You are failing miserably. I'll make it easier on you. Organize the staff to work from home after tomorrow."

He ends the conversation by disappearing around the corner, and I gasp as Chris immediately appears in the alcove.

Twelve

⌇

"What the hell was that?" Chris demands. The fact that he doesn't touch me tells me how pissed off he is.

"I'm not completely sure. He's a live wire ready to explode, Chris."

"That's not what I want to know. How did you get into the alcove with him?"

"He grabbed my arm and pulled me along with him, and I'd have had to make a scene in front of the police to avoid it."

"Why, Sara?"

"He got pissed because I confronted Ryan over Amanda."

"What do you mean, confronted him?"

"He came to pick her up, and he's creeping me out. Why choose now to pursue her, with all of this going on? I can't sit by and watch her be a victim." My throat tightens. "I don't want her to end up being another Rebecca. And though Mark was lecturing me about letting him deal with Ryan, he didn't put my mind at ease. Something is off with Ryan."

"What does that mean?"

"He told the police that Ava told him she saw Rebecca the night she returned, and took her to Mark. He never mentioned this to Mark, though—even though he was a part of their ménage. What sense does that make? I'm worried he helped Ava do whatever they did to Rebecca. And now he's hyperfocused on Amanda."

Chris's jaw tightens. "Or Ava's using Ryan to create an alibi."

"But he and Ava were intimate with Rebecca and Mark. Ryan could've been just as jealous as Ava, for all we know. He could have helped her kill Rebecca. Or he could have done it himself."

"I'll make sure Blake's team keeps an eye on Amanda." He studies me, his gaze probing. "Back to Mark and the alcove. I don't like it."

"I know. I didn't, either. And," I hesitate to agitate the situation more, but I know I have to tell him. "I've had issues with Mark today. "

"That makes two of us. Mine starts with the alcove."

"Mine started with a confrontation in his office, when he confessed that I remind him of . . . of Rebecca. He says he can't be around me. He wants me to prepare the staff to work from home after tomorrow."

"You remind him of Rebecca," he repeats, the words tight.

"Yes." I hug myself. "I don't like it for all kinds of reasons. It feels pretty shitty, actually."

He cuts his gaze away, rubbing the back of his neck, before shaking his head and looking at me again. "We need to leave before they change their minds and try to stop us."

"You're not going to say anything else about Mark?"

"What do you want me to say, Sara? I help the man, and he's constantly trying to bend over my woman. I need to think and figure out what the fuck to do about him. But right now, David wants to meet with us before another client meeting. Blake's joining us at a restaurant by the police station."

"What about the press?"

"Let's hope they're all here. I hired a car in case they're trailing ours."

Ours. The word is a whisper of relief in his present mood. I step to him, twining our legs and wrapping my arms around his neck. "I love you."

His arm wraps around my waist and he pulls me to him. "I love you, too. But, baby, when a man warns you away from him and tells you why, you have to listen before it's too late." He laces my fingers with his and starts walking.

The setting sun has turned into a misty glow when the private car Chris hired pulls to a stop in front of the restaurant. Tension ripples through me and I half expect a swarm of press that doesn't come.

Still, I find myself scanning for cameras as we enter the upscale burger joint with dangling turquoise and blue teardrop lights and stone-top tables. "Try to relax, baby," Chris murmurs as we approach the hostess stand.

She looks up our reservation and we follow her between

the tables. Our destination, no doubt by special request, is a small round booth in the very back that has the luxury of being tucked behind a wall. Blake wears his royal-blue Walker Security T-shirt and his long, dark hair tied at his nape has the kind of edginess that says this ex-ATF agent is a rebel with a cause, while David sports a finely fitted dark gray suit, his bald head glistening under the lights. The one commonality is that they're both garbage disposals who at present seem to be having a "who can eat my bread" faster contest. At our approach, they abandon their food and begin to stand.

"Don't get up," Chris says. "We know how much you two like your food."

Blake settles back into his seat and winks at me. "Empty stomach, empty mind," he jokes, as Chris and I take off our coats.

David, who's already busy buttering his bread again, adds, "Being a calculating asshole burns calories. But Sara already knows that about me." He grins. "Right, sugar?"

Glowering at him, I slide into the booth across from Blake, who chokes on his bread.

"Sorry," he says, reaching for his drink. "The women in the Walker family would have his balls if he called them 'sugar.'" He motions to David. "I think he has a death wish."

Chris sits down and slips his arm over my shoulder. "He does. And full warning, David, Sara had fantasies about pouring a pitcher of beer over your head the last time you called her that."

"Coke's better," Blake offers. "It's stickier. Ask my wife. She once dumped a pitcher over my brother Royce's head."

I laugh. "For what?"

No In Between

"I'm pretty sure he told her his gun was bigger than hers."

The entire table bursts into laughter, and I downright get the giggles. "Thank you, Blake. I needed that."

The waitress appears, and we order promptly due to David's deadline. "So," he says the instant the waitress departs. "What happened today that I need to know about? Aside from the search warrant, which was bound to happen."

Jumping on the topic most on my mind, I say, "Ryan told the police that Ava told him that she took Rebecca to Mark, the night Rebecca arrived."

David snorts. "He told them, and she told him, and who's on first? That's just hearsay, which never holds water."

"Besides," Blake adds, "Mark never talked to Ryan, Ava, or Rebecca the night Rebecca returned. I have the phone records to back it up. And the timeline is clear, too. He flew in from New York six hours after Rebecca arrived. I tapped the database for Mark's home security company, and viewed the taped footage. Based on the time stamps, he went straight home from the airport and no one was with him, nor did anyone visit him. Conclusion? Ava didn't take Rebecca to Mark that night. And believe me, if I know this, so do the police."

"Translation?" David adds. "Ava's a lying bitch. But we knew that already."

"What about Ryan?" I ask. "Did he talk to Ava the night Rebecca arrived?"

"Yes," Blake answers. "It was a ten minute call and again, if I know this, so do the police. The security footage of his apartment says he was at home at the time. He didn't leave home again until his normal morning departure, nine hours later."

"But she could have told him she took Rebecca to Mark's," I press.

"She also could have told him she just baked apple pie," David says. "There won't be a recording of the call. It could have been her way of covering her ass in case she got caught."

"That's exactly what I suggested when I heard," Chris reminds me.

"I know," I say. "I just have a bad feeling about Ryan."

"He's on the police radar," David assures me.

"What about Rebecca's travel dates?" Chris asks. "Any update there?"

"They're just using that bullshit to scare you into talking," Blake replies. "We did that crap all the time when I was ATF. Rebecca used her cell phone the day we know she arrived here in the city, and she hasn't used it since. It hasn't pinged, but that's not surprising considering how long she's been missing."

This punches me in the gut. No one missed her for far too long and I have a jab of anger at Mark for letting his big-ass ego get in the way. He wrote her off, engaging in his typical game of denial. She didn't exist, so her rejection didn't exist.

"And just to be thorough," Blake adds, "I checked with the boyfriend she was traveling with before her return. She didn't have any other phone than the one we had on file. Not that he knew of."

"I forgot about him," I say, glancing at David. "Are they investigating him?"

"They're looking at everyone," he confirms, "but Detective Miller says he's been ruled out."

"Rebecca returned to San Francisco," Blake inserts. "He didn't. That's a pretty solid alibi."

"What about the past boyfriend Rebecca wrote about occasionally?" I ask. "She met him at a bar and he turned a bit obsessive with her."

"Moved out of state before Rebecca went missing," Blake replies, evidently with an answer to everything.

"None of this proves Ava killed Rebecca," I say, my concern about Ava being set free growing. "Is it possible Ava's silly accusations could sway a bail jury, or judge, however that works, into discounting four witnesses to her attack on me?"

"I won't let that happen," David replies, intending to give me confidence but failing.

"So it *could* happen," I challenge.

"I've never lost a case," is his rebuttal.

"You are walking around my question, and it doesn't make me feel better."

"We build a case against her," Blake says. "Piece by piece, we complete the puzzle."

"I do have some good news," David adds. "Tiger and I finally connected on a major issue. He has the club situation contained, at least for now. Mark agreed to turn over a membership list if there was a written agreement that it would never be shared."

Chris leans forward, his hand flattening on the table. "And this is good news why?" The snap to his voice tells me he's not as unaffected by the club's exposure as he's let on. "Can't the court still subpoena the information?"

"Yes," David agrees, "but if the police have what they need, the chance it'll get that far is less likely. And here's the kicker:

That list has high-level judges, doctors, and business owners on it, many who are political contributors. And campaign donors are protected, often to law enforcement's frustration."

"That's the fucking truth," Blake says.

"This is good news, Chris," David tells him. "This assures us there won't be police cars and search warrants at the club in the near future."

"How do we know Ava won't release this information, if she hasn't already?" Chris presses.

"Oh, she will," David responds. "But Mark has the 'Bay City Cigar Club' cover for the operation, and it's pretty damn tight. The media isn't going to break that down easily."

I turn to Chris. "A cigar club? I'm lost. I had no idea."

"It didn't seem relevant, since we aren't involved anyway," he explains, then his gaze shifts back to David. "But money has power. If Ava discusses the club, the press will look for someone to corroborate her claims. And if the price is right they'll find that someone, even if their story's a lie. I'm willing to be slaughtered in the press, but there are a lot of people who won't survive it the way I will."

"I understand," David assures him, "and I think the main concern is trial time, and real members of the club being blackmailed to testify in a way that is favorable to Ava and not to others. That makes time critical. We get her in a real jail cell, not a fluffy hospital, where she feels real pain. Then she'll be willing to take a deal."

"A deal," I say flatly. "What kind of deal?"

"It's irrelevant," Blake says. "I'll prove she killed Rebecca before that's on the table."

"In other words, the deal wouldn't be much of a punishment," I say.

David rubs his head and leans forward. "Trust me. I'm good at my job. If you can't trust me, trust Chris. He picked me for a reason."

"He's an asshole, but he's our asshole, baby," Chris says, repeating what I'd said to him.

"Exactly," David agrees. "The DA's motivated to get murder back on the table. As of tomorrow when they drop that charge, they have not one, but technically, two missing women, and no explanation. I pointed that out, too, believe me. The more pressure they feel, the better they do their jobs."

I swallow the acid the "two missing women" comment stirs in me. "Or they find a fast fall guy. Detective Miller trapped me at the gallery today. She said Ella and Rebecca have the storage unit and me in common."

"That's ridiculous," Blake says. "Seriously, Sara. Your alibi is tight. They're just running scared and terrified of 'serial killer on the loose' kind of headlines. That shit makes law enforcement hide under their beds."

David leans closer, lowering his voice. "No comment—that's your answer to everything. I repeat, Sara: *Stop* fucking talking to them without me. She's messing with your head, and testing how you'll handle yourself during the trial."

Two waitresses appear and start distributing our food. Chris shifts in his seat, leaning on the table, and giving the others his back, blocking me from their view. He studies me a moment, eyes softening with whatever he sees, knuckles caressing my cheek. "Deep breath, baby."

"I'm trying."

"There is no serial killer. Ava never knew Ella."

"What if she was afraid of something she thought might be in the journals, and she killed Ella to get them?"

"We know Ella was in Paris. She's not a part of this."

He's right. "I think what gets me is that everyone has an agenda of their own. It makes me feel so out of control."

"That's why we take control and hire people we trust."

"Excuse me," someone says and I glance over my shoulder to see the waitress holding my salad.

"What about Ava's estranged husband?" I ask after the wait-staff is out of hearing range.

"Unlikely suspect," Blake says, "and I base that on his blond babe of a girlfriend, who seems to have all of his attention. That, and he owns a bar on the Wharf, where he was working the night of Rebecca's return."

"But that's perfect," I counter. "What if Ava took her there? Does he have a boat?"

Blake dips a fry in ketchup. "No boat."

"But he'd have access to people who do, right? He works on the pier."

"Sara thinks Rebecca's at the bottom of the ocean," Chris offers softly, squeezing my leg.

Blake's brown eyes meet mine. "Because of her nightmares."

It's not a question, and it twists me in knots to know he's read those entries and so have many other people. I give him a choppy nod. "It's almost like she was having premonitions about her death."

Blake's eyes glaze over a moment, like he's affected by this in some way, but it's hard to read those journals and not be affected. "I was curious about her father, too. I've tracked down an old friend of her mother's who swears her father is Kenneth Burgendy. Burgendy is a big real estate investor with known mob ties."

I glance at Chris. "Neville," I whisper. "He's got ties to the mob, too."

"In France," Chris reminds me.

Blake knocks on the table to get my attention. "No connection. This reaction is exactly why I almost didn't tell you. I knew you'd jump to conclusions."

Tension crawls through my body. "Serial killers, mobsters, and two people connected to me are missing." My voice is as edgy as I suddenly feel. "Why the heck would I jump to any conclusions?" Feeling claustrophobic, I stand up.

"Sara—"

I lean into Chris and kiss him. "Sorry—I'm fine. My bitch queen and I just need a minute."

"You're sure?"

I see the worry etched in his eyes and I repeat, "I promise."

Looking anything but convinced, he reluctantly orders, "Hurry back."

I follow the signs to the restroom and enter, leaning against the closed door. The sensation of suffocating from uneven breaths makes logical thought nearly impossible. I don't know what's wrong with me. I never snap at people. And David has to leave soon, so I can't stay here long, but . . .

Who am I kidding? I *do* know what's happening. It's been building and I just haven't wanted to admit it. It started again in Paris, soon after Ava's attack. And it's why I ended up hunched over a trash can in Rebecca's office. It's a return to what I'd felt in random spells for six months after Michael's attack.

I lift my face to the ceiling, forcing myself to slowly breathe in and then let it out. I don't want to be back here. I *can't* be back here again. I'm ashamed of myself for being this weak. Ashamed?

I inhale with the realization that these feelings have a purpose beyond me—an important one. *This* is what Chris feels about his need for the whip, and why he tries to hide from me when he does. It's not about fear of what he'll do to me: it's shame. Burned deep into his soul. How will I ever convince him I'm strong enough to handle that part of him, if I'm not strong enough to handle myself?

A knock sounds on the door, and I jump. "Damn it," I whisper, grabbing the counter. I have to pull it together. I have to go back to the table, and I'm going to do it with my shit together. I have to. For me and for Chris, Rebecca and Ella. I *won't* relapse into panic attacks. I refuse to. Once I get past tonight, I'll figure out what my trigger is, and I'll be fine again. Like I've been for almost two years.

Determination in place, I yank open the door and then gape in absolute shock. Ricco Alvarez is standing in the hallway.

Thirteen

"Ah, bella." Ricco's voice is richly accented, his elegant white shirt and black slacks starched. His sharp, aristocratic features and warm brown skin are as familiar and striking as I remember, but unlike past encounters I do not welcome his visit or feel safe in his presence.

"What are you doing here?"

"We need to talk." He advances, clearly intending to back me inside the ladies' room.

"No." I step into the hallway, yanking the door shut behind me. "You want to talk, we talk here." The scent of his musky cedar-scented cologne accents the close proximity of our bodies.

His blue eyes narrow on my face, and several heavy beats pass before he steps back, giving me breathing room. "You're afraid of me. Priceless, when I am here to warn you, to keep you safe."

"You followed me here," I hiss with accusation. "I don't feel protected. I feel stalked."

"I had to find a way to reach you when you weren't under lock and key. I didn't expect you to go back to the gallery. It's not safe. You need to stay away from Mark."

"Mark isn't the problem."

"You're just like Rebecca, so damn blind to that man's evil. I didn't do what I've been accused of doing, and neither did Mary. Why would I do that? I'm a very rich man."

"Because you hate him."

"Yes. I do. I know he hurt Rebecca, and I pressured him at every turn. I made him nervous and that's why he set me up."

I shake my head, rejecting his claim. "Then why include Mary, and damage the name of his family business? He wouldn't do that."

"I'd asked Mary to help me, as I did you. Mark must have found out. Listen to me, bella. He's dangerous. He killed Rebecca. I *know* he did."

"Ava confessed to killing Rebecca."

"She's as guilty as you and Rebecca are of falling for Mark's charms. She took the fall to save Mark, but she's come to her senses. He's going down. Make sure you don't go with him."

"She told you this?"

"I'm telling you this. Stay away from him and the gallery. Do not ignore my warning. You were almost killed once. Don't tempt fate." He walks away toward a rear exit and I stare after him, stunned, uncertain what to do.

"Sara."

I turn at the sound of Chris's voice and launch myself at him, throwing my arms around his neck. He folds me against him and he is safe and warm, and the solidity I need when it feels like the earth is shaking around me.

"What's wrong?" he asks, tilting my face to his. "Did something happen?"

"Ricco. He was here. He followed us. I came out of the bathroom and—"

"Did he hurt you?"

"No." I shake my head. "He—"

"Where is he?"

"He went out the back door. Chris, he's saying Mark framed him and Mary because they were trying to prove he killed Rebecca. He said Ava was pressured into confessing by Mark, and"—I swallow hard—"he told me to stay away from Mark. He said he's dangerous. He knew about me being attacked, and he said he didn't want me to be hurt again."

"Your attack isn't public knowledge. That means he's talked to Ava. Damn it. He's going to pay her bond." He closes his hands over the sides of my head. "Are you okay?"

"Yes," I say and it's true. That's how my stupid panic attacks work. They aren't logical or predictable, and neither is anything Ricco is doing. "I don't know if he was warning me or threatening me."

His jaw clenches and he laces his fingers with mine. "Come on. We're getting out of here."

It's exactly what I want to hear and I gladly keep pace with him. If I'd been nervous scanning for the press earlier, I'm ten times more on edge watching for Ricco's reemergence now. Blake and David must read our expressions because they're both on their feet before we reach the table.

"What just happened?" Blake asks as Chris helps me into my coat.

Chris grabs his jacket and puts it on, giving them a full rundown. "I'm getting Sara out of here, and I'm going to warn Mark in case Ricco heads in his direction."

David nods. "I'll give Tiger a heads-up as well."

"I'm walking you out," Blake insists. "And let me go check out the exterior of the building before you exit." He takes off.

"There are too many unknowns here for me to feel comfortable," Chris tells David. "We'll stay local until after the hearing, but I'm taking Sara to my godparents' place in Sonoma, away from all of this. I expect you to get that approved, just like I expect you to get a restraining order on Ricco, Ava, and Mary. I also want permission to take Sara back to Paris during the wait for the trial. And I want it yesterday, so we can make plans."

"I can't promise I can do that."

"Then you'd damn well better make sure Ava isn't released. And if that means we have to be there to testify tomorrow morning, then we will."

That's a shocker I didn't expect, but it's not nearly as terrifying as Ava being set free. "I'll do whatever it takes," I say.

"They don't want you there," David says, "but I'm headed to the police station now. I'll cancel my other meeting and get on all of this."

"Call me," Chris snaps, closing his hand around mine, and starting for the door, already on his phone as we walk. At the front of the restaurant we step to the side of the door, away from the crowd, and I listen to the short conversation Chris has with Mark.

"Ricco showed up at the restaurant and cornered Sara. Ava's convinced him you forced her into confessing. He's going to bail her out." He's quiet for a moment and glances at me. "She's shaken up, but fine. Look, man. Be careful. His coming here tonight says he's a loose cannon, and I wouldn't be surprised if he came after you." He listens a moment. "I'm not sure yet. I'll let you know."

The instant he hangs up, I ask, "Not sure about what?"

"If you want to go to the gallery tomorrow, or even should."

"We have to go to the hearing tomorrow, Chris. If we don't, I'm afraid things will happen and we won't know what's going on."

Blake walks in the door, and Chris wraps his arm around my neck. "Let's talk about it at home."

Home with Chris is the exact sanctuary I crave right now and I lean into him, welcoming the feel of the hard lines of his powerful body against mine.

"Ricco pulled out of the drive as I exited the building," Blake announces, joining us. "No signs of any other trouble. Your driver is at the door waiting."

Exiting the building with Blake protecting us, I slide into the back of the vehicle.

Blake tells Chris, "I'll follow you to your apartment and have Jacob waiting for you. We'll locate Ricco and Mary, and keep men on them."

Chris joins me in the car and pulls me against him as if he needs me close, holding on a little too hard—or maybe not hard enough. At this moment, I'm not sure he can ever hold on hard enough.

• • •

The short drive home is silent. With the press all over this we don't dare speak in front of the driver, and that suffocating feeling from the bathroom keeps trying to return. It has to be due to Ricco's visit. The extremes he'll go to to destroy Mark are terrifyingly similar to those Ava was willing to take with Rebecca. I'd thought Ricco was arrogant but misunderstood, more protector than aggressor, as Rebecca had said in her journals, but now I'm not sure. I didn't believe Ava could kill, but she did. And I didn't believe Michael, despite being an asshole, was capable of what he did to me, either.

By the time the driver stops in front of our apartment building, I feel as if I'm drowning in "what-ifs" and I am eager to escape. Jacob greets us as we exit and we join him to the left of the building entryway, out of the range of prying ears. "Ricco is in his home," he tells us, "and we have a man watching him."

Relief washes over me. "Thank God," I murmur.

"What about Mary?" Chris asks.

I hadn't even considered that she was also a potential threat. Proof that my head isn't on straight.

"Mary's staying with her parents," Jacob supplies. "We confirmed that she's there now, and we put a man on her as well. I have to say, I'm baffled by Ricco's alignment with Ava. I thought he had feelings for Rebecca."

"He hates Mark," I reply. "And that makes it easy for him to believe Ava when she says Mark killed Rebecca, then threatened her and forced her into a fake confession."

Jacob seems to consider that a moment. "Hmmm."

"Yeah," Chris replies. "My reaction as well."

I glance between the two of them. "What does that mean?"

"From my perspective," Chris replies, "something doesn't add up with Ricco."

"My thoughts exactly," Jacob confirms, "and a number of scenarios come to mind. Ricco's obsession with Rebecca borders on stalkerdom. Maybe he had a fit of jealousy and killed Rebecca himself."

My lips part in shock. "Ricco? No. There's no scenario where Ricco kills Rebecca, and Ava confesses. That makes no sense."

"It doesn't have to make sense," Chris says. "Ava's a crazy fucking bitch and if the doctors who evaluated her don't see that, they're as stupid as she is insane."

I shake my head. "No. Ricco doesn't fit. He just doesn't. Ryan said Ava called him the night Rebecca arrived, and the phone records confirm that."

"Ricco tried to ruin Mark and Allure," Chris argues, "and he did so at the risk and expense of his freedom and success. I'm not underestimating what he's capable of."

He's right. I'm dismissing exactly what I'd thought on the ride over here. Ricco's corrupted by the same irrational jealousy as Ava. This entire scenario is insanity. All Rebecca wanted was to chase her dreams, and to be loved the way she loved. *Will we ever know the truth about what happened to her? Will we ever truly be safe again?* I feel like we are standing in the center of evil, and the ground is an illusion.

Chris's hand settles on my back and I sway in his direction, to the heat, the safety, the rightness that he is to me. "Sara and I are going upstairs," he announces. "Call me if you hear anything new."

"Is there anything either of you need now?" Jacob asks.

I snap, "For Rebecca to be alive, and this to be a big misunderstanding." Jacob's eyes widen, and my cheeks heat. I'm losing it again.

I turn away and walk toward the sliding door entry, tension climbing from my toes to my neck in about thirty seconds. I am tumbling down the hill I'd finally climbed.

I am not this weak. Not anymore. That was the past, the old me. The past. The past. The past. I'll make it stop. I just need space. I need to think about my triggers. I need . . . space.

Chris murmurs something to Jacob that I can't make out and then he falls into step with me as I enter the lobby. "Sara," he says softly, willing me to look at him, and he is a powerful force, nearly impossible for me to resist.

But my need to hide my scattered emotions wins. This is not who he needs me to be. It's not who *I* need me to be.

"Mr. Merit. Ms. McMillan."

The greeting is delivered by an unfamiliar man in a suit and earpiece standing by the front desk. I assume he's Jacob's replacement.

I'm uncharacteristically unfriendly, walking on toward the elevator with barely a glance in his direction. Thankfully, Chris pauses to greet the man, giving me a chance to gain my composure. I continue on to the elevator and punch the call button. When the doors don't open immediately I punch the button again, irritated at the way my hand shakes. Why can't I be one of those people who hides what they feel? Someone who doesn't shake and ramble? Someone who doesn't—

The doors part and cut off my thoughts. I step inside the car and hit the hold button, my chance to pull myself together gone. Chris joins me inside, his fierce male energy shrinking the space, consuming me, and I swear I can no longer breathe. He steps toward me, crowding me with his big, impossibly perfect body.

He glances at the panel, punching in the code for our floor, wisps of longish blond hair teasing his cheek and jawline. Trying to dash an unexpected rush of desire, I lower my lashes before I cave in to touching him, and invite further inspection. I have no idea how I want to run from this man and kiss him in the same moment, but I know this is going to be the longest short elevator ride of my life.

His fingers curve around my waist, possessive and warm, sending darts of awareness all through my body. Flattening his palm on the small of my back, he molds me to him.

My hand flattens on his chest, in that spot over his heart that has come to feel like *my* spot. I don't want to lose this, or us, or him.

"Talk to me, baby," he prods gently, and oh, how those familiar words speak to me.

I want to tell him what I feel, but I know if I love him, I cannot. Not if I want to replace the whip. And I do. I want that for him, and for us. I love him too much for him to see Amber in me any more than he already fears that possibility. That would allow the whip to win.

Chris cups my cheeks, forcing my gaze to his, and the tenderness in his eyes could melt ice. "Talk to me," he repeats, adding a soft command to the words.

"Not now." It's a plea from deep in my soul. "If you love me, not now."

His green eyes narrow, sharpen. "*If?* Where did that word come from?"

"I'm sorry . . . I . . ."

"Sara—"

My fingers curl around his wrists. "I need . . . Chris, I need to think."

"Think *with* me. Talk to me, Sara."

"No." It's out before I can stop it, sharp edged like when I snapped at the table, sure to alert him to how wrong I am right now.

"*No?*"

"Chris." I press on his chest. "You need to let me figure this out."

"Figure what out?"

"I don't know. I need—" The door dings open and I try to dart for it.

Instead of escape I end up over his shoulder, and he carries me into the apartment. I press my hands to my face, the blood running to my head making it harder to think than it already was, his hand on my ass making it nearly impossible. I can't do this now. I don't know how I'll react. I don't know who I'll be.

He sets me on my feet at the edge of our bed, my back to him, and then hits the light, casting us in a dim, seductive glow. "Whatever this is," he says, pulling my coat down my arms, and holding it there, trapping my wrists as he leans into me, "we're going to make it go away."

I inhale a shaky breath and allow him to pull my coat off. "You can't just say you're going to do that and it does. It's not that easy."

He encloses me in his powerful arms, burying his face in my hair, nuzzling my neck, and his smell, that deliciously wonderful smell, surrounds me. "I didn't say it would be easy." His hand caresses up my waist and he tugs my blouse free of my skirt. "Just that we'd deal with it together."

His palms slip under the silk, finding my bare flesh, and his touch is like liquid fire in my veins. Sensations roll through me and collide with emotions. I squeeze my eyes shut to hide what I feel, as if Chris can see my face, but he can't, and somehow I know this is intentional on his part. The way he instinctively knows what I need is both perfection and a trap at the same time. It would be so very easy to tell him what's happening to me, and so very shortsighted and selfish. I'd feel better now, but it would steal his freedom to be free with me, and eventually turn me into an obligation.

With another deep breath, I face Chris, and I do what I would have done sooner, had I been thinking straight. I stop attempting the losing strategy of hiding from the man I want to get lost in, and I seek the kind of escape I trust only him to give me. Wrapping my arms around his neck, I confess everything I dare. "I don't know why I'm letting everything from the past few days get to me. I'm thinking too much."

"You're thinking too much," he finally repeats, and it's not a question. It's doubt, and doubt, like a secret, is poison. "I know you. You aren't saying something, and I want more than that from you."

"I know you're worried and trying to protect me, Chris. It's who you are and I love you for that, but please don't try to get in my head right now, when I'm trying to get out of it. I'm

173

on overload, and the only 'more' I can take is the kind of 'more' only you can give me. That place you take me that leaves no room for anything but you. I need that. I need you."

"And yet you tried to run from the elevator to escape me."

"Not you, Chris. From *me*. I'm all over the place. I'm worried about tomorrow. I'm worried about Ella and Amanda and—" I press my hands to his face. "Fuck me, Chris! I need you to fuck me."

His answer is silence, and I can feel the deep, slow way he's breathing, the calm calculation I sense in him that has me counting torturous seconds. He leans back, his eyes locking with mine. "It won't work."

"Why not?" I ask.

His voice is sandpaper rough. "It would be *so damn easy* for me to tie you to the bed and fuck you every which way, but it wouldn't distract me from asking questions, like you think it would. It'll become the tool I use to get the answers you don't want to give me."

"Even if that's not what I want?"

"I won't be able to help myself. Because the last time I saw this look in your eyes, Michael put it there." Abruptly, he sets me away from him. "But I won't force you to tell me what's wrong, no matter how insane it's making me right now. That would make me no better than he was to you. But be clear, Sara: If you want me to trust you and show you everything, you have to be willing to trust me that much, too."

He walks out of the bedroom, leaving me staring after him.

Fourteen

I stare at the doorway Chris has just exited, stunned. He knows I'm still affected by Michael. *I* didn't know; how did he? Or maybe I did, but I was in denial—and that's a mistake Chris doesn't make. He accepts his scars. More than once he's told me that the way Mark lives is dangerous, convincing himself that extreme control over everything and everyone around him somehow wipes out his past. Chris called it a crash waiting to happen.

And he's right. I see Mark unraveling, pieces of him falling, cracking like glass on the ground he thinks is solid under his feet, but even that's unsteady. Perhaps Mark's ability to live in a façade of rightness is what draws me to him, since I'm also guilty of that, too. That's how I survived Michael, and I've never envied Chris's ability to know himself as much as I do right now.

Kicking off my shoes, I rush to the bathroom and undress,

anxious to explain everything, so he doesn't believe tonight was about a lack of trust on my part. I consider showing up in Chris's studio naked, exposed in every way, to make a statement. But his mood is a swiftly changing vehicle, and I have to drive the appropriate speed. I decide to err on the side of caution, slipping on a long, pink silk robe.

With bare feet and anxious steps I rush through the apartment, and down the long hallway. The studio doorway is cracked open but the lights are out, and there's silence where Chris usually favors music. I don't know what this means, but I rethink playing this cautiously. That's what got me into trouble in the first place. It's all or nothing with Chris. It always has been. I need to make that statement, to declare to him that I am not holding back.

I drop the robe and step inside the studio. Chris stands in the center, his feet bare, his shirt off, his inked skin and defined chest deliciously male.

He is shrouded in shadows, his features dusted with starlight, his blond hair a wild, spiky, finger-tousled mess, and I can almost see him running his fingers through it in frustration. Because of me. I've twisted him into knots, when I was trying to protect him. I wait for him to act or speak but he does nothing, and I slowly become aware of what sits next to him: the painting of me naked, sitting on this floor, my hands and feet bound. It is a sign that he'd expected me to follow him and, no doubt, a warning and a promise of what he has planned.

His gaze rakes over my body, taking a leisurely stroll over every part of me, before lifting to my face. "I see you came dressed for the occasion. Come here."

I don't hesitate. I never do when Chris's dominant side is in control. My feet travel the floor quickly; I want him to know that I'm eager. And I am. The sooner I'm touching him and he's touching me, the sooner I can breathe again.

"Stop," he orders when I reach the center of the room.

I halt and he closes the distance between us, all long-legged grace and confident man. *My man, whom I don't want to lose.* He halts in front of me and I can smell the earthy, wonderful scent of him that has come to mean dominance, power, and home.

His green eyes meet mine in challenge. "Showing up naked is an invitation to get fucked, Sara."

"Yes," I say softly. "Please."

"Do you remember what I said the painting means to me?"

"You said it's about trust."

"That's right. I also told you that if I fuck you tonight, I'll make you tell me why you just tried to run from me."

"I know."

"I changed my mind, though. You want to be fucked, I'll fuck you. But I don't want what you don't give me freely."

"Everything, Chris. I give you all that I am, and I give it freely."

"And yet there's fear in your eyes, and you ran rather than telling me why. Do you know how crazy that's making me, or what I'm imagining the cause might be?"

"I didn't mean to make you worry." I hug myself so I won't reach for him. I desperately want to touch him, but I sense the edge in him, the way he needs control right now. I understand it. I've lived it, and he gives me the freedom to let it go. And that's what I have to do now. Just let go and tell him.

177

"Before Ricco showed up, I had a panic attack in the restaurant. I don't know why it happened. I hid in the bathroom and pulled myself together. I haven't been myself since Ava attacked me. I think you know that."

"And you couldn't just tell me this? *You ran,* Sara."

"No, I didn't. That's what you're not getting—or I'm not getting across. I was trying to make sure *you* don't run."

"Baby, I'm not running. I never have."

"But you just tried to get *me* to, over and over. It's the same thing, Chris. You're finally letting me into those darker places you go. I finally feel like I could win over the whip, but I see the moments when you fear my seeing the part of you it controls. I don't want you to shut me out because you think I'm like Amber."

He drags me to him. "You *are not* Amber. You will never be like her."

My fingers wrap his wrist. "I know you want to protect me, and I love you for that more than you know."

"Yet too easily, you found a reason to shut me out tonight. Trust isn't a fair-weather friend. It's about a willingness to be vulnerable and exposed."

"And I am willing to do that. That's why I'm here now."

He searches my face, and I don't know what he looks for, what he needs, or what he finds. He releases me abruptly. "Hold out your hands and lace your fingers together."

Heat rushes through me with the certainty that I'm about to fully understand the painting he's created of me. This is him sending me a message. He's not holding back. My confession, as incomplete as it is, has changed nothing. I offer him my arms, aware as I haven't been in the past few minutes of my naked body, my breasts pressed together.

Chris reaches into his back pocket and produces a roll of art tape, using it to wrap my wrists. Task complete, he bends my elbows and presses my wrists to my chest, his fingers covering the bindings. He has become dark Chris, the dominant Master who never shows emotion; the Chris who arouses me in ways I would never believe a man could.

"Sit down," he orders, and the way he manages such force with what is no more than a whisper stirs heat low in my body.

My throat is dry and my heart beats so loudly I am certain Chris can hear. I squat and he follows me down, steadying me so I don't fall without the use of my hands. "All the way," he murmurs, gently nudging me until my bare backside is on the floor.

He angles my knees up toward my chest, with my feet out enough to stabilize my body. His long lashes lower, half-moons on his cheeks, and I sense him struggling with what has passed between us. He knows I need to see he won't hold back, but this isn't just for me. I think he really needs this, too, for me to show him, not tell him, how much I trust him.

Chris tapes my ankles and then throws the roll over his shoulder. My nerve endings are so alive, so on edge that the roll hits the ground like a thundering drum that seems to radiate through the room, through my body. His hands come down on my knees and the touch sweeps over me, awakening nerve endings in the most intimate and unforgiving of places. I feel this man everywhere, I want him everywhere. But as if he knows what I feel, and he means to deny me, he withdraws. I shiver with a sudden cold certain to linger. He will torment me, make me wait for him. Make me beg.

He stands up, towering over me, and I stare up at him, trying to read him, the anticipation of what comes next tingling through me. And it's supposed to. I see that in his eyes, and I am reminded of his words when I'd first seen the painting. *It's about trust. The kind of trust I want from you and have no right to ask for.* He's going to push me. He's going to take me somewhere uncomfortable. Somewhere I might not want to go, but I will. With Chris, I will.

He walks behind me and then shows me a red silk cloth, proof that my assumptions are right. He means to take trust to a whole new level. "Have you ever been blindfolded?"

"No."

"Any objections?" he asks.

Nerves dance frantically in my stomach and my nipples tighten to the point of pain. "Yes. I mean, no. No objections."

He lowers his head, his warm breath shimmering on my cheek. "I could do anything to you right now, and you couldn't stop me."

"I don't want to stop you."

"*Anything,* Sara," he emphasizes.

"I trust you, Chris," I say, my voice laced with a breathless quality that he's too observant not to notice. He knows how he affects me and that is part of his power.

"Lean on your elbows," he orders.

I ease forward and he gently presses his cheek to mine as he says, "I'm not going to spank you." He frees me and I sizzle with the certainty that this wasn't meant to comfort me. It was meant to make me wonder what he *is* going to do to me. He's testing me, something I'd hoped we were beyond, but I've put us right back there again. Perhaps we never left. Actually, until the day he has to choose me over the whip, we won't leave.

Leaning forward, I rest my weight on my elbows, the angle lifting my backside in the air. If this isn't exposed and vulnerable, I don't know what is. He doesn't touch me but I feel the heat of his stare, and I hear the rustle of his pants as he rises and the pad of his bare feet on the floor as he crosses the room. With the absence of sight and music, my nerve endings prickle with every sound. I hear Chris's footsteps as he nears again but still I gasp when he is suddenly beside me, his arm wrapping my waist. Heat rushes through me with the touch and he lifts my body, lowering my elbows onto a cushioned pad, then scooting it beneath the rest of my body.

It is this part of Chris that really gets to me. The man who is a contradiction to himself, who can spank me, but worries over my tiniest discomfort. The man who can order me around, but asks how I feel about everything. I don't know how he achieves such a delicate balance, but it's why I can not only be bound, naked, and blindfolded, but do so fearlessly. Unbidden, emotions well inside me. During the end of my time with Michael, just the idea of him touching me had made me recoil. Yet this is where I am with Chris—and that's one of the many things I have to tell him before this night is over.

There's a flickering sound that I try to identify but can't. I'm aware of Chris behind me, the random sounds of him moving about, and then the shocking sensation of some kind of liquid squirting onto my back. I gasp with the cold, the wetness, and then sigh with the relief of Chris's hands dragging it over my skin. *Oil.* I have no idea where this is going or what he plans, nor can I form real ideas when he's touching me, caressing up and down my sides, then over my backside. Over and over he repeats the sensual motion. Again and again. Slowly, my muscles ease, tension sliding away and I relax into the sensations he's creating, my nipples throbbing, sex clenching with the need to feel him inside me.

The thrum of pleasure is jolted when more liquid splatters over my skin, but this time it's warm, almost hot, and thicker. Much thicker. Then, shockingly, icy cold replaces the heat as Chris rubs ice all over my skin. "Cold."

"What is it?" he demands.

"Ice. It's ice."

Hot liquid splatters over me again. "And now?" he demands.

"It's heat." More of the splatter, and I know what it is. "Wax."

His answer is a caress of ice, then more hot wax. I can hear myself panting. No. Moaning. I don't know these sounds that I'm making. There are too many sensations, too much happening. I'm disoriented. I'm aroused and my skin is tingling all over. I want him to stop. I want him to keep going but he stops abruptly, without any warning or explanation. And then nothing. There is nothing. Stillness overcomes me and the room. There is no sound. No movement. No hot or cold. Just the ache inside me that I'm desperate for him to fill.

Time ticks by and my heart starts to race again, wild, so wild. I need him to do something, anything, and when I think I might lose my mind and shout with anticipation, oil covers my back. His hands move rhythmically over my skin, my nerve endings screaming with tingly, achy sensations as the wax begins to crumble away. On and on this goes, and I feel as if my back can take no more when finally he caresses lower, over my hips, my backside. In no rush, he lingers there, touching me, soothing me. Arousing me. Knowing there is no spanking to follow, the tension I didn't know was there slips away. As if that's the moment Chris has been waiting for, he shocks me with the intimate invasion of his fingers tracing the crevice of my cheeks. I stiffen, a thrill of anticipation and renewed arousal overwhelming me, but his fingers don't move to my sex. They linger in that intimate part of my body where no man has been.

The realization of what he intends hits me and I arch my back. "Chris—"

His hand flattens on my lower back. "Easy, baby. Have you ever—"

"No," I say quickly. "Never. Chris—"

"Deep breath, baby. Just like last night. Nothing but pleasure."

"Yes," I breathe out, panting to bite back further objection. This is about trust, and I trust him.

"Pleasure," he repeats, and he begins stroking again, only this time his other hand teases my sex, distracting me from my fear. His fingers stroke through the liquid heat of my arousal, all the ways he is touching me, all the sensations, overwhelming me. I am climbing to the edge of orgasm, so lost that it takes me a moment to realize that his fingers have entered me front and back. I still can't process. I can't protest. I don't want to protest. "Chris, I—"

My words are lost to the deep stroke of his fingers, an arch of my hips. "You what?"

I don't even remember what I'd been going to say. Sensations spiral through me, a wicked wonderful darkness consuming me. I think he asks me something else. I don't know. There are only his fingers pumping into me, sensations spiraling inside me.

"Oh," I gasp. "I . . . I'm going to . . ." I spasm around him with intense, amazing pleasure that seems to last forever, yet leaves me panting for more when it ends. Exhausted from the intensity, I sink deeper onto the pad beneath me. Chris slides his fingers from inside me, his hands momentarily resting on my hips. Something soft and silky rubs over my back, drying the oil, and then I'm being scooped up in his arms and carried.

I curl against his chest, my bindings making it impossible to hold on, but I'm completely secure that he won't drop me. My nostrils flare with the rich, warm scent of our room, and I expect to be laid on the bed. Instead, I am sat down on our bed as he pulls away my blindfold.

The instant I see his face, emotions burn in my chest and damn it, my eyes. I want to blame it on adrenaline again, but this time, I'm not sure it is. It's the past bleeding from deep in my soul, refusing to be buried.

Chris reaches in the nightstand and produces a pocketknife, slicing my bindings free. The instant I'm free, I wrap my arms around him and press my lips to his. His hand comes down on my head, his mouth angling over mine, but it is me who is kissing him, me who is crazy hungry for this man I do not want to lose.

"What haven't you told me?" he demands, tearing his mouth from mine.

"I need you to know something first. Our first night together, I hadn't let another man touch me in two years. I felt no fear with you, Chris. No hesitation. It felt right with you, freeing in every way. And you know what I'd been through now. So you know how huge that was for me."

"Why are you telling me this?"

"Because tonight's panic attack wasn't just a panic attack."

"What does that mean?" he asks quietly.

A shiver races over me, and he wraps the throw blanket at the end of the bed around me, holding on to the edges. "Talk to me, Sara. I need to understand."

I nod. "Back when Michael . . . when . . ."

"He raped you."

"Don't call it that."

"You need to face what it was, to deal with it. And if that means going to that counselor we talked about in Paris, then we go."

"I suggested it; I know. And we should. But right now, I need to start with you."

"I'm listening, and I'm in all the way, baby. Whatever it is, right or wrong, I'm here."

"I know. I just hope you don't end up regretting it." He starts to object and I touch his lips. "Just listen." He gives a short nod and I let my hand slip away. "After I threatened Michael with the protection order, I was terrified he'd come back. I hid inside my apartment a lot and kept to myself. A couple of weeks later, while I was teaching a class, a sudden panic came over me.

I ended up in the bathroom in a cold sweat, not knowing why. There was no obvious trigger. And so it began—one panic attack after the other."

"How often?"

"Daily, for six months. I was alone and had no one to talk to that I trusted. I thought about seeing a counselor then, too. But knowing how Michael operates, I also knew I was being watched, and he would have seen seeking counseling as a weakness that made me fresh prey all over again. I dealt with it on my own, and thankfully the attacks stopped as abruptly as they began."

"You know why they started. Do you know why they ended?"

"It was when I finally felt in control for the first time in my life. I have an ex-student to thank for that. Elizabeth's father was beating her and her mother. She often came to school with bruises, and I'd made efforts through my superiors to get her help. She and her mother denied there was a problem, but I bonded with the girl. Gradually, she shared small details."

"You saw yourself in her."

"Yes. I was never beaten, but the pain both my father and Michael had caused me was very present for me. And the way her mother didn't get her out of the situation was a hot button, too. I loved my mother, but she accepted my father's abuse."

"So you got stronger for Elizabeth?"

"Oh yes. Teaching brought out this mama bear quality in me."

"What happened to Elizabeth?"

"Her mother showed up at the school one day with the car

packed up to leave. When I walked them to the parking lot, the dad showed up." I shake my head. "It was bad. He was violent, and he lunged at the mother. She'd finally stood up for herself and her daughter, and I couldn't let him hurt her. I jumped between them."

"Oh fuck, baby, what happened?"

"He broke my nose. I sent him to jail. Elizabeth and her mother left town, and I never heard from them again."

Understanding seeps into his expression. "And the panic attacks stopped."

"Yes. And from that point on, I swore no one else would ever control me again. But you . . . you are the one person who makes me feel I can let the walls down without any repercussions. That's trust, Chris."

"But you didn't let the walls down tonight."

"And I told you why."

His hands slide around my neck. "You aren't Amber. You will never be Amber. She sought out the whip to get my love. You only need to breathe, and you have it. What you see as flaws, I see as perfection."

"Chris," I whisper, too choked up to manage more. I love him with all my heart and soul.

"No one," he adds, his tone raw, "most especially Amber, is *ever* coming between us." He kisses me, a deep, passionate kiss that has my head spinning. "Let's get out of town after the hearing tomorrow," he says, tearing his mouth from mine. "We'll go see Katie and Mike. We have a wedding to plan."

His message is clear. Nothing I've confessed changes his intent to make me his wife.

"I don't want to get married in the middle of this hell," I say. "I want the day I marry my best friend to be special."

"Best friend?" he asks, his eyes lighting.

"You are. You know that, right?"

"And you're everything to me, Sara. Screw everything else; we're planning our wedding. We can set the date later. And I'm going to have the jeweler I told you about meet us at Katie and Mike's." He brushes his lips over mine. "I want to show you something." He leans back and reaches between the bed and the dresser, producing a sketch pad. "The ring I designed."

I straighten, eager to see his creation. "Yes. Please."

Mischief fills his eyes. "That's twice you've said that to-night." My cheeks heat and he laughs. "I'm planning on making it three before the night is over."

I give him a scolding look and reach for the sketch pad. "Stop teasing me. I want to see the design."

"Hold on." He turns a page and then allows me to see the sketch. I blink down at the ridiculously large round stone sur-rounded by an elegant design, momentarily mesmerized by his gift for detail. But as I study the wide band, I blink again and tell myself I'm not seeing what I think I am. Yet it is. He's designed a delicately woven vine of roses, and now that I look closer at the stone, it too, is a rose.

Shocked, my gaze lifts to Chris's, but my questions fade when I see a rare anxious uncertainty in his eyes. He has no idea that this is a connection to Rebecca; he'd refused to read the journals and I've never talked about the roses. This means something else to him—something special I don't want to ruin.

He strokes my cheek. "If you don't like it—"

I smile tenderly. "I love it. I absolutely love it."

His brows knit. "You're sure?"

"Yes, I'm sure." I want to ask him what inspired the roses, but he sets the pad aside and lowers me to the bed, his big, wonderful body covering mine. A moment later he is kissing me. Another moment later and his hand is traveling to my waist, my breasts, and my neck.

I don't care about the roses. I care about the man who created a masterpiece for me.

Fifteen

It's nearly dawn when I fall asleep in Chris's arms, but I awaken instantly with the alarm and reach for the remote to tune in to the news. Chris quickly removes it from my hand and drags me to the shower, where he successfully distracts me from my worries about the bail hearing.

But an hour later I'm a ball of nerves again, and I begin pacing under the awning of our apartment building while we wait for our car to be pulled around, somehow managing to trip over my own feet. Tumbling forward, I'm thankfully saved as Chris shackles my waist and steadies me. "Stop fretting or I'm going to turn you over my knee."

I gape. "What?"

He laughs, a deep, sexy rumble. "That's the amazing thing about a spanking," he says, his voice a naughty whisper near my ear. "Just the threat makes you forget everything else."

I glower fiercely at him. "That's not funny."

"No." His hand slides under my trench coat, fingers flexing on my hip. "It's a lot of things, baby, but funny isn't one of them."

The car pulls up behind us. "You really are—"

"Mr. Merit," the attendant announces.

Chris arches a brow, focused on me. "I really am what?"

Sexy. Amazing. "Bad."

He laughs again, wrapping his arm around my neck, and the sound is a balm soothing my nerve endings. "Let's go get this day over with so I can show you just how bad." He holds the door for me and I've already slipped back into stress mode, reaching for the radio to try and find the news.

"I hope David told Tiger that Ricco accused Mark of setting him up," I say as Chris claims the driver's seat. "Your call with him was too short to say much."

"I didn't," he says. "I have no idea what David told him, but we can confirm what Mark knows when we get to the gallery."

"I can't believe he'll be in. Not after he pretty much told me he doesn't want to see me again."

Chris shifts into gear. "He'll be in. He has to be in the eye of the storm; that's his control. And just to be clear, the only reason I'm letting you near him, after his confession yesterday about you and Rebecca, is because I'm going to be your personal bodyguard."

"So you said when you picked out my outfit today," I comment of the high-necked, knee-length basic black dress. "And I'm not complaining about having you around today, considering everything going on, but you also need to be clear: I don't need a bodyguard to protect me from Mark. I can handle him."

"You have a big heart. Even Amber managed to get to you. It gets you into trouble."

"I'd like to argue, but I try to fight battles I can win."

Chris pulls into the alley leading to the newly fenced parking lot, keying in an entry code, and I'm surprised at the absence of press. "No Mark," I say, as we park, noting the absence of his Jag. "I only see Ralph's car, and what looks like the security crew."

"Anything happening we should know about?" Chris asks Jacob as he opens the back door for us, obviously alerted to our presence by the gate entry.

"Nothing beyond Blake and Kelvin are at the courthouse, and it's a media madhouse. Blake's keeping me apprised. I'll let you know as I get updates."

Chris nods and we make our way to the office where, judging from the sound of Ralph swiftly keying his calculator, he's already hard at work. Amanda is nowhere to be found. "I'd say good morning, but it's not," Ralph calls out. "Coffee is made and no, she hasn't called." He never stops keying.

I hang my coat on the rack behind Amanda's desk, while Chris shrugs out of his leather jacket and does the same. "Don't read into this," he warns, and when I'm momentarily, impossibly under the circumstances, distracted by his hotness in faded True Religion jeans and a light blue "Matchbox 20" T-shirt, I decide every girl needs a man who can distract her this easily under this kind of stress.

Chris steps to me and brushes hair over my shoulder. "She's only late a minute or two."

"Yes, but—"

"She's never late," Ralph says. "Yesterday she was distracted by Ryan, and then left with him. Now she's not here. I don't like it. Not one bit."

Jacob pushes through the door and motions to Chris, and he must read the instant concern in my face because he quickly holds up a hand and says, "Nothing new, and nothing to worry about. Blake's brother, Royce, wants to talk to Chris."

Chris squeezes my hand. "I need to take this. Royce has some FBI contacts with links to Paris. He's using them to help find Ella."

"Oh, thank you. Thank him."

He motions to Ralph's office and mouths, "Get him out of here." I nod and he disappears into the gallery with Jacob.

I head to Ralph's office, pausing in his doorway. "Did you try to call Amanda?"

"Not yet." He laces his fingers on the desk, his orange bow tie practically glowing. "I sense something in the air. What do I need to know?"

"Mark's going to have us work from home for the next few weeks. I'll coordinate everything with you by phone."

"Fine by me, but I can't do that until I finish these reports for Mark."

"How long will that take?"

"With Amanda's help, all day. Without it, today and tomorrow."

"You can't finish at home?"

"Are you kidding me? The police made a mess of my files. I can't find half of what I need. Moving things will only make it worse."

"I really wanted you gone before the hearing is over today and the press invasion happens."

"Unless Bossman wants me to forget these reports, I can't. And since he called about them this morning, I'm assuming that isn't the case."

"He called? Did he say if he'll be in?"

He snorts. "Like he tells me anything. He just wanted to know I was on the reports."

As much as I understand Mark's stress, I don't understand how completely he's ignored the gallery. "I'll help," I volunteer, sitting in his visitor's chair. "Let me call Amanda, then you can show me what to do."

"I'll call," he offers, punching a button on the phone and letting it ring on speaker. It goes directly to voice mail. Grimacing, he punches the End button. "Same as yesterday. I'm telling you, her obsession with Ryan has changed her. She's ready to bow at his feet, if you know what I mean."

I barely stop my eyes from going wide. Just what does Ralph know about Ryan, and even Mark? "Yes, I got that from her, too. She's young, and he's older and rich. It must have her in some sort of Cinderella fantasy."

He smirks. "Fifty Shades of Prince Charming."

My heart skips a beat. "What does that mean?"

"Well." He leans forward and falls into one of his conspiratorial whispers. "She told me he's all kinds of dominant, in that kinky kind of way."

My lips part in shock. "She told you that?"

"Yes, but nothing more. I tried. Oh baby, I tried. He's hot. I wanted details."

My stomach churns. He'll get more details than he wants once the press frenzy starts, and I'm suddenly glad Mark decided to shut the gallery. I motion to the files and change the subject. "Speaking of details, tell me what I need to do to help."

An hour later we still haven't been able to reach Amanda, and aside from popping his head in to check on me, Chris has spent most of his time with Jacob. Carrying my Ralph-assigned workload, I make my way to my office. Rounding the corner to my doorway, I flip on the light and then stop dead in my tracks, stunned.

It's bare. Completely, utterly bare. No books. No rose-scented candle on the desk. Not even a computer on the desk, just a phone. I walk inside and turn to the wall, surprised to find the painting of the roses remains, but it's sitting on the floor. I can only assume there was some insurance reason it had to stay. It bothers me that it's been moved, to the point it's like a grinding in my belly. It's part of her. It's part of *them,* of her and Mark. If it's gone, what's left? Without the journals, the painting is all I have of Rebecca.

Shaking off my emotions, I stack the files on top of the desk and set my purse in the drawer. As I claim my chair a low whistle draws my attention to the doorway, where my jeans-clad Fifty Shades of Prince Charming appears. "Talk about taking everything," Chris comments, stepping inside and shutting the door.

"I'm surprised they left the furniture."

"This isn't a bad thing," he points out, coming around to my side of the desk, and leaning against the edge beside me. "The more they know about Rebecca, the better chance they have of finding her."

I can smell that earthy, freshly showered scent that is so Chris, and so not Rebecca. Her roses are gone. Like she is. "Why'd you shut the door?" I ask. "Did you get some news about the hearing?"

"There was a bomb threat at the courthouse. The hearing has been postponed until two."

"*Bomb* threat?"

"David and Blake think it was Ava's legal team. Blake's trying to prove it, but he says her people are pretty smart about covering their tracks."

"Why would they do that? Don't they want to get her out of jail sooner?"

"Speculation is they're waiting on a witness that didn't show up."

"What witness?"

"It doesn't matter. I took care of it."

"What does that mean, Chris?" He just stares at me, and it's making me crazy. "It's about me, isn't it? Just tell me. I'm not a delicate—"

"Flower. I know." He inhales and lets it out. "There were phone exchanges between Ava's counsel and Michael."

I laugh without humor and I think it sounds a little crazy. I feel a little crazy right now. "David was right. Ava's people are all about character assassination." My eyes burn.

Chris's fingers slide under my chin. "I took care of it. I called your father."

"My father." My tone is flat, my emotions wild, but at least the threatening tears have dried up. "I'm sure that was a real success. What did Daddy dearest say?"

"He fired Michael, who's now working for a competitor."

I feel like I'm in the Twilight Zone of Hell. "So my father has no control over him now. Not that I thought he would do anything to help anyway."

"Yes, he does. He put a loophole in Michael's exit contract linked to residual income for just this reason. He says the fine print will handle this swiftly and effectively."

"Of course it will. Why would I doubt him? If his daughter looks bad, he looks bad. I guess there's a bright side to having an egomaniac for a father."

"What's important is it's handled. I found out about this yesterday and took action, and we wake up to the bomb threat today. Michael had to have backed out, and Ava's team is buying time to get him back on board."

"You knew yesterday and you didn't tell me?"

"I was going to tell you, but—"

"You were afraid I'd freak out. Which was what *I* was afraid would happen if I told you about my panic attacks." I sigh. "Is Michael in town?"

"Sara. I didn't think you were going to freak out."

"You can't tell me you aren't worried about when I'll have another attack."

"I'm not. But if you do, I'll be here to hold you up."

"I don't want you to have to hold me up."

"That's what we do, baby. We support each other. We made that decision when we decided to get married. For better or worse. End of subject. Okay?"

I nod, and damn it, my eyes are burning. "Okay."

"Good. And yes, Michael is in town, and in a few hours

we won't be. The sooner we leave for Sonoma, the happier I'll be."

"He's going to go into that courtroom and lie about me. God. He's such an asshole. I have to be at the hearing."

"Forget it. They don't want you there and I don't want you there."

"I need to defend myself."

"Your father assures me Michael won't be there. And even if he was, the DA would defend you as their primary witness."

"So far I've been attacked on all fronts. Did my father say anything about me nearly being killed? No. Don't answer that. I know I won't like the answer."

He rests his forehead on mine and says nothing, his silence the bitter confirmation I expect. My father didn't care about my safety. He cared about his reputation.

I can't think about this now, and I look at Chris. "I assume Blake has men watching Michael?"

"Yes. If he heads to the courthouse, we'll know. Any word on Amanda?"

"Nothing. I've tried to reach her and so has Ralph. I have a bad feeling about her, Chris."

"It's easy to have a bad feeling when you're in the middle of a murder investigation. If it'll make you feel better, I'll have one of the security guys run by her house."

"I think I should go. She knows me, and she'll be freaked out by a stranger showing up at her door."

"No, baby. I know doing something, anything, makes you feel more in control right now, but we have to think about Ricco and the press."

"Ricco's angry at Mark, not me."

"Jealousy and vengeance make people do crazy things. We talked about this. So we aren't underestimating Ricco. I'll go check on Amanda. She knows me, and I can call you and put her on the line with you while I'm there."

"I'll just go with you."

Chris shakes his head. "You stay and help Ralph get out of here. I want to pay Ryan a little visit after I check on Amanda, and I'm not taking you along for that ride."

"Good. Just call me as soon as you get to her apartment."

"Of course." He runs his hand down my hair. "I don't think you'll see Mark today. My understanding is they called him in for last minute questioning this morning, but text me if he shows up." His voice lowers, roughens, and he tugs me to my feet. "Just remember. You're mine, baby, and I protect what's mine. I won't let anyone hurt you in any way." He kisses my forehead and leaves.

Thirty minutes later I'm on pins and needles waiting to hear from Chris, but I've managed to be productive, sorting files and righting papers that are an absolute mess. How can the police justify leaving the gallery's records like this? I'm about to head to Ralph's office again when I hear the exterior door open.

Hoping for news, I reach my doorway just as Mark stops in front of me. We are toe-to-toe, a lean away from touching, and I am captured by those icy gray eyes. For several moments I can't breathe, and he knows it. I see it in the narrowing of his eyes, the hint of satisfaction that tells me he misreads my reaction as something it is not—and never will be.

Jolted back to sanity, I step backward.

"My office, Ms. McMillan," he snaps, and leaves me staring after him.

My shoulders slump. So much for not seeing him today. My fist balls at my chest, where my stupid heart is racing. I hate that he can still do this to me; that any man can do this to me.

Mark hits the same hot spots that Michael and my father do, both of whom are very much on my mind today. I respond to him more out of conditioning than by free will, like I do with Chris.

I walk down the hallway toward Mark's office with trepidation, replaying his words from yesterday. *You remind me of her.* It's rather ironic, how I remind him of his past, and he of mine.

Entering his office, I find him leaning against the front of his desk, his arms crossed over his chest, looking every bit the powerful, unapproachable "King."

"Shut the door," he orders.

"I'm not sure that's a good idea."

"*The door,* Ms. McMillan."

I hesitate, but my worry for Ralph's uncanny ability to overhear things wins. I shut the door, and hope it's not a mistake.

Sixteen

Mark's spacious office shrinks the instant I'm sealed inside with him. His energy and power radiate through the room, a sharp, familiar sensation that I now realize always stirs a bit of my past, and my defenses with it.

"Why are you and Ralph still here?" he demands.

I force myself to stand my ground. "Ralph can't do the reports you want from home. I'm helping him since Amanda was a no-show today."

"Jacob told me about that."

I wait for him to express concern or offer a game plan or explanation, but he just gives me silence. "It's not like her to not show up. Chris went to check on her."

"I made sure she won't be given entry into the club, should Ryan choose to take her there."

"Did you talk to Ryan?" I ask hopefully.

"I told you, Ms. McMillan; it's not in my or Ryan's best interest for me to communicate with him at present."

I bite back a snarky remark that would only lead me into a battle I won't win, opting for an information dig instead. "You think he's involved in Rebecca's disappearance, don't you?"

"You asked that yesterday."

"That's right," I agree, "and I'm asking again."

"You really don't know your limits, do you, Ms. McMillan?"

"I most certainly do," I say, my sureness returning, my hands finding my hips. "It's yours I'm pushing. You said Ryan knew that Rebecca returned to San Francisco."

"Correct."

"But you didn't."

"Correct again."

My mood softens again with the certainty that this is a betrayal of friendship to Mark. "Could he have thought it was a difficult subject for you?"

"I don't allow Ryan to know what difficult means for me."

"You call him a friend."

"A socially acceptable term, better described as a business acquaintance."

"But one you trust," I counter.

"*Trusted*. Past tense." He changes the subject. "I understand Ricco paid you a visit last night."

"He showed up at the restaurant and cornered me by the restroom door."

"And he did this why?"

"To warn me away from you."

His lips twist wryly. "At least he and I agree on something."

I ignore the reference to our conversation yesterday and push forward with what's important. "He hates you, and he thinks you killed Rebecca. That spells dangerous to me, especially when you consider he threw away more than most people have in a lifetime to try to ruin you."

He arches a brow. "Worried about me, Ms. McMillan?"

"Yes, Mark, I'm worried about you," I say, refusing to be baited. "And I know you and Chris have had issues, but he's worried, too."

"Issues," he repeats flatly. "Are you referencing his warning to Rebecca to stay away from me? Or mine to you, to stay away from him? Or perhaps the 'issues' lie in the way he left you alone and miserable, and I tried to fuck you to your senses."

If he intends to shock me, which I'm certain he does, he fails. I cross my arms and level him with a frosty look. "What is it with you being crass all of a sudden?"

"I wasn't aware you had such delicate sensibilities. I'd have thought Chris would have remedied that by now. I certainly would have."

My hands go back to my hips. "Stop it, Mark."

"I'm pretty sure that's what Rebecca said to Chris. We see how well that worked out for her."

"That's enough," I snap, and it's all I can do not to say more, to remember he's hurting and motivated by who knows what emotion. "Ricco accused you of setting him up. If that's what he's saying to me, that has to be what he's using as a defense to the police."

"Not a very subtle change of subject, Ms. McMillan. But then, subtlety isn't exactly your strong point. Tiger told me about the accusations and they aren't surprising. Ricco's entire objective is to ruin me and he has deep-enough pockets to make a valiant effort. Do I care? No. Ricco Alvarez is the last thing on my mind right now."

Though his expression and tone are as unreadable as ever, there's an unspoken message in his words. Nothing Ricco can do to him comes close to what losing Rebecca has, or what fearing for his mother is doing to him now. "When do you go back to New York?"

"I'm flying back this evening to attempt to head off any bad press that might land on Riptide's doorstep today."

"I warned Crystal about today's events and the potential media frenzy to follow. I didn't want to risk her being surprised and walking out on you."

The ice is back in his impenetrable gray eyes. "Go help Ralph finish the reports and then leave, Ms. McMillan."

I'm stunned by the sharply spoken dismissal. "But—"

"Don't argue, Ms. McMillan."

I want to, but he's stone now, and I might as well have already left the room. I turn on my heel and go to the door, before I do something insane like try to shake some sense into the man.

"Ms. McMillan."

My hand freezes on the knob in a déjà vu moment. This is reminiscent of the many times in the past when Mark sent me fleeing his office in a mess of mixed emotions, only to stop me to land one final blow. I pause, holding my breath with the expectation this one will rock my world, as he always intends.

"Chris and I are far more alike than you think," he says,

repeating what Chris himself has said to me on more than one occasion. "Rebecca held on too long. Don't make the same mistake."

Anger begins to burn through me, fiery and hot. Afraid of what I might say, I yank open the door and exit into the hallway. I am not Rebecca, and Chris isn't Mark. I refuse to let him mess with my head.

My pace and my erratic heartbeat don't slow until I'm in my office, behind the desk. I stare at the painting of the roses that's so much a part of who Rebecca and Mark were together, and I can't help but think of the roses on my wedding band.

My cell phone beeps with a text, and I grab it to read the message from Chris. *She's not home. I'm on my way to Ryan's.*

It's not the news I'd hoped for, but expected. Knowing what I have to do, and dreading his reaction, I type, *Mark's here.*

It takes about three seconds for my phone to ring. "I knew I chose that dress for a reason," Chris says, and while it's spoken playfully, there's an undercurrent of tension.

"He's more overbearingly impossible than usual," I tell him, "and as eager to get me and Ralph out of here as we are. I dared to ask him about Ryan and he shut me down, of course."

"Well, I'm no fan of his silence, or Ryan's timing with Amanda. If we can get her out of the center of this, I think that's smart. I'll be at Ryan's office in about fifteen minutes."

"What about his apartment?"

"I bribed the doorman into telling me Ryan left hours ago, and he was alone."

"That's not good. Where's Amanda?"

"I'm hoping he can tell us. I'll call you as soon as I know

something. In the meantime, stay away from Mark." While I don't regret returning to the gallery, since it still feels like the window to finding Rebecca, I'm ready to leave.

I make a coffee run to the break room and catch a glimpse of Ralph disappearing into the gallery with Jacob on his heels. Frowning, I set my coffee on my desk, grab my cell phone, and head to the showroom to find it empty. The sound of voices draws me toward the front door and I see Ralph and Jacob standing outside, their backs to me. Crossing the display floor, I push open the door to find two of Blake's men flanking the entry. I start toward Ralph and Jacob's direction, only to stop dead in my tracks when I realize who's with them.

Seventeen

"There she is," Detective Grant says, looking far from court-room ready with a two-day beard and a navy blazer he's paired with jeans and a loosened tie. "Just the woman I was hoping to talk to. Your bodyguard here said you weren't available."

"She's not," Jacob snaps tightly, his spine ramrod straight, his jaw set hard. "Go back inside, Ms. McMillan."

"Yes," the detective agrees. "Go back inside, Ms. McMillan. I'll chat with Ralph."

The look of utter terror on Ralph's face tells me how direly he needs saving, and I squeeze his arm. "Go finish your reports."

"He's already agreed to talk to me," Detective Grant insists.

Irritated at the way this man throws around his power, my gaze snaps to his. "Schedule a meeting so he can have an attorney present."

"I need an attorney?" Ralph exclaims. "Since when do I need an attorney? I barely knew Rebecca. I liked her, though. I really liked her."

Oh, crap. "Relax, Ralph," I say quickly, stepping in front of him, my hands coming down on his upper arms. "Don't over-react. It's just a precaution. You're fine."

"You're not a suspect," Detective Grant assures him from behind me. "I just want to talk to you about this."

Certain that I don't want to know what "this" is, I turn to find him holding a book. My stomach plummets as I recognize it as my journal.

"What is it?" Ralph asks.

"Sara's journal," Detective Grant answers, his hard stare boring into mine. "Interesting that you started one at the same time you were reading Rebecca's. It's really quite interesting reading. Deep thoughts, Ms. McMillan. For instance," he pauses, and flips it open to a flagged page, "right here where you say that Mark—"

"I'll talk to you," I interrupt, all too aware that I've referenced intimate details about his relationship with Rebecca. "But I need to call my attorney first."

"No time for that," the detective counters. "He's at the courthouse where I need to be in," he glances at his watch, "an hour. In fact, let's save time and the three of us can talk right here." He glances at Ralph. "Sara wrote a note I'd like to get your opinion on." He glances down at the page. "It says, and I quote, *'If there is a fine line between love and hate, where did Mark walk then and now?'*" His gaze lifts from the journal. "My question to you, Ralph, is in your observations—"

"Enough," I snap, in disbelief he's gone as far as he has with my private property, and wishing I knew my rights. "I'll talk to you."

"Ms. McMillan—" Jacob begins.

"I'm fine," I assure him, knowing he will call either David or Chris, or maybe both. I just need to get the detective and that journal away from Ralph and then buy time until the cavalry arrive. I cut Ralph a look, and instruct, "Go back inside, please."

"We're through, Ralph," the detective adds.

"I don't have to be told twice," Ralph mutters, already backing up and moving away.

"So here we are," Detective Grant says, rocking on his heels, and giving Jacob a judicious once-over that thins his lips. "Let's walk next door to the coffee shop, Ms. McMillan. We need privacy."

"The coffee shop?" I say in disbelief. "You *want to go* to the coffee shop?"

"Yes, I do. What better place to jog your memories of the past?" He motions me forward and I take a step, only to have Jacob grab my arm and warn, "Don't do this."

"I'm okay."

"I'm sure Mr. Merit won't agree," he argues.

"No," I concede. "I'm sure he won't, but I'm still doing it."

His jaw clenches and unclenches and he releases me, stepping to my side. "I'm going with you."

"I talk to you alone, Ms. McMillan," Detective Grant replies, as if I'm the one who made the declaration that Jacob is along for the trip, "or we bring Ralph back out to talk."

211

My blood boils with the threat, but there's no room to argue. I turn my attention to Jacob. "I won't let Ralph be harassed over me. Stay here, please."

"I'll wait outside the coffee shop."

"Fine with me," Detective Grant says, and we start walking into a gust of bitterly cold November wind.

Hugging myself, I feel exposed to far more than the cold air. When Jacob steps away from me to open the shop door, I'm unnaturally chilled to the bone. "I'll be right here," he assures me.

"Thank you." I intend to rush into the shelter of warm walls, but somehow my feet are planted and I'm sinking in the quicksand of memories. Ava's smiling face, her laughter, her funny comments about Chris and Mark. Her raging anger when she'd held that gun on me and fully intended to kill me. I know she had. I'd seen it in her eyes.

"Problem, Ms. McMillan?" Detective Grant asks and something in his tone hits a raw, angry nerve.

My attention snaps to him and I shove Ava back into that hellhole I reserve for all the crap in my life. "You know very well there's a problem, and what it is. And you, Detective Grant, are a familiar breed of manipulator. Very familiar." I lift my chin and walk inside.

Passing the many displays of coffee and mugs, my nostrils flare with the rich, nutty scent of coffee brewing. I'd once eagerly inhaled and savored this scent in the past; today it burns my nose and throat, and turns my stomach.

Pausing to scan the dozen rather packed tables for a vacancy, my gaze settles on the counter, where an unfamiliar man with longish dark hair and heavily tattooed arms rings up a customer.

"Ava's husband, Raphael," Detective Grant supplies, stepping to my side. "The rock band he plays in calls him Raf, I believe."

"Ava's husband?" I ask, surprised. While good-looking in the rocker bad boy kind of way, he's far from what I'd imagine for the refined beauty. He's Mark's polar opposite.

"Estranged husband, I guess you'd call him."

"I thought he owned a bar?"

"He does but he plays in a band, too. And now it seems he owns a coffee shop." He motions to a table. "Let's sit. I don't have time for coffee."

Glad to get this over with, I follow the detective to the table and claim the seat by the wall. Feeling like I'm being watched, I look around and am locked in the beam of Raf's stare, and choking with the unpleasant sensation of being naked.

Detective Grant slaps the journal down on the table and I nearly jump out of my seat. "Let's talk," he says, and now I'm stuck in *his* probing, always judgmental, stare.

"Should we do a read-along of your opinions of Mark Compton?" he asks. "Or do you care to simply share them with me?"

Angry with him all over again, I set my cell phone in my lap, and lace my fingers together on top of the table. "Why share them if you read them?" I challenge. "And is it even legal for you to show my personal items to Ralph?"

"Feel free to use all that money your boyfriend has and sue me, and I guess we'll find out."

"My rich boyfriend? Are you *trying* to alienate me, or is being a jerk so natural for you that you simply can't help yourself?"

He chuckles. "Oh, Ms. McMillan. I think I see why all these men find you so appealing."

"All these men?" I demand. "I'm with Chris, and only Chris. And for the record, Detective, you're living up to my manipulation expectations. Even that comment was meant to lure me into saying something I'm not going to say."

Unfazed, he taps my journal. "Let's talk about Mark."

"He's not guilty of anything but loving Rebecca," I say before I can stop myself.

"There's a fine line between love and hate. You wrote that yourself."

"Because Ricco Alvarez said that to me. He's the one to be worried about. He loved her, too, and he was insanely jealous over Mark." I lean back. "That's all I'm saying. I'm done."

"This isn't about you or Chris Merit. I've cleared you both."

"You have?"

"Yes. You both have rock-solid alibis." He leans forward. "I need to find Rebecca, Ms. McMillan. Help me."

"I want to, but I can't help you without my attorney present."

"I told you I've cleared you."

"I know, but you think Mark is guilty. And I'm not helping you convict an innocent man."

"How can you be sure he's innocent?"

My phone vibrates and I know who it is before I even

glance at the caller ID and see Chris's number. Knowing he'll be worried, I hold up a finger and say, "Give me one minute, please."

He leans back in his seat. "By all means. Take your time. The only place I have to be is in court to testify against your attacker."

The snide remark makes me ignore my phone call. "My attacker is exactly right—yet you insist on meeting here, at her coffee shop? No one looking out for my well-being would do that."

"Just because you don't understand my reasoning, doesn't mean it doesn't make sense."

"Just because you think you're a hero, doesn't mean you're not a jerk." My phone starts ringing again and I hit Ignore, but I don't put the phone down. I punch the auto-dial Chris programmed for David.

"Ms. McMillan," Detective Grant begins, just as David answers the call with, "What the fuck is going on, Sara? Chris just called and told me you're with Detective Grant."

"That's why I'm calling. He's right. I'm with Detective Grant right now."

"You *only* talk to him when you're with me. No other time. What part of that don't you understand?"

"He threatened to show my personal journal to Ralph if I didn't go with him—"

"What journal, and go where?"

"Notes I took on people Rebecca knew. He acquired my journal at the gallery during yesterday's search. And he took me to the coffee shop."

"The coffee shop that's owned by the woman who tried to kill you?"

"Yes."

"Put that lousy piece of shit on the phone."

I hold out my cell phone to Detective Grant, who looks amused rather than irritated. "Smart lady. I'm impressed, Ms. McMillan." He puts the cell to his ear and says, "Hello, David." There are several moments of silence before he chides, "Calm down. I'm aware of all of that."

They begin going back and forth, and I can't make heads or tails out of who is winning what battle. Afraid the detective is getting a little too loud, my gaze lifts and lands on the counter again. Frowning, I watch Corey, the college-aged kid who's worked here as long as I've been around, and Raf in a deep, animated conversation. Corey seems to be getting more agitated, swiping his hands around to make his point. Raf holds up his palms stop-sign fashion, as if trying to calm the kid down.

The detective nudges me and hands me the phone back. "Your turn."

Reluctantly, I drag my attention from the counter and accept the phone. Detective Grant glances over his shoulder, immediately moving his chair to the side of the table where he can observe the action.

The moment I speak, David launches into a rant. "I'm not sure what kind of Jack and Jill trip he thought he was taking you on, but get up and leave. He snuck over there and pulled that shit knowing I was here. He won't be showing your journal to anyone." It's hard for me to believe that, after my conversation with the detective, but I'm not going to argue. David doesn't give me time to anyway. "Text me when he's gone or if there's a problem. I won't be able to take the call unless it's critical."

"Yes. I will."

"Good. Now get up and leave. Oh, and you did good calling me, babe. Kudos, sister."

Babe and kudos, sister. I almost laugh. Really, what else can I do at this point? It's like I'm living in a soap opera with really bad writers. I stand up and the detective follows me. "I'm sure you know I can't talk," I tell him.

"We'll talk," he assures me. "Maybe not now, but we'll talk."

A loud crash thunders from the counter, and suddenly Raf is on top of it with Corey straddling him. Raf manages to kick him away, and the next thing I know, they're both tumbling behind the displays.

"Well, well," Detective Grant murmurs, "isn't that interesting. I was hoping our little meeting would stir up some sort of reaction, but this is even better than I hoped for. I might be a jerk, Ms. McMillan, but I'm a calculating jerk. Sometimes you have to put flames under a pot to make it boil.

"And just so you know, Ava will likely get out on bail, but I'll get you your restraining order and I'll get you a conviction. I'll be in touch."

He dashes toward the counter and I stand there stunned, watching as he climbs over the counter and throws himself into the scuffle. He grabs Raf and Corey hits him, and I dart for the door for help, bursting through the exit for Jacob.

"Fight," I pant. "There's a fight inside and the detective needs help."

Jacob curses and opens the door. He takes one glance inside and grabs the walkie-talkie on his belt. "Kelvin, I need backup. Come get Sara now." Then to me: "He's two blocks away. Don't move."

"Okay. Be careful."

He enters the coffee shop and I turn to watch for Kelvin, whom I've met before and trust, only to discover instead that I'm staring into the eyes of the worst mistake of my life. "Michael."

Eighteen

Michael presses against me, his hands shackling my waist, and the feel of his hands on my body makes my skin crawl. "Let go of me," I hiss, shoving at his unmovable chest. I hear the sound of sirens nearing in the background, but they aren't here to rescue me. I need to rescue me.

He dares to slide his hand down my waist to my hips, and anger explodes from some deep, pent-up place I had forgotten existed. "I said, let go," I growl, swiftly lifting my knee and fully intending to plant it in his groin. He captures my leg, the touch wrong in every way.

"You have two seconds before I start screaming," I warn.

"You don't want that attention right now."

"Try me," I challenge. "Go ahead."

His eyes narrow and he seems to sense just how dangerous the ground he walks upon is, and he moves his body from mine. But his hands flatten on the wall beside me, his arms caging me in. But I don't want to escape. I want to finally face him, and the past that's haunted me for far too long.

"Why are you here?" I demand. He looks so civilized in his perfectly fitted black suit and deep blue shirt, no doubt chosen to match his eyes, yet he's such a barbaric asshole.

"I didn't come to San Francisco to testify against you," he claims, lying as easily as he has a million times before. "I came here to protect you, since your 'boyfriend' can't seem to get the job done. I'll be right here in town until the trial is over, no matter how long I have to stay. You can count on it."

I laugh and I sound a little insane, but it's controlled insanity. My kind, and I'll unleash it my way, in my time. "That's truly priceless, Michael," I say. "You've managed to turn this into a way to get back into my father's good graces."

"I didn't ask to be called into this, but I'm here now, and it's clear I'm needed."

He's so damn believable in the role of Mr. Tall, Dark, and Perfect, that it makes me sick to my stomach, thinking of all the people he takes advantage of. And I was one of them.

"You know what?" I demand. "Fuck you, Michael. Fuck you. Fuck you. And *fuck you.*" Shock slides over his face, and I revel in it. "If you think hanging around with the threat of butchering me in court is going to scare me into helping you get your job back with my father, you're wrong. I'm already going to be sliced and diced by the press, so it doesn't matter what you do."

There's a movement to my right, followed by Jacob's harsh command. "Step. Back."

Michael's eyes glint with irritation but he's smart enough to listen, pushing off the wall. A moment later I have Jacob on one side of me and Kelvin on the other, but Michael's cold, calculating blue eyes don't move from me.

"I'll be at the Fairmont," he says with barely contained anger. He pauses, for effect no doubt, and adds, "Indefinitely."

"Go home, Michael," I bite out. "There's nothing for you here."

His lips twist evilly. "I guess we'll see about that," he replies, a snide arrogance in his tone that makes me want to slap him, but he's already turned away. He's leaving, but he's not gone. I have failed to get rid of him.

"Are you okay?" Jacob asks. If he's been in a fight, his perfectly pressed suit and flawless face show no sign of it.

"Did he hurt you?" Kelvin asks, stepping closer, and I realize I've never seen him in a suit before. He heads the local Walker Security team, which makes him Jacob's boss.

"I'm fine," I assure him, and it's remarkably true. "And I have Jacob to thank for that. He refused to leave my side even when I was with the detective."

"Good thing he didn't," Kelvin comments. "Michael was supposed to be on a plane out of the city."

"Apparently his travel plans and departure from his hotel were meant as a distraction," Jacob says.

"That doesn't surprise me," I say, shivering against a gust of cold wind. "Is Chris—"

"On his way to kick my ass for letting this happen," Jacob assures me, his frustration evident.

"It's not your fault this happened, Jacob," I assure him, "and I'll be the first one to tell Chris that."

"When I'm protecting you, anything that goes wrong is my fault," he corrects. "I should have let the detective get his ass kicked."

The coffee shop doors open beside us, and Corey and Raf are marched out in handcuffs. Kelvin rests a hand on the wall and lifts his chin at Jacob. "What the hell happened in there?"

"The kid, Corey, seems to have the hots for Ava, and apparently called Sara a lying bitch."

I blanch. "Me? He doesn't even know me."

"Out of the mouths of babes," Kelvin says. "Sounds like he was speaking Ava's kind of language. How'd that turn into a fight?"

"Raf, who in case it wasn't explained is technically still Ava's husband. Sara wasn't the lying bitch," Jacob says. "He claimed Ava's the lying bitch. Then it was all fists."

I think back to the Chanel store, when Ava took a call from her Raf. "I thought he wanted Ava back?"

"That is *not* a man who wants his wife back," Jacob assures me, cutting a look toward the police car as the back doors are closed. "I need to go talk to the detective before he leaves."

"Go," Kelvin orders. "I have Sara."

Jacob takes off in a jog and Kelvin is already herding me toward the gallery, eager to escape reporters. As we walk, a sudden wave of emotion overcomes me. Fortunately, I have the short hike to beat it back down. I *won't* let Michael have the power of destruction over me—not even in the form of a few worthless tears.

Once we're inside the gallery, Ralph darts out of his office. "What happened? Are you okay?"

"I'm fine," I say, though the dull throb starting behind my eyes and in my head argues differently. "I handled the detective. But you," I add, "need to stop letting the police intimidate you. What time is it?"

He glances at his watch. "Ten to two; time for food. How about pizza?"

"Sure," I say, though I'm certain I won't be able to eat since Ava's hearing is about to start. "You know what I like. Can you order?"

"You got it. Extra cheese coming your way."

I shut myself in my office. Leaning against the door, I squeeze my eyes shut, only to have someone start shoving their way inside.

"Sara."

Relief washes over me at the sound of Chris's voice. I move away from the door, giving him space to enter. He steps inside the office, shutting us in, and the deliciously wonderful power of him consumes the room, and me, with it.

"I heard about Michael," he says, dragging me against him, and he is warm and hard and wonderful in all the unexplainable, perfect ways that are Chris. "I hate that I let him get close to you." He leans against the door and frames my face. "I swore I'd never let him hurt you again. I thought he was on a plane. Blake's team confirmed his travel, and watched him get into his car."

My hands go to his. I will never get tired of having Chris hold me like this, or look at me like I'm the beginning and end of his world, as he is right now. "Jacob told me they thought he was leaving, but I'm fine. This isn't his fault, Chris. He got sideswiped. And this isn't your fault, either. You're the man I love, not my personal bodyguard."

"The hell I'm not, and Michael will find out that his bullshit doesn't change anything. You don't have to worry."

But *he's* worried, and well beyond the normal, bossy, protective man I adore. I see it in his eyes, and I fear my confession last night is why. "I wasn't afraid, and I'm not about to have a panic attack, if that's what you're thinking," I say. "I told you. They never happen at a logical time."

He turns us, claiming the dominant position by pressing my back to the wall, framing my hips with his, his hands going to the wall by my head. "Don't do that, Sara. Don't assume I think you're weak. I don't. You were afraid for Ella's safety last night. If that's not a logical reason to have a panic attack, I don't know what is."

"And don't *you* make excuses for me. That's denial—the very thing you swear destroys anyone it touches." I try to duck under his arms.

He shackles my leg with his. "No one's making excuses. That's not how I operate and you know it."

"You must wonder when, and where, I'll have an attack again."

He shakes his head. "You're creating a problem that doesn't exist, but know this. If you have another attack, I'll be there to catch you."

"This is *exactly* what I didn't want. I don't want you walking around trying to catch me."

"That's what we do, baby. We catch each other. I've accepted that with my meltdowns; now you have to accept it with this. I'm not entertaining any other version of who we are to-gether." He runs a gentle finger down my cheek. "Understand?"

While his tone is hard, his eyes are not. He means what he's said. He really doesn't seem to be letting this new knowledge cloud how he sees me, or us. "This is where you agree with me," he encourages.

"I do. It's what I want, too."

"Good. Now tell me what happened with Michael."

"He says he's staying until the trial. And the real kicker? He says he's doing this to protect me and my father."

"A way to intimidate you with the threat that he'll smear you in court."

"And a desperate play to get back in my father's good graces, which is exactly what I told him—right before I screamed 'fuck you' at him a few times."

He gives me a deadpan look. "You screamed 'fuck you' at Michael?"

"Several times, quite fiercely. And considering it was in a very public place, not one of my most shining moments."

"Well," he says thoughtfully, "you did need to make sure you got your point across." His lips quirk in that sexy, kissable way, and the tight ball of tension in my head dissolves into laughter.

"Yes," I agree. "I guess I did."

His hand settles possessively on my hip. "You kicked some ass today on all fronts. David was laughing his ass off at the way you called him and put the detective on the spot."

"Did you hear that Grant used me to start a fight next door?"

"Yeah, I heard. Interesting development. I wonder what they know about those two that we don't."

"He gave nothing away to me. He made me think he wanted to know more about Mark and Ricco."

Chris brushes some hair from my eyes, his mood doing one of those dark shifts, his fingers lingering on my cheek before falling away. "Your panic attack last night means nothing, Sara. Fighting back today, does. It proves you're putting the past behind you. You know that, right?"

"Yes," I say, realizing as I speak that he's right. "The panic attack scared me because it made me feel out of control, but that's not how I felt with Michael today. Not at all. I'm not the same person I was when I was with him, or even a month ago. Or even before that last night in Paris. Because of you. Because of *us*."

"Us," he repeats.

"Yes." I confirm that bond we share. "Us."

His fingers flex into my backside where they've settled, and his gaze lingers on my mouth. When it lifts, his stare is as hot as I suddenly feel. "I want to fuck you right here and now," he shocks me by announcing.

"Oh no," I say quickly. "Not here. We can't."

"We can," he assures me, and his fingers begin to inch my skirt up.

My hand goes to his, stilling his actions. "No," I insist. "Not here, Chris. And the hearing has already started; we have to be ready to deal with the results."

"It'll take a while to end," he says, his fingers tunneling into my hair as he drags my mouth a tantalizing breath from his. "Didn't we just decide it's better to focus on what we can control? And I choose to control all the things I can do to you while we wait for David's call."

"Chris—" His lips brush mine, a featherlight touch that sends a rush of sensations along every nerve ending in my body. "You're so unfair."

"How's this for fair?" He turns me and walks me backward until I hit the desk. "I'm going to fuck you right here, right now." His hands go to my waist and he lifts me, setting me on the desk and caressing my skirt up my thighs. "Any objections?" He opens my knees and fits his hips between my legs, nestling the thick ridge of his erection in just the right spot.

"Since you put it that way," I say, sounding as breathless as I feel, "no objections."

His dangerously perfect mouth quirks and he leans in, nuzzling my neck, my arms wrapping around his neck. His tongue flicks wickedly over a delicate spot behind my ear that he somehow makes me feel in the deepest part of my sex. My thighs clench his hips and his hand cups my breast, strokes my nipple, and my lashes flutter, lowering. And then somehow, I'm staring over his shoulder at the painting of the roses resting on the ground.

Unbidden, random entries from Rebecca's journal flicker into my mind. I can almost hear her voice in my head, feel her need for Mark in my need for Chris. Because of this room, which was her office. It's their place, their past. It's Mark's loss and pain and Rebecca's murder. It's them, not us. A desperate need to escape rushes over me, and I shove my hands against Chris's chest. "Wait," I say, straightening. "Wait, Chris. Wait."

He leans back, giving me a heavy-lidded stare, his hands

coming down on the desk next to me, his breathing heavy. "What just happened?"

My mind races with a million things I want to say to him, about the roses and Mark and Rebecca, but all I can see in my mind is the ring he designed for me. I don't know what those flowers mean to him yet, and I can't ruin what he's done for me over a wrong thing said in the wrong moment. Finally, I say, "This place is them."

"Them?" he asks.

"Rebecca and Mark. It's . . . them. I don't want it to be us."

Understanding shows in his eyes and he drops his head forward, as if he's scrabbling for control. His cell phone rings and he straightens, reaching for it. "David," he announces, answering the call.

"Is it over?" he asks, listening a moment and then giving me a nod.

Scooting off the desk, I tug my dress back into place, my eyes not leaving Chris's impassive expression as he listens to David. I watch the tick in his jaw get faster, until he abruptly turns, giving me his back. "She'll have a monitoring device?" he asks, leaning a hand on the door.

My pulse leaps, and my fist balls on my chest, where my heart is now thundering. Ava's getting out of jail. She's going to be free. I drop my face in my hands, trying to calm the white noise in my head and listen to Chris's conversation, but I can't seem to make it happen. *Calm down,* I tell myself. *Calm down!* Finally, Chris's voice comes back to me.

"Me?" I hear him ask. "When? Fuck, David. Yeah. Okay. I'll be there." Silence follows, and I realize he's ended the call.

Letting my clammy hands drop to my lap, I say, "They let her go."

"Yes." He stuffs his phone in his pocket and comes to me, his hands settling on my knees. "She'll have an ankle monitor, and we have a restraining order in place as a condition of her release. David's still working on the approval for us to go back to Paris until the trial, which will be months away."

"They dismissed the murder charges?"

"For now, but David seems to think that might change. They want me and Mark down at the station."

"Why you? Detective Grant told me he cleared you, Chris."

"That's the first I've heard of it, but either way, if I can help them lock Ava back up, I will. Hopefully it won't be long, but I'll take you home first."

"No. I'll stay. Blake's team will be less spread out with me here, and I'll know more of what's going on."

"That might actually be better. I know you knew this was coming, but your name did end up getting released in court with the press present." He grabs my hips and settles me against the desk again. "It gets worse, though. For starters, Ava's counsel stuck to the giant conspiracy story about the four of us framing her to shut her up over Rebecca's death, so that theory went out to the press."

"Detective Grant told me he's completely cleared us. Can't they speak up for us?"

"Truth or fiction, it's not really relevant in the bond hearing. Unfortunately, Ava's crazy claims, along with the dropped murder charges, muddied the prosecution's case enough to lower her bond."

"This is all stuff I expected," I say, and I cannot help but notice the subtle tension tightening around Chris. There's something he's dreading telling me. "What else, Chris?"

"Ava's counsel claimed you hated Rebecca because she was my lover."

Nineteen

"I never touched Rebecca, Sara," Chris says, his legs capturing mine as if he's afraid I'll try to escape.

"I know you, and I know the defense is doing their job—no matter how sleazy their tactics. That doesn't mean it's not hard to hear the things they're saying."

"Believe me, baby, I know. And it's all the more reason for us to get out of town."

I sigh. "I suddenly wish I were back at the chateau in France."

"If I could charter a plane and make that wish come true tonight, I would."

"I know. But we're trapped in the middle of this mess. Can't the police just clear us publicly, to take some of the pressure off of us?"

"Don't get your hopes up. David cautioned me that they often give people room to hang themselves. We have to remember that they're playing dirty ball with people who play dirty

231

ball. They don't know whom to trust until they discover the facts; facts we want them to find. And remember, too, that even if we're cleared, the press nightmare won't end. We're targets to these fame whores Ava has representing her, and if they can make this their O.J. Simpson case, they will."

"That's exactly what they seem to be doing."

"It's going to be a hundred times worse after that news special tonight, and I want us out of town before it airs. We'll have Blake send us a recorded copy to watch after we're away from the city."

"Won't the press find us at Katie and Mike's?"

"We're staying at a private house I rented. We'll be fine."

Any relief I feel is washed away by an upsetting realization. "We *can't* go to see Katie and Mike. I can't even imagine what they'll think about what's being said in the press. How am I ever going to face them again, Chris?"

"I called and warned them—fully. I told them how dirty this was getting. The first thing Katie did was ask how you were holding up."

"Because she's proper about everything. That doesn't change what she might be thinking about me, or us. I'm too embarrassed to face her and Mike."

"Don't be. They know how the press operates. They had an issue with the press over a competitor-created scandal years back. They know how things are twisted for other people's benefit."

"Still—"

He cups my face and kisses me soundly on the lips. "I promise, baby. If I thought it was a problem, we wouldn't go there." He steps back and glances at his watch. "I need to get moving so I can get back here at a reasonable time. I'll ask Mark to walk out with me so I can pick his brain about anything he knows that we don't. I'll call or text you if I'm going to be more than an hour." He disappears into the hallway.

It's going to be hard to hear the accusations about Chris and Rebecca; my heart aches just thinking about it. I want all of this to go away and I can't make it happen. Nothing I do changes anything, and I'm left with a clawing sensation inside me—like I'm supposed to do something before it's too late, but I don't know what it is, or why.

Three hours after his departure, Chris still isn't back from the police station. Judging from his numerous text messages, he's doing a lot of waiting in between a lot of talking, and I have no idea when he'll return.

Thankfully, inside the gallery things have been calm, though Jacob has warned Ralph and me that there's a circus outside.

I'm just about to deliver the last of the data I've collected for Ralph, when Jacob walks into my office. "Amanda's safe and at her parents' place in L.A." He sets a piece of paper with a number on it down on the desk. "Thought you might want that."

Relief washes over me. "Oh, thank goodness. But why in the world is she in L.A.?"

"No idea. We tracked her travel data. We have no other details, but I'm guessing someone or something spooked her. We need to know who or what, and people talk more openly to those they trust."

Understanding, I nod. "I'll call her and let you know what I find out."

"Remember you're all over the news. She's going to know what's being said."

My belly clenches. "I figured as much."

"I'll be in the break room in case you need me. I never ate my lunch. You might want to consider joining me and eating yours."

"Yum," I say. "Cold pizza."

"A microwave works miracles."

"A microwave makes soggy crust."

"Which is better than nothing." He disappears into the hallway. My attention shifts to the phone number he's given me, and I do what I've avoided all day: I google the local news. I know from the first sentence I'm going to wish I'd skipped the story, but it's like I'm transfixed by a bad horror movie, and I keep on reading.

Guilty, or a victim of a sexcapade gone wrong? That's the question about Ava Perez. Accused of murdering Rebecca Mason, who has been missing for months, she now claims her confession was brought on by blackmail. Those charges were dropped today, but she's still accused of attacking Sara McMillan and trying to kill her. So who is this Sara McMillan? She works for Mark Compton, said to be the kingpin of a high-end sex club. Ms. McMillan is also dating acclaimed billionaire artist Chris Merit, who is rumored to be a member of said sex club. Both men were allegedly intimately involved with Rebecca Mason, the missing woman who once held Sara McMillan's job.

I can't take any more, and I hit Escape and press my fingers to my throbbing temples. But I had to know what's being said; denial is dangerous. And I'm okay. I won't be a victim to anyone, including the press. Nothing in this story is unexpected.

Grabbing my cell phone, I punch in the phone number Jacob has given me to reach Amanda. After three rings, a man answers. "Hi," I say. "I'm looking for Amanda. This is Sara. I work with her."

"Hold on."

The line goes silent and I wait for what feels like forever.

"Sara?" She sounds awkward, like she doesn't really want to talk to me.

"Amanda. Hi. I was worried when you didn't show up at work."

"I meant to call you."

"What happened? I was afraid something happened to you."

"I know." She's silent a moment. "You were right. I was in over my head."

"What does that mean?"

"Ryan. He's into all that kinky stuff you guys are into, and I'm just not."

"There is no 'you guys' to this. I told you the news was going to report a sex scandal today. Ava's people are trying to make me look bad so the DA will drop the charges."

"I heard she attacked you."

"She did. I had stopped by Mark's to ask his advice about something, and she was there with Ryan. She started screaming that she was going to kill me, like she did Rebecca. It was horrible."

"Oh God. I had no idea."

"It was beyond horrible. But maybe we can at least get justice out of this."

"Now I feel bad for leaving."

"Don't feel bad for getting out of this mess. I'm sure you can keep your job if you want it."

"No. No, I can't come back. Ryan—he did things, and I started crying, and it was horrible. I can't face him and then Mark and you, and—"

"Sweetie. I'm not into the things Ryan is. Neither is Chris. I tried to warn you."

"I know. I should have listened."

"This isn't about I told you so. What's important is you're safe, and you're okay. Are you staying there a while?"

"I don't know. I haven't had time to think it through."

"Call me and let me know. Please."

"I will, Sara. Thank you, and I'm sorry all this happened to you."

"I'm strong. You be the same."

"I will. Bye, Sara."

She hangs up and I look up to find Ralph gaping at me by the doorway. "I googled. I'm guilty. I'm weak sometimes. I admit it."

I squeeze my eyes shut a moment and when I blink Ralph back into view, he's sitting in the visitor's chair in front of me with an expectant look on his face. Sighing in resignation, I share the same details with him that I have with Amanda. "Wow," he says when I'm done, shaking his head. "Just . . . wow. The bitch tried to whack you."

"Whack?"

"Don't you watch *The Sopranos*?"

"No."

"Where have you been, honey? When Tony had a problem . . ." He drags a finger across his neck. "Head gone, and body and feet in concrete blocks in the ocean."

"In the ocean," I croak, replaying Rebecca's nightmares of drowning.

"In whatever water is convenient." His eyes widen. "You think—"

"No." I hold up a hand. "Stop. I don't want to talk about this."

"You think Ava put her in the ocean." His expression turns fierce, his voice crackling with anger. "That would explain why she's missing." He slams his hands down on the desk. "You can't let that bitch get away with killing Rebecca. You make her pay. You put her in jail."

Shocked by this side of Ralph I've never seen, I nod. "We're trying."

"Good. And screw the press and their scandal. You keep your chin up. You're a butterfly, Sara. Spread those wings and let them see your bitch colors if you have to."

Laughter bubbles from my throat. "My bitch colors?"

"That's right."

"I love you, Ralph. I really do."

He stands up and comes around the desk, wrapping me in a hug. "I love you, too." He leans back and studies me. "You need to go home to your hot artist lover. I'm far enough along to finish my work at home now."

"My hot artist lover will be happy to hear that," I reply, barely containing more laughter. "He'll be here soon. You go on home."

"You're sure?"

"Positive."

"I don't have to be told twice." He rushes to the doorway, pausing to give me an exaggerated wave. I'm still staring in his wake when Mark walks past my office door without a glance in my direction. Hoping this means Chris is soon to follow, I call him, listening to it ring five times before it goes to voice mail.

I punch in a text message to him and Jacob interrupts my useless staring at the screen, waiting for his reply, by poking his head in the door. "Kelvin's going to escort Ralph home to protect him from the press. Anything on Amanda?"

"Yes, I just talked to her. The bottom line is that she was in over her head with Ryan, and embarrassed about it."

"He didn't hurt her, did he?"

"I didn't get that impression. I knew she was in over her head and that's why I tried to keep her away from Ryan. He knew it, too, and that's what really upsets me. It's like he wanted to upset her."

"Or maybe he was sending Mark a message."

"What do you mean?"

"Ryan knew Amanda for at least a year, and chose now, the most illogical time, to pursue her. He also knew Mark was counting on her here at work, and that a sex scandal would be highly unfavorable."

"And Mark had shut him out," I say, following where he's going. A chill goes through me. "I have a very bad feeling about that man."

"I think we all do—and we know he's intimately involved with Ava. Have you heard from Chris, by chance?"

"No. Not yet."

"Well, I'll be up front if you need me. If you're bored, you could try eating that pizza you never ate."

My lips curve at his concern. "I'll think about it."

He gives me a look that makes me think he might insist, then leaves. Tapping my fingers on the desk, I stare at the painting of the roses on the floor, starting to feel irritated by how much it haunts me. I dial Chris again with no success. After ten more minutes, I'm officially getting worried. I decide to try David, but of course he's with Chris, and doesn't answer. I try Blake. No answer. Another ten minutes and I buzz Jacob, with no news.

My cell phone rings and I don't even look at the caller ID. "Chris?"

"No, sorry. It's Crystal."

"Oh hi, Crystal. Is everything all right?"

"As okay as it can be, with the press suffocating us. I'm sure it's a hundred times worse there."

"I've been hiding from it. If you're dealing with the press, I'm sure you've heard my name."

"Yes, but I knew about Ava attacking you. Mark called me last night and told me the whole story. He wanted me to be prepared. But more than anything, he was worried about how his mom was going to deal with all of this, and he wanted to be here. Yet now he's saying he's not coming this weekend."

"He told me a few hours ago that he was flying out tonight."

"So you don't know why he would make this decision?"

"No. I had no idea he'd changed his mind."

"Sara," she says, worry thickening her voice, "he told me he needs me to just handle it."

"That doesn't sound like Mark."

"No, it doesn't. That man doesn't say 'need' to anyone, and he sure doesn't say 'handle it' where Riptide and his mother are concerned. He didn't sound good, and I'm not there to figure out why. Is there news on Rebecca?"

"I'm not certain. Chris is at the police station, and Mark just arrived back here at the gallery."

"So he's there with you?"

"He's in the same building but I wouldn't say he's with me. He didn't even speak to me when he came in."

"Can you try to figure out what's going on, and call me?"

"Yes. I will."

"I know you're going through hell, but it's hard to be here with my hands tied. I have this family's livelihood in my hands, and I'm terrified of letting them all down."

"You won't," I assure her. She clearly cares for Mark, and I hope she doesn't end up hurt. "Let me go talk to Mark. If I don't call you right back, it's because Chris and I are trying to get out of town to escape the press."

"I understand. If you get the chance, please tell Mark his father knows what's going on, but his mother doesn't and we aren't going to let her. We have a plan. I left him a voice mail to reassure him, but I have no idea if he'll listen to it anytime soon."

My phone beeps. "I will. That might be Chris calling, so I need to take this call."

"Okay, 'bye, Sara."

I quickly click at the sight of Chris's number, only to have the line go dead. "No. *No*." I dial him back and the call goes right to voice mail. My phone immediately rings again and it's Jacob.

"Did you talk to Chris?" I ask. "He just tried to call."

"Yes. He said to tell you he's going to your apartment to get your bags, and then he'll be here to pick you up. He's with David and he'll update you when he gets here."

"Is everything all right?"

"You're approved to leave town. That's a good sign."

"Okay. Thanks."

I have limited time to talk to Mark, so I push to my feet and head to his office. With a deep breath, I prepare myself and knock. And knock again. Frowning, I'm surprised to hear music coming from inside. That's unlike the Mark I know. Whatever the case, I'm not sure he can hear me knock. So holding my breath, I open the door to the lion's den.

"Say Something"

Say something, I'm giving up on you
I'm sorry that I couldn't get to you
Anywhere I would've followed you
Say something, I'm giving up on you

And I will swallow my pride
You're the one that I love
And I'm saying goodbye

A Great Big World

Twenty

Cracking Mark's office door, the searing lyrics I'd been playing on my phone two nights before when Mark abruptly left my office reaches my ears, warning me all is not well. In fact, I'm fairly certain something is very, very wrong. Easing inside, I see his empty desk.

Mark is sitting on the black leather couch to my right. His jacket is gone, his tie is loose, and he's holding a glass of amber liquid, and still he manages to give me a superior stare. "Limits, Ms. McMillan," he berates me. "Knock on the damn door."

"I did knock. You didn't hear."

"That doesn't constitute an invitation. I didn't *want* to hear." He refills his glass and I swear there is a slight tremble to his hand.

A swell of emotion fills my chest and I cross the room, stopping in front of the coffee table where his laptop, the source of the music, sits.

He downs another gulp and fixes me in a bloodshot stare that's void of emotion. He says nothing and I think he might be waiting for me to say something, like the song says, but I could be wrong. Maybe he wants me to say nothing, because it's not me he truly needs to speak to. It's Rebecca.

"How are you?" I blurt out when I can take it no more.

"I'm fucking wonderful." He refills his glass. "I had good news so it's a good day."

"What good news?"

"I'm cleared of Rebecca's murder. So are you and Chris, but I'm sure he told you already." He holds up the glass. "Celebratory drink?"

I can't celebrate anything with the word *murder* attached. "I didn't know you drank."

"Only when my joy reaches a point of zero containment."

The pain in his words is so bitter, I think it might make them crumble into tiny pieces and take his heart with them. I move forward and sit on the other end of the couch, angling toward him. "Did they clear Ryan?"

"Yes. Seems he's got a rock-solid alibi."

"Blake's still trying to find a connection."

He turns to face me. "You don't know yet, do you?"

A tremor of unease goes through me. "Know what?"

He motions to the computer, and I turn it toward me and bring the screen to life. A news story fills it and I read, *Police search the Muir Woods beachfront.* "Oh God," I whisper, and read the article in more depth. *While police stay mum on the reason for the search, an insider says it's related to missing local woman, Rebecca Mason.*

The rest is a recap of the day's hearing, and when I'm done reading I turn to Mark. "What else do you know?" His eyes collide with mine, and the torment in them is like a blade slicing through my heart.

"I have no idea," he replies. "They aren't telling me shit, and Tiger's vicious reputation isn't doing shit for me right now. They aren't talking to him, either."

"They arrested Corey today. He must have told them something."

"Obviously. More good news, by the way. That 'tell-all' news story that was going to run tonight isn't running. The police offered the newsperson an exclusive on something big coming soon, to hold it off."

"Do you . . . do you think they found her?"

"No. I think she's at the bottom of the fucking ocean, and they don't have enough evidence yet to prove how she got there. And I don't believe for a second that Ava pulled that off on her own."

"You think Corey helped her?"

"He had some involvement. I'm not sure he's smart enough to do it on his own."

"Ryan?"

"Yeah. I think it's Ryan."

"Ava will give him up once she feels trapped."

"That's to be seen, I guess." His voice lashes out at me, brutally sharp, angry even. "Why are you in my office?"

"Crystal called and—"

"I told you to let me handle Crystal."

"Like you handled Ryan and Amanda?" It's out before I can

stop it. "He scared the crap out of her, and she ran home to her parents."

"That's probably the best thing that could have happened to her. Look what happened to Rebecca when she stayed. Look what happened to you."

"Nothing has happened to me."

"Hasn't it?"

"No. I don't know what you mean."

"Who owns you, Sara?"

Adrenaline surges through me and I stand up. He follows me, his body too close. "Answer the question."

"What are you trying to prove, Mark?"

"Friends don't let friends make mistakes." Suddenly I'm yanked against him as he adds, "Waking you up is doing you a favor."

I flatten my hands on his chest to push him back. "Let go, Mark. You're drunk."

"I need you," he murmurs. "You know that. That's why you're here."

I shake my head. "Not in the way you—"

His hand goes to my hair, and now his mouth is near mine. "I've wondered how you would taste." He dips in to kiss me, and my knee instantly lifts and lands hard in his groin.

He grunts, cursing under his breath, and lets go. I stumble backward and put the table between us.

"Really, Sara?" He sinks to the couch. "You had to fucking *knee* me? It was a kiss, not an act of war."

"I told you to stop. You weren't listening, because you're drunk on more than booze. You're drunk on pain and guilt.

"And I see what you were doing. If I had let that happen, then Chris and I would have been nothing, and love would mean nothing to you—which is what you want to believe right now. Because then you don't have to deal with what you lost with Rebecca.

"But you *have* to deal with it, Mark. She's gone. I hate saying that to you, but you have to stop denying the truth. Admit it, and admit that you loved her. She deserves that."

He stares at me with unreadable eyes for several long moments. Then he reaches for the bottle and refills his glass, then just sits there, staring at the liquid inside.

"Aren't you going to say anything?" I demand.

He downs his drink. "You're saying enough for both of us. Go."

I walk toward the open door, then turn and meet Mark's eyes. "If his owning my heart and my body means I belong to Chris," I say, "then I belong to him. I'm not afraid to admit that, because he's worth the risk of getting hurt that comes with love." I turn and leave, pulling the door shut, only to gasp as I nearly run into Chris.

He pulls me to him, framing my face, his mouth near mine, his heart thundering beneath my hand. "You heard," I whisper.

"Every single word." And then he is kissing me, and I sink into the taste of him, the taste of us, and it is good and right in ways nothing else in my life ever has been. When our lips finally break apart, our eyes connect, a million silent words passing between us.

He takes my hand in his and we start walking toward the exit, but suddenly I can't just leave, knowing that Mark is in that room alone. Chris must feel the same because we both halt at the door, staring at it. I see his struggle in the tight lines of his body, the dip of his head between his shoulders.

God, I love this man. He is so much more than the paintbrush he masters with such incredible talent. So much more than his past, and his pain. I know even before he does that he can't walk out of here and leave Mark like this, either.

He faces me, inhaling heavily and letting it out. "I'll be back."

I push to my toes and kiss him. "You are the most amazing man I have ever known."

"Don't give me more credit than I deserve. I still may punch him, but I'll give him an ice pack for the ride to Sonoma if he wants to come."

I smile. "Kick him like I did. Safer for your hand."

I exit into the gallery and decide a walk through his art might be exactly what I need. I seek out the Chris Merit sign and stare at the ten pieces of art arranged in a box shape, all visions of San Francisco through the eyes of the man who will soon be my husband. I walk to the center and sit down, shut my eyes, and let the memories flow.

That first night when I'd come to find Rebecca, during a Ricco Alvarez show. The way I'd helped an elderly couple pick out a Chris Merit picture, which earned me a job offer from Mark. Meeting Chris. Spilling my purse in front of him. I laugh with the memory, and suddenly Chris is squatting in front of me.

"What are you doing?"

"Remembering the 'Man with One Red Shoe.'"

His lips quirk. "On the floor?"

"Yes, in the center of your universe."

"Baby, we have a lot of world to see, and as soon as this mess passes, I intend to show it to you." He stands up and pulls me to my feet. "The news story isn't running after all. The police convinced them to hold off in exchange for a bigger exclusive when they're ready to go public."

"I heard that. But can't Ava's people just call another station?"

"My understanding is the police told the rest of the stations they'd get shut out completely if they didn't wait."

"I wish I could say that's good, but it's happening because bad news is coming."

"Justice is coming," he says. "The bad news came weeks ago."

A lump forms in my throat. "Yes. But whatever they find on that beach is going to make it all feel very real."

"Yes, it will. Let's get out of here. Katie and Mike are eager to see us."

"What about Mark?"

"He wants to stay close in case the beach search turns up any news."

"I'm worried about him being here alone if they find something."

"He won't be. When I walked in, he was arranging a private jet to fly in company."

"Crystal? She really cares about him and the family. I'm concerned she's going to get hurt."

"He says she has open eyes. All we can do is hope she's seeing clearly enough for both of them." He laces his fingers with mine and we retrieve my purse and coat, then head for the car Chris has hired.

"Michael's gone," Jacob announces at the back door. "Kelvin watched him get on a plane himself."

I'm comforted, but part of me isn't sure he'll ever really be gone. Just like part of me still isn't willing to believe Rebecca's gone. "Thank you, Jacob."

His gaze remains on me a moment longer, then he glances at Chris. "If you decide you need me to come out to Sonoma this weekend, I can make it happen."

"I'd rather you stay focused on helping Blake here. The local operation my godparents hired seem to be working out."

"They had to hire security?" I ask.

"As a precaution until the trial," Chris says, his hand settling on my back. "I don't want them getting overrun with press."

Jacob holds the door open and Chris is about to usher me into the backseat of the black sedan, when I hesitate and turn to stare at the gallery.

"What is it, baby?" Chris asks.

"I have this sense of a book that I'm not quite ready to end, ending."

"And so we start a new chapter to our story."

"Yes." But I feel heartache and loss for a woman I never met, but feel as if I did. Rebecca helped me find myself, and she will always be a part of me.

I turn back to get into the car, when Jacob suddenly pushes through the doorway. "Hold up. Ava's out. I thought you'd want to know. Ricco paid her bond, and she has a friend acting as her supervisor. A woman who happens to be a friend of Ricco's as well."

My stomach knots. "The restraining order?"

"Blake confirmed with David that it's in place." Jacob glances at Chris. "My understanding is that David's about to call you."

"And she'll have one of those leg monitors?" I ask.

"Yes," Jacob says, "but that usually takes a day or two. A contract company will go to the residence she's staying at and connect it to that phone line."

Chris turns me to face him, his hands coming down on my shoulders. "Don't freak out. We're leaving the city. She could be back in jail before we even return."

"That's overly optimistic, Chris. I'd rather face reality."

"I don't do fluff. You know that. The police believe whatever they're searching for will lead to re-charging her, and quickly."

"How do you know?"

"Detective Miller told David."

"I'm ready to get out of here." I give Jacob a nod and slide into the backseat.

"What are you thinking?" Chris asks when we're inside the car, the driver taking us to pick up the 911.

"Ava is free, and Rebecca is really gone." And in my mind, I hear one of the lines from the song Mark was listening to: *I'm sorry that I couldn't get to you.*

Twenty-one

Chris's plan to dodge the press works, and at nearly 7:00 p.m. we retrieve the 911 he'd parked in a garage several miles from the gallery without incident. We're both starving but eager to get out of the city, so we choose the gourmet delight of Taco Bell on the go, and eat in the car by a parking meter. I've barely opened my burrito when I squirt taco sauce all over the dash and steering wheel, barely missing Chris.

He laughs and holds up his hands. "Whatever I did, I won't do it again."

Red-faced and giggling, I clean the dash, and when I reach for the steering wheel, he grabs me and kisses me. When I settle back into my seat, it's with a warm glow instead of the deep chill of hearing about Ava's release. And sitting there with him, wrapped in the cozy cocoon of the car, I have an "I'm so very blessed" moment. I'm alive. I'm with a man I love. And while that love stems from all the incredible things that define his character, and I certainly can't complain about his hot factor, his easygoing humbleness gets to me. His ability to be this gorgeous, talented man, with money and power, and yet he loves Taco Bell in the car, the way I do. With so much loss and heartache in the air, it's that small thing that fills my heart with emotion.

When we're finally on the road exhaustion begins to take hold, and I snuggle on my side facing Chris, his leather jacket draped over me. "Are you tired?" I ask, feeling bad that I can rest and he can't.

"Not yet, but I've done the time change from Paris many times. You haven't. Rest."

"I feel guilty."

"About too many things," he says.

"Did you hear about Amanda?" I ask, and it's really not a change of subject. It's about that word. Guilt.

"You are not Amanda's keeper, Sara."

"I know."

"I know you know, but you're letting worry over Ella and the connection you feel to Rebecca turn you into everybody's mother. Save your strength."

"My concerns for Ella and Rebecca may have led me to be gullible with Amber, but I'm not sure I care. She was crying for help."

"You're right, and I was enabling her instead of helping. Maybe your going to Paris was the catalyst that led to her finally getting help."

"I hate to think that I pushed her to the final edge, but I think she was close to being there anyway. I could almost feel her struggles pulling her into hell. It's hard to hate someone who makes you hurt for them."

"I get that, and the connection to me. But you barely know Amanda."

"It's the Rebecca connection, and the way Ryan was trying to make her his next conquest. I don't trust him. I know he has an alibi, but somehow, some way, I know he's involved in Rebecca's disappearance."

"If he is, Ava will sell him out," Chris assures me. "The good thing about people with no morals is that they gravitate to other people with no morals; then they undo each other."

"She hasn't so far, and he's supposed to testify against her for attacking me."

"She hasn't felt any pressure yet. The murder charges were dropped, and her team is working to tear down the witnesses to get her off the charge of attacking you. But from what Detective Miller told David, the kid from the coffee shop is talking and he has a lot to say."

I sit up straight. "Like what?"

"I don't know, but it led to the search on the beach. I have a feeling Ava's going to be talking real soon, and the truth is going to come out."

I melt down into the leather seat and stare into the inky darkness outside. The truth is about to be discovered. And isn't the truth what most people fear more than anything?

The sprawling country home that Chris has rented sits atop a hill with a gated entry. "The views are supposed to be magnificent in the daytime. There's a heated pool, gym, and a private vineyard. More important, it has a space I can use as a studio, and room you can set up as an office to work on your consulting business if we decide to hide out here awhile."

"It sounds fabulous," I say, as we exit the car in the garage.

"I figured we'd want to stay at least until we get some of the media frenzy behind us." He crosses to the door to the house and grabs the large envelope propped against it, opening it to hand me a key. "You also have the gate access code, and the garage remote they left us by the gate is over the visor on the car."

I accept the key. "You already told the Louvre you can't do the charity event?"

"Yes. I made it up to them in cash. Don't worry about it; we'll be there next year."

"But maybe now that we're cleared, we can go?"

"If we do, I can still attend the event, but at least now they can make plans if I can't."

The buzzer by the door goes off, and he scrubs his blond hair into a spiky, sexy mess. "That'll be Katie and Mike."

I glance at his watch. "Nine o'clock," I say. "Right on time."

"Sorry, baby. You heard me trying to convince her to wait until tomorrow, on our way here. But she was insistent she see us tonight." He hits the intercom and Katie comes on immediately.

"We're here and so are you. Wonderful!" she exclaims.

Chris tells her, "I'll open the gates and you can pull into the garage next to us." He reopens the garage and glances at me. "A little longer, and we can crash."

"It's okay. I love Katie."

"Good, because you should be prepared for a wedding explosion. She's going to lay one on you, I promise. Details will be planned and rehashed a million times. Just keep stressing small and intimate, like we talked about, or she'll have several countries here."

I smile at the idea of Katie's excitement. Headlights flash in the driveway and I have the sense of how my life has changed—how I'd been alone six months ago, and now I am not. Emotion overcomes me and I turn to Chris, wrapping my arms around his neck. "I love you, too, and . . . and I can't lose you."

"You won't. I'm not leaving again. It was a mistake I won't repeat."

"I don't mean that. I mean, I can't lose you the way Mark lost Rebecca."

"You won't."

"No one can promise that. She was going back to him. They had a chance and in a blink of an eye, she was gone."

His hands rest on my shoulders. "You're right. None of us can promise that we'll live another day. But you can't lose me the way Mark lost Rebecca, because you have nothing to regret with me like he does with her. And when I buried Dylan and came back to you, I knew it was all or nothing with you; no regrets." The headlights flicker and a car pulls in next to the 911, but Chris doesn't turn.

"No in between," I whisper.

"That's right."

Car doors open and I hear, "Sara!" and I turn to find Katie and Mike coming toward us, both as distinguished and warm as I remember. They're in their sixties and her gray hair is long and sleek, though his is getting a bit sparse on top. Both are elegantly dressed in casual, obviously expensive dress slacks; Katie's are loose, flowy black satin.

Mike shakes Chris's hand and then pulls him into a hug. I'm smiling when Katie goes straight for a big squeeze with me, and the distinct scent of roses reaches my nostrils, shaking me to the core.

Leaning back, she inspects me. "You look pale." She gives Chris a reprimanding look. "Why is she so pale?"

Because you smell like roses, and I must be losing my mind.

Chris replies, "It's been a hell of a day, Katie."

She turns back to me. "It has been a bad day, hasn't it? Life gets so messy sometimes, and people will do and say anything to get on top. Once, I was accused of sleeping with a reporter to get press for the winery. A bastard competitor made me look like a tramp. So I want you to know that nothing anyone says can sway us. You are your own story, here."

"I'm with Katie," Mike agrees and gives me a big hug, and dang it, now I know I'm nuts. He smells like roses, too, the cloyingly sweet scent staying with me after he steps away.

"Thank you both," I say, touched by the story she shared to make me feel comfortable. And I do. I have zero sense of being judged by them. Chris was right; I had nothing to fear coming here.

"You can thank me by letting me help plan the wedding," she asserts.

I laugh. "I wouldn't have it any other way."

She smiles. "Excellent." She motions to their shiny black BMW. "We brought some groceries so you can settle in and relax tonight." She cuts Chris a knowing look. "See? We saved you starvation until the stores open tomorrow."

Chris chuckles. "I should have known you'd come prepared. Thank you, Katie."

She snaps her fingers. "Both you men." She points to the cars. "Unload."

Then there's the unloading of bags and suitcases, followed by the stocking of the refrigerator in the gorgeous country-style kitchen with a dramatic stainless steel range hood above the stove.

"Coffee's almost done," Katie announces once we are almost settled. "We should go round up the boys and talk about the wedding. We can go shopping tomorrow."

"We want small and intimate," I say. "Just a handful of special people."

"We can do that. At the chateau, right?"

"That's what Chris and I talked about."

Her eyes light with pleasure. "Excellent. Tomorrow we can pick the spot on the property. I'm so happy, Sara. You've been so good for Chris."

"He's been good for me."

"That's when you marry someone—when you make each other better."

"We do," I say, unable to keep the gravelly quality from my voice. "In every way."

I hear Chris and Mike's voices a moment before they appear, and Chris comes up behind me, wrapping his arm around me, as Mike does with Katie. A sense of being a part of a family washes over me, a warm blanket I've never had before. I'm in this safe place for the first time in my life.

"Do I smell coffee?" Chris asks.

Katie beams with satisfaction, and in a few minutes we're all sitting around the table with steaming cups, chatting. "I'm so excited that you're getting married," she says. "Sara says you both want small and intimate."

"Yes," he says firmly. "*Small,* Katie. I know how you are. Don't keep adding names once the list is together."

"I won't, but we need to work quickly if we're going to set a date before you return to Paris."

"Look out," Mike says, holding up his hands. "She's about to start talking a hundred miles an hour. I might need wine, not coffee."

"I'm just excited," Katie says. "I've waited Chris's whole life for this. And frankly, at thirty-five, I was starting to think it wasn't going to come."

"Well, you can take a deep breath," Chris teases. "With everything going on here we canceled the Paris event, so we aren't in a rush. We have plenty of time, and Sara wants the trial behind us before the wedding."

"Good decision," Mike agrees. "You can't deal with legal issues split between countries."

"So, for a date," Katie says, "how about Valentine's Day?"

"I'm not sure the trial will be over by then," Chris answers, sipping his coffee.

"Why don't we plan for Valentine's Day," Katie suggests, "and then we can move it if we have to. We can work through the rest of the details in the meantime."

I lose track of time as we chat about anything and everything, until Chris's cell phone rings.

He glances at it, and I see the subtle tension in his face even before he looks at me and says, "David."

"Our attorney," I explain to Katie and Mike.

Chris answers the call with, "Tell me something good." He listens for a few seconds, then says, "Give me a second." He stands up and walks to the counter for the remote to a small TV hanging under a cabinet. I push to my feet and join him as he turns it on and finds the news, then says, "Got it, David. I'll call you back."

He turns up the sound and Katie and Mike join us to watch a male newscaster standing on a beach, wind gusting around him, the sea behind him.

"All we know at this point is that boxes have been carried out of the residence of Tom and Dorothy Merdock, whose son is Corey Merdock—an employee of Ava Perez, the woman who had confessed to killing the missing woman Rebecca Mason. Those charges were dropped after she said that her confession was coerced and there evidently wasn't enough evidence to hold her. Ms. Perez is still being charged with attempted murder against Sara McMillan, who worked at the same gallery as Rebecca Mason. Police are mum on what they know about the whereabouts of Rebecca Mason, or what Corey Merdock has to do with this case. There was some talk of a seedy sex scandal wrapped around the case, but at present we haven't been able to confirm or deny those details. The police are telling us they'll address all issues in a news conference that may come as early as Monday morning. We'll keep you posted as developments hit our news desk."

Chris turns off the TV and silence surrounds us. Then his phone rings again and he answers it, doing more listening than speaking. When he ends the call, he runs a rough hand through his already tousled blond hair.

"Well?" I urge.

"David doesn't know much. Detective Miller is staying close-lipped for the most part, but she let one big thing slip. They found another journal, and it's believed that Rebecca wrote in it the night she returned to San Francisco."

My hand goes to my neck. "They found it on the beach?"

"She wouldn't say where they found it. David says she'd get her teeth kicked in if they knew she even told him what she did."

"And Rebecca? Did they find her?"

He shakes his head. "David doesn't think they'll find Rebecca."

My knees are weak, and my stomach isn't much better. "Because she's in the water."

"Apparently there is reason to believe that is the case."

I sink back against the counter and replay her journal entry that I'd dreamed about. *I try to swim to the surface but the trolley is over me, shoving me down, down, down. . . . I cannot get to the surface. I cannot breathe. And my mother is nowhere. She is just gone. Like me.*

Chris and I sleep late on Saturday morning, and wake with coffee on the patio overlooking the Palisades Mountains and our own vineyard. David and Blake assure us they'll call if they have news, and Chris convinces me to try to let it go and enjoy the day. By two o'clock, Chris and I head to the garage to make our date with Katie and Mike at their winery. Since shopping is on the menu for Katie and me, I've gone casual dressy in dark navy jeans and a rich emerald silk blouse, with adorable boots

I bought in Paris. Chris wears an "Imagine Dragons" T-shirt paired with black jeans and biker boots, which he makes look hotter than any cover of *GQ* magazine.

At the chateau, Mike and Chris take off to tour some changes to the vineyard, while Katie and I spend a fun girls' afternoon at the local specialty stores shopping for a dress.

By early evening, the four of us have met up at the chateau for dinner before the jeweler arrives to talk about my ring. And we do dinner in amazing style, in a private dining room that's complete with a dungeon door, a round stone table, and dimly lit lanterns on the concrete walls. My pleasure is dimmed only by the huge centerpiece of freshly cut roses. I can't escape those flowers. They haunt me.

Somehow I manage to enjoy the fabulous four-course meal. We've just finished cheesecake and coffee when one of the waitstaff whispers to Katie and she announces, "The jeweler is here. Are we allowed to stay and see the design?"

Chris glances at me and I nod. "Yes. Of course."

A few minutes later, Everett, a tall, dark, curly-haired man who is as renowned for his craft as Chris is his, has joined us at the table, and begins measuring my ring size.

"Done," he says, after logging sizes for each of my fingers, though I have no idea why. "We are ready to design you a gorgeous ring."

Chris opens the sketch pad sitting on the table and slides it in front of Everett. Katie and Mike crane their necks to see the draft, but Everett picks it up and studies it long and hard. "Ah, Mr. Merit," he says finally. "It's spectacular, an absolute original I would be honored to design. Let's talk about the stones." He sets down the draft and reaches for a booklet of his own to show me images of jewels.

"I'd rather Chris pick," I say, glancing at him. "I want it to be your vision. That's what makes it special to me."

"I want you to love it," he insists.

"It's a Chris Merit original," I say, determined to get past the way the roses remind me of Rebecca. "I already love it."

Katie slides the sketch over to look at it, then makes a slight sobbing sound that draws my gaze. "Roses," she whispers. "For your mother."

Chris's expression turns solemn and he nods. "Yes. For my mother."

"It's a wonderful gesture, son," Mike adds.

My brows dip and I glance at Chris. "I don't understand."

He stands. "Walk with me and I'll explain."

"I'm sorry," Katie says. "Did I give it away?"

"Nothing to be sorry about," Chris assures her and then glances at Everett. "Can you leave the stone charts?"

"Of course. And I have what I need for the other project we discussed as well."

"Excellent," Chris says. "Thank you."

Mike and Katie stand. "We'll show you out," Mike tells the jeweler.

The three of them leave the room and Chris offers me his hand. "Let's grab our jackets and go outside," he says, and there's a raspy timbre to his voice, an emotional quality to his energy that he normally reserves for those intimate moments when everything between us combusts and explodes.

I twine my fingers with his. "Yes," I say. "Let's go outside."

A few minutes later we walk hand in hand across a small brick walkway to a wooden bridge that arches over a large pond. The same bridge we'd stood on the night he'd confessed his father's drinking problem to me. Just like that night, there's a glow from the orange lanterns dangling from poles mounted in the wooden rails, and stars dot the black, cloudless canvas above.

As he had then, Chris leads me over the bridge toward a gazebo, and I catch the sweet scent of roses, their stems entwining in the wooden overhang, delicate buds clinging to the leaves. Once we're in the gazebo, he leans on the railing and folds me against him. "Look up."

We tilt our heads and look up at the blossoms quilted like a beautiful blanket above us. "This is where I'd like to get married," he says, drawing my gaze to his. "Right here, under the roses my mother helped Katie plant."

My heart squeezes. "Your mother?"

"Yes. She convinced Katie that everything was better with roses. She loved them. Katie cuts at least one fresh flower every evening in her memory." He laughs, a tinge of sadness in it. "Or she picks a ridiculously impossible blossom, and makes Mike find a way to reach it for her."

I tear up with the deep feelings this stirs inside me: memories of my own mother, of reading about Rebecca's heartache after losing hers. "That's why they both smelled like roses last night."

"I'm sure that's why." A tear slides down my cheek and Chris wipes it away. "Why are you crying?"

I grab his hand and hold it to my chest, like I want to hold him in my heart. "Because it matters. This matters. *We* matter, and the way you invited your mother into our life through the ring is special beyond words."

The love in his eyes is like a new day's sun, waking the parts of me that were buried in the darkness of night. He is my other half, my soul mate, the person who knows me even better than I know myself at times.

"I'm never letting you go," he declares.

My lips curve. "Ditto."

He smiles, and the heartache of his past slides away. Because of me, I think—and it's the most amazing feeling in the world, that I can do that for him. He leans in to kiss me, pausing as we hear Katie's voice. "I guess the kiss has to wait."

My lips curve. "Anticipation makes it better, right?"

"But it's torture in the process," he admits.

"Remember that the next time you decide to unleash it on me."

"With pleasure," he promises, and the mischief I adore is back twinkling in his eyes.

"You heard the story of the roses?" Katie asks as they join us.

"I saved that for you," Chris tells her, just as his cell phone rings. He pulls it from his jacket and glowers at it. "I really want to throw it in the pond right now."

"Me too," I agree, fearing our perfect night is about to be ruined.

Glancing at the screen, Chris tells me, "Blake," then answers. I want to listen in, but Katie immediately links her arm with mine and pulls me to the center of the gazebo, launching into a story I barely hear. Chris has just walked down the bridge, and the rigid line of his back says something is wrong.

He finally turns around and swiftly crosses the bridge. When he stops beside me, he laces his arm with mine and pulls me close, as if he needs to hold on to me. "Sara and I need to leave," he announces. "Blake and his team will be here in the next five minutes."

"Who's Blake?" Mike asks.

"Our security team," Chris explains.

"Chris, why?" I ask urgently.

He pulls me in front of him, his hands on my shoulders. "We're handling—"

"Oh God, just *say* it."

"Ava escaped, and they can't locate Ryan or the kid from the coffee shop."

Twenty-two

The world spins around me, and I sway. Chris wraps his arm around my waist, catching me to him. He glances at Katie and Mike. "Give us a few minutes."

"We'll go watch for your security team," Mike says.

"And Ryan?" I ask. "Is he with Ava?"

"All they know is that Ryan took a flight to Los Angeles."

"Oh God. That's where Amanda is." I push away from him. "I need your phone to call her. No, I need my phone to call her. I have her number."

"Sara." His hands come down on my shoulders. "They know Amanda's in Los Angeles. They're on it. And now that we're cleared, the DA's contracted Walker to help with the investigation. We're well-informed, I promise you."

"Still, I need to call Amanda. I need—"

"Baby, you have to deep breathe and trust me to handle this.

And Blake. He's good at what he does. He and his brothers have extensive law enforcement experience."

"Why is he coming here?"

"Ava's on the run, and he doesn't want to take any chances of her making a beeline for us."

"How would she even know about this place?"

"We don't know if she has help with money and resources, or if she's simply on the run, trying to survive. To be cautious, we have to assume she has resources."

"So where do we go?"

"For now, we're going home to the city."

"But the press?"

"They're the least of our worries right now. Blake feels the apartment is the most secure place for us to be. From there, we'll decide what to do. We might go to Paris. We might not."

"I need to deal with my work visa first."

"It's fine. The consulting work can be run through the States, or one of my corporations in the meantime if needed. We'll work it out. Right now we just need to get to a secure location, and look at what we know then."

I glance up as Blake, Kelvin, and Jacob walk toward us, and the sight of these three powerful men closing in on us has a choking effect. How bad *is* this that they feel we need all three of them? Chris must see my expression, because he turns to look over his shoulder, then back at me. "The odds of Ava coming after you are next to zero. She's going to run. But I'm not taking any chances; I told Blake to come prepared." He cups my face. "I protect what's mine, baby."

A moment later I'm surrounded by men, a protective shell around me. Chris is my shelter. He is my strength.

An hour later, Chris and I have said our good-byes to Katie and Mike, and Blake has assured us that their security team has them covered. We've returned to the rental house to pack up, and we're in the kitchen listening to the news when Blake appears.

"We've confirmed that Ryan's with Amanda."

I stiffen, going on high alert for about the tenth time this hour. "What? Where? Is she okay?"

"She's still in Los Angeles at her family home, as is he. She told the police she invited him and he's her guest."

My brow furrows and I shake my head. "That makes no sense. She told me he scared her."

"Her family confirmed her story, which gives him an alibi for the time period during Ava's disappearance. He's claiming he wasn't anywhere near Ava to help her escape, and his travel times support that conclusion."

"So he's not involved?" I ask, leaning on the kitchen counter next to Chris. "That can't be right. Surely that kid from the coffee shop doesn't have the resources to help Ava escape."

"I didn't say Ryan wasn't involved," Blake corrects. "I said he's got an alibi. I have concerns about this kid Corey. He was going to testify against Ava. So he could be in danger from her, or anyone helping her."

Chris drapes his arm around my shoulder. "Are you suggesting that's Ryan?"

"I'm not ruling out anyone," Blake says. "And I've learned

something interesting from working with the police. There's a woman named Georgia O'Nay who—"

"She's a local artist," I say. "She created the rose painting in Rebecca's office. That painting's been on my mind. What about her?"

"She was involved with the club and came forward," Blake explains. "She said she had problems with Ryan and dropped out of the entire club scene because of him. He turned obsessive on her. She threatened to go to Mark, and he backed off."

I shake my head, frustrated. "I must have read something in one of Rebecca's journals about this. That has to be why I kept thinking about the painting."

"You said the kid was going to testify against Ava," Chris says. "What did he have against her?"

"He loaned her his parents' boat. He claimed she said it was to impress a potential investor in the coffee shop, and she banged the kid as a thank-you. Now that he's taken off with her, we're assuming he was more involved. Either way, the extra journal was in the boat under a seat. And there's plenty of DNA evidence that Rebecca was in the boat."

The news blasts through me, overwhelming me, and I bury my face in Chris's chest, tears welling in my eyes. "I knew, but I didn't want it to be real."

His hand closes on my head. "I know, baby. None of us did."

Anger starts to burn in my chest and I turn to Blake, tears streaming down my cheeks. "Ryan has money. Couldn't they have hired someone to help Ava escape? Could they have kidnapped the kid?"

"Certainly an option we're looking at," he confirms. "But

Ryan's smart. If he's involved, he's covered his tracks, including any money trail."

"What about Ricco?" Chris asks. "He got her out of jail and he has deep pockets."

"Yes," I agree. "And he believes she's innocent."

"We're looking into that, too," Blake confirms.

"Maybe I can make him confess," I argue. "Can we record a call?"

"He's smart, Sara," Chris warns. "He's not going to admit anything."

"I have to try," I insist. "He's a more logical choice than Ryan to help her escape. He really believes she's innocent. He believes Mark isn't. He's angry and jealous and bitter."

"It's not a bad idea," Blake agrees. "If we want to try, there's an app you can download to your phone to record the call. It's legal since you're part of the conversation. Where's your phone?"

I turn to grab my purse from the counter, but Chris's hand comes down on it. "No," he says. "No matter what his role is in this, Ricco's not behaving sanely. You don't want more of his attention."

"I know you're worried, but Ava running around free isn't the answer, either."

"If Ricco helped her, he has a plan, and you can bet it involves Mark."

"Then *he* could be in danger." I turn to Blake again. "Can I tell Ricco Mark was cleared of all suspicion?"

"You may," he says, his eyes meeting Chris's over my head. "This is your call, Chris. I think she's okay, though. I don't think Ricco's targeting Sara."

My gaze meets Chris's. "This isn't your decision. It's mine."

He shakes his head. "Not yours. Not mine. Ours. We make decisions together now."

"Yes. I know." I flatten my hand on his chest. "But Ava on the loose is far more dangerous to us than Ricco, who really wants Mark."

A tic starts in his jaw.

"Chris," I plead. "I'm safe. You have a small army protecting me."

"Okay. Make the damn call. But we're talking about what you can say in advance."

"Of course." He releases my purse and I dig out my phone, giving it to Blake, who starts searching for the app to download.

"Let's sit at the table," Blake suggests, glancing up to find Jacob in the doorway.

"What's our exit timeline?" Jacob asks.

"Are we still feeling secure?"

"We're clear," Jacob confirms.

"Give us fifteen minutes." Blake sits at the table next to me and across from Chris, and shows me how to use the recording app. "Just activate it before you dial Ricco."

For the next five minutes, he and Chris throw out warnings and things I shouldn't say to Ricco, to the point where they're making me crazy. "Stop," I say. "I'll handle this. I'm ready." I don't give them time to argue. I dial Ricco.

Three rings and he answers. "Bella. I would say I'm surprised to hear from you, but really, I'm not. Today has been an interesting day, has it not?"

"Did you help her escape?" I demand. Chris and Blake throw their hands in the air as I throw caution to the wind, but I go with my gut. "She's guilty. Not Mark. They cleared him."

"I've heard nothing of Mark being cleared or her being charged."

"They found evidence, Ricco. It was Ava. She wanted Mark, and when Rebecca came back, she knew she'd lose him. Please, I'm begging you. If you know where she is, turn her in."

There is complete silence on the line, and every muscle in my body is tense as I wait. Finally, he says, "I didn't help her escape. But you, and whoever is listening in on this call, can be assured that if I find out that she killed Rebecca, and I find her before the police do, she'll never make it back into custody alive."

The line goes dead and, stunned, I can barely breathe. It takes me a moment to set the phone down on the table.

"Sara," Chris says. "Baby, what happened?"

"I think he might kill Ava."

Blake takes the phone and hits Replay on the app and he and Chris listen to the call.

We leave the rental property in a black sedan with Jacob as our driver and Blake and Kelvin driving the 911. That they feel we're a target in the 911 does not make me feel good. Chris and I huddle together, talking very little, and you can almost hear our minds working. Worse, we hit some sort of traffic jam heading into San Francisco, and after an hour of sitting still, and my impossible-to-ignore need to go to the bathroom, we decide to pull over to a diner and eat.

Once we're inside, I take one look at the group of alpha men waiting for me to slide into the center of the booth, and decide to use the bathroom first.

"I'll go with you," Chris says, determined to be my number-one bodyguard.

As we walk down the small hallway he asks, "You okay?"

"As long as I'm with you, I'm okay." His furrowed brow says he's not convinced, and I push to my toes and kiss him. "I promise."

"Just remember that people make their own choices, and then they live with them. We can try to change them, but we can't make their choices for them. If you do everything you can to help, you have to accept the outcome they bring on themselves."

I nod. "I'll be right back." I enter the bathroom, locking the door. I'm washing my hands when my cell phone rings. I pull it from my purse, surprised to see Chantal's number.

"Chantal!" I say eagerly, answering the call, missing my friend in Paris.

"Sara." Her voice is a rough, strained whisper.

"What's wrong?"

"Tristan is here. He wants to talk to you. He said he doesn't have your number, and I didn't know if I should give it out."

My stomach knots at the name of the man who tried to replace Chris with Amber, and failed, foreboding tensing my body. He's in Paris dealing with Amber's rehab that Chris is paying for. Why is he calling me?

"Sara?" Chantal prods.

"Yes," I say. "Okay."

"Sara," he says, his voice hard.

"Tristan? Why are you calling me and not Chris?"

"Amber killed herself."

I fall against the door. "No. No. No." My eyes burn. "When? How?"

"She hung herself at the treatment center. I can't talk to Chris. Maybe never again." His voice cracks. "She left a note. She wants to be cremated. No funeral. Absolutely no Chris. She died hating him. I hate him. Keep him away or I . . . I don't know what I'll do. I have to go. Just . . . keep him the fuck away." The line goes dead.

I sink down against the door, tears streaming down my cheeks. Amber is dead, and I have to tell Chris.

Twenty-three

I'm sitting on the floor, my cheeks streaked with tears, when Chris knocks. "You okay, baby?"

"Yes. Sorry, I'm coming." But I can't move. What am I supposed to do? I can't tell him. Not now, in the middle of a pack of men, in a public place, when he's about to be trapped in the back of a car. I have to wait until we're alone.

I push to my feet and wobble to the sink, and stare at my red, puffy eyes. Even cold water won't hide the fact that I was crying. I'll have to make him believe this is due to all this hell we're living.

He knocks again. "Sara. Open up."

"Just another minute." I open my purse to grab my makeup and the tears start again. I thought we got her into rehab in time. She was *supposed* to be okay.

"Sara."

I give up trying to pull myself together, turning and

opening the door. The minute I see my amazing, damaged man, the tears start flowing again. He comes in and shuts the door, folding me into his strong arms.

"Hey. Baby." He frames my face, stroking wet hair from my cheeks. "What happened? I thought you were okay?"

"I was. This isn't a panic attack. Those don't come with . . . tears. This is . . . This is just . . . It hurts that she's dead." Amber. Rebecca. I can't tell him. "And it's real, and I didn't want it to be this way."

He rests his forehead on mine. "I know. It's a lot, but it'll be better. We just have to hang in there."

My hands cover his, and I want to hug him and comfort him. The day we've both feared is here, when we must face his demons, and we have to do it while we're already standing in the fires of hell. And I have to be strong enough to keep him from burning alive.

I swallow my pain and nod. "Yes." I force my gaze to his. "We do. We will. I love you."

He strokes the dampness away from under my eyes. "I love you, too, and we can get through this. We can get through anything."

Emotion overwhelms me and I press my hands to his cheeks. "Yes. We can get through anything."

Going back out to that table of men and managing to stay dry-eyed is almost unbearably difficult, but I do it for Chris. And the ride home is even harder, filled with empty space that allows my mind to replay every moment with Amber, and question every action I took, every word I spoke to her. I know Chris will do the same, multiplied in every possible way. It's nearly eleven o'clock at night when we finally pull into the garage of our apartment building, and it feels like I have lead in my stomach and a vise on my chest. I can barely breathe for what comes next.

Chris helps me out of the car and walks over to the 911, joking with Blake about riding the gas too hard. Jacob shuts the front door of the sedan and stretches, and I take the opportunity to quietly tell him, "We put Chris's ex-girlfriend in Paris in rehab before we left. She just killed herself. I have to tell him."

"Holy fucking shit." He scrubs his jaw.

"I found out in the diner. I have to tell him in private, and I need to know we won't be interrupted until I contact you again."

"Consider it done."

"Thank you." My eyes burn. "I'm barely holding it together, so . . . if we can speed things up and get everyone gone quickly?"

"I'm on it. You did the right thing by waiting." He steps around me to join the other three men.

I need a breath I can't seem to manage to pull into my lungs. I stand there, my back to the men, and I am not sure how much time passes. Then Chris's hand is on my shoulder and I reach up and cover it with mine, and that breath fills my lungs.

I turn to face him. "Any news?"

"We just missed a police press conference about the manhunt for Ava and Corey. They said they'd have more details on the investigation tomorrow morning."

"So it's all public now. No sign of Ava?"

"No. No travel activity. No sightings, but the press conference will change that. Blake says leads will flood the tip lines." He motions to the elevator. "Jacob just took our coats and bags upstairs. Let's go try to get lost in our own little world."

If only that were possible. His arm settles over my shoulder, when it's he who needs shelter from the firestorm I'm about to deliver. We ride the elevator in silence, and I wonder if he's thinking about how to help me escape the torment I'm feeling. I know he is. That's Chris. My dark knight. My hero. God, please let me be his now.

The elevator doors open and Jacob is there, his eyes meeting mine. His expression is carefully schooled but I feel his awareness, his understanding, and it's a whisper of comfort. "Your bags are in the bedroom," he says as we step inside the foyer. "We'll have the building well covered. We don't expect much to happen overnight, but if Ava or Corey is located, I'll call. Otherwise, we'll meet you here before the press conference at nine a.m."

A storm of emotion hits me and I quickly leave them to say their good-byes, running down the stairs to the living room. I drop my purse on the chair and stop at the window to stare out at the inky black night, the stars and moon sucked into the darkness of clouds and an impending storm. My hands flatten on the cool glass and I drop my head forward. I don't know how to tell him.

I feel the moment the room shifts with his presence and I squeeze my eyes shut, waiting for his touch. It comes with a hot spike of more emotion. So much emotion. I turn and grab his waist. "Lean back against the window."

His brow furrows but he does as I say, allowing me to trap him with my body. I need to hold him. I need to try to control how this happens. Swallowing, I stare up at him, and I wish I'd turned on the lights. There are too many shadows, too little light.

"Sara—"

I press to my toes and kiss him. "Just . . . listen. Okay?" He gives me a nod and I settle my hands back on his waist.

"Tristan called." The words are a pained whisper, and I feel Chris's body harden.

"How did Tristan call you?"

"He went . . . to Chantal. He said he can't talk to you. Chris—"

His hands come down on my shoulders. "Just say it, Sara. Whatever it is, say it."

"Amber . . . killed herself."

He doesn't move. He doesn't speak. I don't know how much time passes but I feel the eruption bubbling just beneath his surface a moment before he turns us and steps back. Withdrawing. He's withdrawing. "When?"

"Tristan called me while we were at the diner. I didn't want to tell you in front of everyone, and then have you be locked in a car, unable to react."

He squeezes his eyes shut. "Thank you."

I want to touch him, oh God, how I want to touch him, but I sense he's not ready.

"How?" he finally asks.

"She hung herself."

"And the fucking rehab facility let it happen? I was paying to have her protected, and where is my phone call? They're probably too busy talking to their attorneys for fear I'm going to sue their asses."

"I know. I thought the same thing."

He pulls his cell phone from his pocket and dials, surprising me when he leans on the glass next to me, though we're still not touching. I listen as he talks to the rehab facility and then to David. He's calm. Controlled. The way he handled an awards banquet for the Children's Hospital when he was bleeding inside.

He finishes the calls and drops the phone to the floor. And then we just stand there side by side against the window, hanging over the city. Time stands still. There is only his pain, which slices and burns through the room like boiling acid.

Eventually, without a word or a glance in my direction, he pushes off the window, crossing the room, and I fear the moment he will walk to the elevator, the moment he'll seek the whip and I'll have to stop him.

But he doesn't turn for the elevator. He turns right and makes a path to his studio. Relief washes over me. He's staying. He's fighting this with me. I don't know if he wants me to follow now, but I have to. I have to know he's okay.

I follow and tentatively enter the studio, stopping inside the doorway. The windows surrounding the U-shaped room deliver all darkness, and no light. There's a rustle of clothing, a flicker of movement, but I can make out nothing but the outline of Chris's body.

Then a small light flickers on, a barely-there glow casting the studio in shadows, and I'm relieved when I see that he's removed his shirt, shoes, and socks. This is how he paints, and his art is how he's going to deal with his pain. Certain he knows I'm here, I sink down the wall and watch as he steps to an easel and starts to paint in silence.

I watch him stroke paint onto the canvas and I know fairly quickly that he's creating a dragon, his symbol of strength, and one that Amber had inked permanently on his body. Hours pass, I think, and I take off my own shoes and socks, curling my knees to my chest. Ready to act the moment he needs me, I watch Chris's grief bleed onto that canvas. I'm entranced by every flip of his hand, every tease of color, as the dragon becomes the one on his shoulder and arm. Abruptly he steps back and drops the brush, and just stands there staring at his work. And then, he crumbles. He falls to his knees, and his head drops forward.

I'm crossing the room to him in an instant, and rest my hands on his shoulders. He pulls me onto my knees in front of him, his hands coming to my face as I stare into his bloodshot eyes and tear-streaked face. "I don't need the whip. I need you."

"I'm here," I promise, heartbroken but relieved. "I'm here."

He tangles his fingers in my hair, letting his pain spill out. "I can't lose you."

"You won't. Never. I promise."

He drags me down to the floor with him, holding on to me like he's afraid I'll escape and be lost forever. "You can't promise that," he whispers into my hair. "None of us can."

I cup his face, forcing him to look at me. "We also said no regrets," I remind him. "We won't ever have any."

"I have so many with her. Too many. I thought . . . I tried . . ."

"I know you did. Remember what you said about Ricco and Ava: We choose what we do with the life we're given, and we live with the results. Free will. You choose to help other people. You helped her."

"I fucked her life up."

"No, you did not. She had problems and we were getting her help."

"Too late. I knew she needed that kind of help, but I didn't act on it until you saw it, too."

"Don't do this to yourself, Chris. Don't."

His fingers find my face, my hair, and my lips and then he's kissing me, salty tears trailing down my cheeks and his. We end up on our sides facing each other, undressing each other right here on the hard floor. But it doesn't matter. We gasp in unison when he enters me, and I cling to Chris, holding him a little too tight, like I plan to do for the rest of my life. I don't know where he begins and where I end, but maybe that's the glory of who we've become. We begin and end together. We're a puzzle that fits perfectly together, where we fit nowhere else. And right now we're seeking peace in the only place we know to look—each other.

When the wild frenzy of passion passes, we don't move. Thunder rolls outside the windows, rain starts to patter on the glass, and we just hold each other, finally falling asleep.

A week later, Chris and I sit at the kitchen table surrounded by windows, the ocean glistening like blue silk beyond the glass. I'm in his T-shirt and he's in his pajama bottoms that I insisted he wear to allow me to focus on cooking breakfast. We've just finished our omelets and the news is playing, reporting nothing we don't already know.

Ava and Corey haven't been seen or heard from, and Corey's parents' are making regular TV appearances claiming he's an innocent victim. Mark has been in New York, finding sanctuary with his family, as has Crystal. Crystal doesn't tell me much, and I pray she's not getting in too deep.

"If Ricco's involved with Ava's disappearance," Chris says, "I'd think the trial will stir anger toward Mark, and pressure him to crack."

"I still feel Ryan's involved, but maybe that's because I don't want to think about what Ricco said about killing Ava."

"Free will, baby," he murmurs sadly, words we've spoken often this past week. "She made her choices like he is, and they're responsible for them. But it makes me damn glad we're leaving for Paris tomorrow. I want space between us and here, with her still on the run."

My heart squeezes and I lean closer, teasing his hair with my fingers. "What you're doing for Amber, by bringing back your dragon paintings and auctioning them off for the Children's Hospital in her name, is an amazing way to honor her."

He catches my hand in his. "I need to make this all matter to someone."

The buzzer rings and I frown, still expecting bullets where there are no guns.

He kisses the frown mark. "Stop that. I'm expecting a delivery."

Relieved, I sink back into my chair. "Thank goodness." I think I see a glimpse of a smile, and maybe even some mischief in Chris's eyes before he turns away. I hope so. That man needs to smile again.

Pushing to my feet, I refill our coffee cups. I've just returned to the table when Chris returns, and there's definitely a light in his eyes that I'd feared long lost. He joins me at the table, sitting down and turning our chairs to face each other.

"We won't have your engagement ring for another month because of some of the stones I ordered, but it'll be ready in plenty of time for the wedding in February. But my first vision for the ring wasn't the roses. And I've had that first ring created and sized for your right hand—the same side as my ink." He holds out a black velvet box and lifts the lid, and I gasp at the sight of a ring twinkling with reds, yellows, and blues.

"A dragon," I whisper.

"To represent the strength you are to me."

Tears prickle in my eyes and he pulls the ring from the velvet and slips it on, an intricate dragon's tail wrapping my finger. "I love it." I wrap my arms around him. "And I love you."

And he holds me to him, molding us close, hugging me a little too tight, just the way I like it.

Epilogue

Ricco

"Hello, Alvarez," I hear as A.J. Wright falls into step with me in the center of the busy Saturday Pier 39 crowd, meant to disguise our meeting from prying eyes.

"The kid?" I ask, glancing at the stocky ex-mercenary whose new job is doing my unavoidable dirty work.

"Badly beaten but alive, just as you ordered," he replies. "The police will get a call to locate him later this evening."

"A shame we had to do that, but he shouldn't have helped Ava with the boat. And what of her?"

"As requested," he replies. "Suffering terribly."

My lips curve. "Excellent."

"How long do you want this to continue before I kill her?"

"Drag it out. I have plenty of cash to pay for your time.

We'll discuss her conclusion in our next meeting. What about Mark Compton?"

"Operation 'Fuck Mark Compton' is well under way. You have nothing to worry about."

I smile.

To be continued in *I Belong to You,*
coming from Gallery Books in September 2014.

The wedding is on!
Find out what happens on the day Sara and Chris say "I Do"
on Valentine's Day, in February 2015.

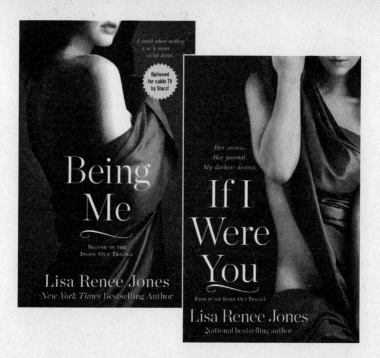